BAD BLOOD

Bad Blood

....

P. M. CARLSON

A PERFECT CRIME BOOK

DOUBLEDAY

New York London Toronto Sydney Auckland

A Perfect Crime Book
PUBLISHED BY DOUBLEDAY
a division of Bantam Doubleday Dell Publishing Group, Inc.
666 Fifth Avenue, New York, New York 10103

DOUBLEDAY is a trademark of Doubleday,
a division of Bantam Doubleday Dell
Publishing Group, Inc.

To the memory of my mother

To the memory of my mother

The author would like to thank friends and experts Patricia King, Robert Knightly, K. T. Anders, Kay Williams, Joanna Wolper, and David Linzee.

"What do you call yourself?" the Fawn said at last. Such a soft sweet voice it had!

"I wish I knew!" thought poor Alice. She answered, rather sadly, "Nothing, just now."

"Think again," it said: "that won't do."

—LEWIS CARROLL, *Through the Looking-Glass*

Thursday, September 13, 1979

I

Arms folded casually across a blond chest as furry as terry cloth, the young man in Rina's guest bathroom smiled: well muscled, relaxed, and totally naked. Rina froze, her hand still on the doorknob.

"Ginny, Ginny!" she murmured, horrified at her daughter's joke.

"Did you say something, Rina?" her mother called from the kitchen.

"No, Mamma." But thank God I got here before you did, she thought. Headed off your usual Vesuvius act. Mamma's spitfire temper had not mellowed, not even now that she was in her seventies. Rina charged across the bathroom, feeling a bit like Vesuvius herself, and folded the naked young man back into the magazine. *Playgirl.* Ginny, you idiot. There ought to be a rule: all offspring must be confined to padded cells between the ages of twelve and twenty-one. The world was a tough enough place without having to put up with teenage humor.

The room was still clean, at least. No toilet paper wrapped around the sink, no graffiti soaped onto the window. Look on the bright side, right? No bombs in the wastebasket either. No dead rats in the soap dish. Nothing unfixable that could cause Clint to storm around about getting tough once and for all. A lucky day all around.

Rina adjusted a towel on its ring and glanced in the mirror.

Dark hair pinstriped with gray, and worry lines seaming her fifty-two-year-old face. Ginny saw to that.

But this was just a phase, of course. Ginny was bright. And God, she loved her daughter despite her faults.

The doorbell rang. Hastily, Rina rolled up the magazine and held it out of sight as she went back into the hall. Mamma had answered the door already. With short iron-gray hair erupting from around her heart-shaped face and dark snapping Italian eyes like Rina's own, she was helping her friend remove her trench coat. "How are you, Marie?"

"Fine, Leonora," Marie Deaver said to Mamma. "My, it smells wonderful in here! An Italian banquet again!"

"Not really. Can't get good cheese around here. You'd think this close to Washington you could get cheese! And the bread is hopeless!" But Mamma beamed at her friend.

Marie Deaver wore a pink bouclé suit that set off her angora-fluffy white hair. "Then you've worked your little miracles again." With one white-gloved hand she touched Mamma's salmon-colored knit dress. "Lovely dress! Oh, hello, Rina, dear."

"Hello." Rina smiled and nodded, feeling foolish, the magazine clutched behind her.

"Is Bobby's quilt done?" Marie Deaver asked eagerly. She had purchased one of Rina's cheeriest works, but had asked Rina to add a wide border echoing the reds of the design so that it would cover her son Bobby's bed.

"Oh, yes, I finished it this week. I'll bring it right out!" Grateful for the excuse, Rina fled to her room, hiding the *Playgirl* under her workbasket before she pulled out the bright red-and-white quilt rolled in a protective plastic sheet. She carried it out to Marie Deaver.

"Wonderful! Here, Leonora, take my cheese puffs. My humble offering to this feast." Marie handed a foil-wrapped baking pan to Mamma and accepted the bundle from Rina.

"I'll just take the quilt out to my car now so I won't forget it. Bobby will love it. His teachers say he's very sensitive to art."

"Oh, good. I'm glad to hear it, Mrs. Deaver."

Bobby Deaver was in his forties. Autistic since infancy, institutionalized for most of his life, he would never be much better. His mother heard the note of doubt that had been in Rina's voice and said, "Well, it's a difficult problem. But they're trying. And you can't give up hope."

"Of course not," Rina agreed quickly. "And they learn more about it every year."

"Yes. And already he's happier. I'm sure of it."

"That's the important thing." Platitudes, but true all the same. Happiness: what we all want for our children.

"I'll be right back, Leonora." Marie Deaver was opening the door. "Then we'll warm up my cheese puffs."

"Oh, Marie, you're a dear!" Mamma's face, the skin as soft and thin as crêpe, crinkled into a smile. She carried the cheese puffs up the half-flight of steps from the entry hall to the living room and kitchen level. An act of kindness, Rina knew, smiling to herself. Cheese puffs weren't real food, not by Mamma's standards. Mamma was definitely more cheerful these days. They'd had months of moping at first, after money problems had forced her from her longtime Hoboken home to live here in the Maryland suburbs of Washington, D.C. with her daughter.

Hastily, Rina dodged back to her room, retrieved Ginny's magazine, and hurried across the hall and into Ginny's room, next to the bath. She closed the door firmly. There was a ragged stack of magazines in the nightstand. Needlework magazines, *Seventeens*, and one or two others with features on the dancer Baryshnikov. Rina tucked the *Playgirl* into the stack. Ought to make Ginny burn it. But this wasn't the time for a scene. She straightened and glanced around the room. Books crammed onto the bookshelves, almost as many more on the floor. Bed hastily made, little stuffed animals and dolls tumbled on the pillow. "Looks like a bomb site," Clint would grumble, "and they're the casualties."

"I keep the door closed, Dad," Ginny would reply frigidly, tossing back her long black hair and disappearing into the room with a slam.

There was a half-finished sewing project on the worktable, scissors and thread and scraps of muslin and broadcloth strewn across it. A box of kitty litter sat under the table. The cat himself lounged on the windowsill, well cared for, glossy as gold brocade in the sunlight, looking sleepily at Rina. Whatever Ginny's faults, she was a model mother to her adored pet.

"We try, Kakiy," said Rina to the cat, who remained royally unimpressed. And she had tried, fighting to overcome her handicap, to remake her life. "But you see, there's a generation gap."

Another platitude, another truth. Mamma was mercurial as a teenager herself these days, sometimes hugging Ginny and praising her art projects, other times lashing out at the girl's clothes, at her boyfriend, at her beloved cat. Not that Rina didn't agree with some of Mamma's complaints, but scolding wasn't the way to convince a willful teenager to change. Not today, not in 1979. Rina's teen years had been in World War II; she'd lost her older brother then, her parents' pride and hope, and at such a time of personal grief and national crisis, the rebellions of coming of age had been dwarfed, somehow, or at least muted by other problems.

Ginny, of course, made no attempt at all to understand her grandmother's frustrations, the natural resentment that came with losing your own home of fifty years and having to move in with your daughter's family. Rina and Clint had given Mamma the big room on the lower level with a private bath and a sliding glass door. It opened onto the garden that Mamma loved so much, and she had adapted well in some ways. She'd made her own friends at church. She was deferential to Clint, and left them plenty of privacy when he was home. From time to time she even tried to reach Ginny, with old family stories of immigrant days that usually concluded, "In America you can be anything!" But lately Ginny responded with boredom or with sarcasm, and it was no wonder that Mamma in turn flared back with Italian gusto.

And Rina, the middle generation, was buffeted by the constant angry flow and counterflow of their clashing demands. The carefully stitched fabric of her family had become a crazy quilt of conflict, stretched and strained until sometimes she felt that her own terrified grip was the only feeble thread that kept it from ripping apart at the seams.

Another dream of her youth was dying.

Ginny was thinking about her mother. A graceful, dark-haired young woman long ago, a dancer before Ginny was born. Ballet. Frail and lovely, headed for stardom before the tragedy. In her mind Ginny pirouetted with her mother in that once-upon-a-time spotlight, jetéed with her across the stage, graceful as a doe. In the audience her father, rich and young, burned with love for the pale vision in the light.

"Ginny Marshall!"

Shit. That tone meant that Mr. Hunt had already called her name once. Ginny gave Mr. Hunt a gentle, regal, ballerina smile and said, "Yes?"

"Number fourteen," whispered curly-haired Jan behind her.

Ginny glanced at the unread page open on the scarred desk before her and skimmed the question. "Um . . ." Oh, yeah, Browning. She looked straight into Hunt's rheumy yellow eyes and explained, "That means he had the duchess put to death. He was jealous because she enjoyed people and things besides him."

"Fine." Mr. Hunt didn't sound pleased. Well, screw you, Hunt. Ginny went back to her dream.

After school Buck stopped by her locker. She had just decided grudgingly to take her books home, three quizzes tomorrow, when she felt his tongue on her ear. "Hiya, Blue-Eyes." He was stoned already.

She pulled her fedora on firmly. "Hi."

"Got a present," he murmured, handing her an envelope. *Happy birthday, love, Buck,* it said.

"Can't wait till tomorrow, huh?" She smiled at him and looked inside. A handful of white pills. "Ludes?"

"Ludes. Lemmon. The best on the old man's shelf."

"Hey, wow!" She tucked them into her black vest.

"Tomorrow we really party." A flicker of uncertainty as he chucked her under the chin. "Wanna go for a ride now?"

"No way. I'm about to flunk math," she lied.

"Okay. Maybe I'll swing by about five, see if you can handle it then."

Linda, her eyes hungry, was waiting for her beside the door. "What went down with Buck, Ginny? What'd he give you?"

"Vitamin Q."

"Oh, my God! All I have is a joint."

"Okay. Trade you." Feeling generous, Ginny pulled out several pills. "You better go easy, Linda."

Linda was already swallowing one. "These can't hook you."

"Yeah, that's what my mother thought too," said Ginny ominously.

"Your mother?"

"Whiskey back in those days. She thought she could handle it too, and then one day she took an axe to her five children in a drunken fit."

"Oh, come on!" Linda frowned uneasily. She wasn't very bright.

"Except the baby. I was the baby," explained Ginny matter-of-factly. "She tried to strangle me."

"You're goofing on me!"

"Listen, I can see it all as clear as yesterday," Ginny insisted. "Good old Mummy, and my brothers cowering against the wall, and Mummy swaying a little with a whiskey bottle in one hand and the axe in the other. Wow! And then just hacking away."

"Jesus, Ginny!"

"And I only am escaped alone to tell thee. I hid under the bleeding bodies. She was smashed out of her gourd and thought I was dead."

"Your mother's no drunk." Cheeks flushing, Linda gave a sudden drugged giggle. The lude was beginning to lift her above worried thoughts, out of Ginny's reach.

"Well, after that she joined AA. See you around." Ginny slung her backpack over one shoulder and bounded out to climb on the bus.

It was getting late. Rina went to her room to pack her workbasket and her demonstration project, a quilted landscape of hills and trees called "Autumn." In the corner of the room, a stack of brightly wrapped presents waited, a frail tower of hope for the future. Ginny would be sixteen tomorrow. Maybe time would help. Transitions were confusing, and what transition was more complex than the one from child to adult? Like being hurtled from fireside to angry open sea. She and Clint had done their best, surrounding Ginny's girlhood with music, laughter, books, love—oh, hell, what did she expect? The Spock Award for Excellence in Parenting? Some days she thought she should never have tried to be a mother at all.

"Mamma?" Pulling on her trench coat, Rina hurried up the half-flight and peeked into the kitchen. It was a delightful array of mouth-watering plates: a hot anchovy dip surrounded by fresh cherry tomatoes and cauliflower and broccoli, crostini toasted and bright with a sun-dried tomato spread, a cold meat platter starring velvety mortadella brought back from her last visit to Hoboken, flaky triangles filled with prosciutto and fragrant with rosemary. The little bridge party would never finish it all, but that meant wonderful leftovers for the rest of them. Rina sampled the broccoli and dip. "Mmm! Wonderful! Have fun, Mamma. I'm going to the college now. Back in a couple of hours."

"Okay, *cara*, good-bye." Her mother kissed her exuberantly, invigorated by the upcoming party. "We'll save you a bite of everything."

"Good! It's wonderful! Oh, hello, Ginny."

Ginny dropped her backpack by the front door and pulled the battered fedora from her black hair. She looked tired, Rina thought, the dark-blue eyes haunted, the leggy young figure drooping. "Hi, Mom," she responded, leaning back against the door to close it before walking slowly up the stairs to kiss Rina and Mamma. "Hi, Gram. How are you, Mrs. Deaver?"

"Fine. Ginny, show me your new soft sculpture. We have time, don't we, Leonora?"

"The others will be here soon." Mamma's brows twitched a warning.

"It won't take long." Marie Deaver urged Ginny ahead down the half-flight to the bedroom hall level, and she and Rina followed the girl to her room. Kakiy bounded joyfully from the windowsill to greet them, and Ginny, cooing, scooped him up. With her free hand she picked up her scissors from the work table, snipped a thread, then offered the ugly muslin baby to the white-haired woman. Marie Deaver understood Ginny's work better than most of Mamma's friends, Rina thought, watching from the hall. Marie loved art, opera, the symphony, and she frequently accompanied Mamma to Wolf Trap. She knew that the purpose of art was not necessarily prettiness. She wouldn't say politely, like another of Mamma's friends, "What a sweet doll!" only to have Ginny reply just as politely, "Yes, ma'am. It's called 'Auschwitz Baby.' Very sweet."

Marie Deaver's brows rose, but she inspected it thoughtfully. Its embroidered eyes were squeezed closed, its mouth unhappy between gaunt muslin cheeks. The thin little body was not floppy, but stuffed taut, hands and legs extended rigidly, except for one bent knee curled tense against its stomach. "She'll have a short red shirt," said Ginny. "Tight around the neck."

"Yes." Marie Deaver nodded in satisfaction as she replaced the haunting little figure on the worktable. "That'll be perfect. It's a good piece, Ginny. Tough."

"Thanks."

Mamma came in with Ginny's hat and backpack and dropped them on the chest of drawers. "I still like the bears best. She used to make real cute ones." She shook her head in distaste at the odd, ugly little stuffed baby lying in the midst of Ginny's scraps of muslin and padding, needles and scissors. Rina tensed, but fortunately Ginny held her peace, cuddling the cat against her flame-red sweater.

"Oh, but Leonora, this is Art," said Marie Deaver lightly.

"That's what Rina says too," admitted Mamma.

"And the Crafts Fair jury." Marie Deaver smiled at Rina and waved a hand at one of Ginny's dolls, framed and hanging on the wall next to the door, a red ribbon still attached to the frame. "Come on, Leonora. She's too clever for us old folks." She herded Mamma expertly from the room.

Rina kissed Ginny good-bye, then Mamma, and hurried out to the car. Gloomy cool day, rain coming. But the begonias Mamma had planted were still vivid, scarlets and pinks as bright as glazed chintz against the dark-stained cedar of the shingled house. Her dream house. She and Clint had planned and saved for years for this house, had chosen every handmade tile in the kitchen, every lighting fixture. And it was lovely, a graceful friendly split-level nestled into the trees of this wooded suburb. A house with room for beauty and love, she'd thought. Illusions, illusions.

She backed out of the driveway, waving at Delores Gallagher, who was just arriving. Someone was with Delores. A man. Rina turned toward the University of Maryland. Rina was teaching a quilting course at the crafts union. Today she wanted to show the students the importance of relationships. She had a scrap of calico, a muddy gray-brown print, ugly to look at; but it would spring to life and become rich and lovely when she pieced it into the shadowed side of a fruitful hill.

That at least was true.

"Keep that cat in your room," warned Gram over her shoulder as Mrs. Deaver led her down the hall.

"I always do, Gram." Ginny closed the door behind them, then put Kakiy down and looked unhappily at the muslin baby.

Oh, God. Oh, God, she thought, help me, whoever I am.

Mrs. Deaver was a pretty good sport. Ginny decided to remove the *Playgirl*. She slipped hastily into the hall and into the bathroom next door. But the magazine was gone already. Mom, probably. Bad scene coming up, especially if she told Dad.

The doorbell rang. More of Gram's friends arriving.

"Hello, Delores," said Gram warmly. "How are you?"

Oh, shit, thought Ginny, seeing Kakiy dart past the bathroom door toward the living room. She should have checked to make sure her door had latched. Ginny eased into the hall to pursue him furtively.

"Hello, Leonora." Mrs. Gallagher was a tall, jolly woman, not as bright as Mrs. Deaver but popular with Gram and her friends. She enjoyed knitting, a waste of a good skill as far as Ginny could see, because she favored garish garments of clumsy design. Today her magenta raincoat came off to reveal a creation of lemon-yellow, with a pair of purple iris emblazoned across the ample Gallagher front. They were done in a bulky yarn that gave the edges of the flowers a stepped effect, as though they'd been built of cinder blocks. But Gram didn't comment on the sweater, because her eyes were glued to Mrs. Gallagher's companion. Mrs. Gallagher, her hand hooked possessively in the crook of his elbow, said, "I'd like you to meet John Spencer." He was a thin man with a paunch, strands of gray hair combed back to cover his bald spot, a yellowish complexion, a pleasant smile.

"Pleased to meet you," said Gram, with what looked to Ginny like a simper.

"Delighted." Mr. Spencer bowed his head politely as he handed her his trench coat. His light tweed suit looked expensive and neat.

"Please come in," Gram said. "Marie is here already."

Mr. Spencer walked up the half-flight rather stiffly, but at the top exclaimed, "Mrs. Rossi, what a perfectly lovely home!"

"Yes. My daughter has done very well," said Gram graciously. Actually she complained periodically that they needed brighter colors. Ginny, annoyed, had once suggested that maybe Gram should move in with Mrs. Gallagher. Mom had shut her up, of course. But thank God, Mom remained adamant about the decorating, and managed to keep Gram's heart-shaped pillows and Grand Canyon paintings limited to Gram's own room. Just as Kakiy was supposed to be limited to Ginny's. Ginny edged up the steps, seeking the cat.

"Leonora! What a feast!" Mrs. Gallagher had peeked into the kitchen. "Oh, you Eye-talians are so extravagant!"

"Just a little snack, Delores," Gram said modestly.

Mrs. Gallagher laughed and squeezed Gram's shoulders.

Mr. Spencer had made his way across the room to the glass doors that led to the deck. Mrs. Deaver, who had been looking out, now turned to meet him.

"Why, Mrs. Darcy, isn't it?" he asked.

"Deaver," she said, smiling. "Marie Deaver."

"Yes, of course," he said. "What a lovely suit you're wearing."

"Oh, you've met before?" caroled Mrs. Gallagher, flouncing out of the kitchen, lemon-yellow sails billowing.

"Just casually," said Mr. Spencer. "In the supermarket out at Eastland mall, wasn't it? How wonderful to have this chance to know you better!"

An old gallant, thought Ginny disgustedly. But it seemed to be working: Mrs. Deaver was smiling at him warmly, and Gram and Mrs. Gallagher were looking on with something remarkably like jealousy. Love among the ruins.

Then Ginny spotted Kakiy. He was crouched behind the big terra cotta pot that held the rubber plant, watching them all. Ginny began to sidle along the wall behind the piano toward him. Gram, fluffing her iron-gray hair, was saying, "Mr. Spencer, would you help me with the chairs, please?"

"I'd be delighted to help you with *anything.*" He beamed at her. Mrs. Gallagher fidgeted with her garish garment, looking uncomfortable. Mrs. Deaver merely eyed them narrowly as he and Gram went to the hall closet where the chairs were kept.

What if Gram wins and marries him? Ginny thought with a sudden lurch of hope. But she quashed the idea quickly. Mr. Spencer would not be that dumb. In the light from the glass doors she could see that his suit, of expensive tweed, was wearing a little on the seat and elbows. Well, none of them were rich, not even Mrs. Deaver. Gram certainly wasn't. If Gram were rich, she wouldn't be living here.

Ginny had almost reached Kakiy when Gram, returning with the cards, spotted her. "Ginny, what are you doing?" she asked, annoyed.

"I'm sorry, Gram. Kakiy got out. I'm getting him now."

"Ginny, I told you and told you to keep that cat in your room!" Gram bristled, her dark eyes snapping, her explosion of gray hair flaring out, making Ginny think of the feisty schnauzer next door.

Mr. Spencer, bringing across two chairs, sneezed. "Is it a cat?" he asked apologetically. "I'm afraid I'm allergic to cats."

Gram lost control. "Scat, scat!" she shouted, running at Kakiy. He darted from behind the planter out into the room and paused, confused.

Mr. Spencer sneezed again. Gram kicked at Kakiy.

The sharp corner of her heel grazed the cat.

Gram looked astonished and started to apologize, but Ginny was already screaming, "You old bitch! Can't you even wait for me to get him?"

Kakiy, yowling, was streaking for the bedroom hall.

"Ginny, be calm," soothed Mrs. Deaver.

"Young lady," said Mr. Spencer severely, "you should never, never address your grandmother that way!"

"Yeah? Why don't you tell her how to address a helpless little cat, you old fart!"

She was running back down to the bedroom corridor after Kakiy. Shocked comments from Gram and Mr. Spencer and Mrs. Gallagher crackled behind her. "I'm so sorry, John! That girl was born rotten!" Gram fumed. "She might as well stab me in the back, she's so thoughtless!"

"Hey, let's not let a silly cat spoil a good party!" sang out Mrs. Gallagher.

Kakiy had fled into the den. Ginny closed the door tightly and inspected him, swallowing her sobs. He was licking a patch on his side, but the skin was scarcely scratched and he was calming down. She stroked him, and eventually he began purring.

The horrified exclamations from the living room had subsided, and the old people were at their bridge game now, discussing each hand with animation. Mr. Spencer was complimenting Gram's cooking. Ginny heard Mrs. Gallagher pass the den door on her way to the bathroom across the hall, and later Mrs. Deaver, and finally Mr. Spencer. Old flabby bladders. And still flirting like the kids in study hall.

Kakiy had gone to sleep, but Ginny still seethed with guilt and fury.

She pulled Buck's birthday present from her pocket, looked at it, and swallowed half a lude. Her eye fell on Dad's desk. The bottom drawer, she knew, held the little metal strongbox.

Shit, why not? She was born rotten, right? Besides, tomorrow was her birthday.

Rina knew when she arrived that something had gone wrong. Her mother's eyes were stormy, the cheerfulness of the others a little forced. Rina greeted them all, then asked, "Where's Ginny?"

"Den," said Mamma tersely. As Rina started down the steps, she added, "I begged her on bended knee not to let that cat out."

"I'll talk to her, Mamma." Rina the go-between. Why didn't they warn you that you had to be a diplomat, chief ambassador, *before* you decided to become a mother? The job description was grossly inadequate. Rina took a deep breath and opened the door. "Hi, honey."

Ginny, her cat dozing at her knee, was sitting cross-legged on the floor looking through the strongbox. "Hi, Mom," she said dreamily. "Kakiy's better. Gram kicked him."

Rina inspected the scratch. "She did that?"

"Yeah."

"Oh, dear." Rina sat down on the floor next to Ginny and put her arm around her. "I'm sorry, honey. What are you looking for in the box?"

"Why is she sho—so mean to him?"

"She's never done anything like this before, honey. But you know the cat upsets her. And she did have guests."

"She shouldn't be so mean."

"I think she's unhappy because she misses her own home."

"But she's been here in Maryland two years!"

"She was there for fifty. In charge."

"Well, she still shouldn't kick Kakiy." Ginny smiled beatifically.

The smile cut cruelly at Rina's heart. A few weeks ago, stumbling in after a movie with Buck, Ginny had been like this. Giggling, she had denied Rina's accusation of being drunk. "Ludes, Mom," she'd explained, half confiding, half cruel, and Rina's world had ripped apart.

But what could you do? Rage about it and lose the close relationship that was so important, and so hard to maintain these days? Or smile politely as though it were okay for your daughter to waste her shining young life?

Clint had raged. "That does it! We'll ground her, Rina. No daughter of mine—"

"Please, Clint. She probably hasn't thought it through. Let me try to explain to her."

Rina had waited a day, found a booklet on the dangers of drugs, and faced her daughter. "Honey, I don't want to make a big thing out of an experiment. But drugs are off-limits in this family."

"For sure, Mom. No problem."

The ironic flash in the blue eyes hurt Rina. She had exclaimed, "Ginny, think of your future! You're bright and talented. You can do anything you want!"

Ginny had smiled tauntingly. "Like you, Mom?"

But at least she hadn't come home high again. Till now.

Rina couldn't trust herself to mention it directly today. She said, "Honey, if you have problems, please tell me about them. Don't run from things. You have to face them."

"Oh? You tell me to face them? You? Funny old Mom!"

"Yes, damn it! I've faced problems!" And a hell of a lot bigger than whatever you think yours are, she almost added. But she swallowed her rage; Ginny was high, so arguing wouldn't help now. She said more calmly, "It's just that you could be hurt. I don't want that."

"Yeah, for sure. I could be hurt." That shining, cruel smile again. "Or I could be an addict. Or I could be a movie star. In America I could be anything!" Ginny pushed herself to her feet, scooping up Kakiy. She carried him steadily enough into her bedroom. Rina followed as far as the door. Ginny had made an insert for her backpack, a sturdy cardboard cat carrier with a round porthole window. She put Kakiy into it, took her waterproof poncho from the closet, clapped the fedora onto her head, then frowned at her cluttered table for a moment. Finally she picked up a box of cat treats.

"Where are you going, honey?" asked Rina.

"Library."

Rina sighed. Better to talk to her later. "Okay. See you at dinner."

"Yeah. Save the whales." She kissed Rina almost contemptuously, then pushed by and swung down the hall. Kakiy, unapologetic, gazed back serenely through his porthole as she marched out the door.

She wasn't back for dinner. Rina fought down her worry. But when her mother finally excused herself and went downstairs to her room, she said to Clint, "Maybe Ginny thought we'd be eating late, because of the bridge game."

"Maybe." Clint, silvery-haired and blue-eyed, paused with a last forkful of cherry pie halfway to his mouth. "You're worried, though."

"Yes."

He tried to be comforting. "She's probably just throwing her weight around."

"Maybe."

"Rina, I hate to see you worrying like this! It's time to get her back in line. It's no favor to go easy on a kid these days. But it's up to you, Rina. I'll back you up, but I'm not here much of the time, damn it."

"She had reason to be mad today."

"Half her fault," he pointed out. He was too much the lawyer, she thought, always ready to see both sides of a question and argue whichever suited him. Rina busied herself cleaning off the table.

But when the doorbell rang at eight-fifteen Rina ran to it, her anxious heart a staccato counterpoint to her footsteps. Two men stood there: stolid faces, intelligent eyes. The older one held out a shield. Police.

"Ginny?" she blurted before they could say anything. "Has something happened to Ginny?"

"No, ma'am," said the older policeman. His voice was flat-pitched, unexcitable. "We're here to ask about a John Spencer."

"Spencer?"

Behind her, Mamma laid a firm hand on her arm. "John Spencer was here this afternoon. Is there a problem?"

"Yes, ma'am. Are you Mrs. Marshall?"

"I'm Mrs. Rossi. Leonora Rossi," Mamma corrected him. "My daughter here is Mrs. Marshall. But I'm the one who knows John Spencer. Not well—we just met this afternoon."

"I see. Well, ma'am, I'd like to ask you a few questions."

Clint had come up behind them. "We'd be glad to help," he said. "What's the problem?"

In answer the policeman held up his identification again. "Just a few questions, sir," he repeated. "I'm Sergeant Trainer. Homicide."

II

"Homicide!" exclaimed Mamma.

Clint said, "Please come in," and Rina showed them up to the living room. Trainer was middle-aged, skin weathered to the rough texture of burlap, shrewd light-blue eyes a bit like Clint's. The other detective, Carmody, ruddy-faced and younger, deferred to him.

They settled themselves on the leather sofa, and Carmody produced a little notebook. Trainer said, "Thank you. We're trying to find out something about Mr. Spencer, about what he did today."

"I'm afraid I can't help," said Clint. He had settled into his favorite chair, next to Rina's. "I commute into Washington, and they'd all left before I got back from work, so I never met him. Can you tell us why you're asking us about him, Sergeant?"

"Yes, sir. He had an appointment book. It gave this address for three o'clock this afternoon."

"Yes, that was my bridge party," said Mamma.

"That was the last thing in his book for today. At two-thirty he had written the name 'Gallagher.' Does that mean anything to anyone?"

"That would be Delores Gallagher," said Mamma. "She drove him over. He doesn't have a car."

"I see. Could you give me Delores Gallagher's address?"

Mamma did so, and added, "She met him through a

church friend a year ago. But Sergeant Trainer, you said homicide. Is John Spencer dead?"

"Yes, ma'am. He was stabbed."

Stabbed. Rina saw the word working on Mamma, the horror slowly seeping into her expression. Rina reached over to take her hand. It was trembling. Mamma shook her head. "No, no! It can't be true! I just saw him!"

"Yes, ma'am. Now, you say this was a bridge party?"

Trainer's calm voice helped. Mamma concentrated on his question. "Yes. Delores and Marie Deaver and I usually play with Marge Buford, but she's away visiting family for a couple of weeks. So Delores said she'd invite a man friend from her church. She knew he enjoyed bridge."

"And they arrived when?"

"Before three," said Mamma. "I don't know exactly. Marie Deaver got here first, then they came."

"I was driving away as they arrived," said Rina, thinking back. "It must have been about twenty to three, because Ginny was already back from school."

"Could I have this Marie Deaver's address?" asked Trainer.

Mamma gave it to him, and Trainer waited until Carmody had written it down before he continued, "So Mr. and Mrs. Marshall, you didn't meet Mr. Spencer?"

"I was at work, as I said," said Clint.

"I met him. I got back around four-thirty," said Rina. "I saw him very briefly. They all left a little after five."

"Did he indicate where he was going next?"

"Home, I thought. Delores was to drive him," said Mamma.

"Did he seem excited, or depressed?"

"Well, I don't know what he's usually like," said Mamma. "But not depressed. I suppose if anything we were all a little excited."

"Oh? Any special reason?"

Mamma's dark eyes snapped. "Ginny. Her cat. Her stupid boyfriend."

Mamma, shut the hell up, prayed Rina; but there was no stopping her. The detectives heard a full account of the altercation, of Ginny's insults to Mr. Spencer. "I didn't mean to hurt the creature. But it's going to give me a heart attack someday! She knows the cat isn't allowed in the living room. And right when I was having a party! In my own home! And poor John is allergic to cats, and she was yelling insults—" For a moment Mamma's lips trembled. She concluded more quietly, "Oh, I'm too hotheaded sometimes, I know that. She's young and selfish, we've all been young and selfish. Anyway, finally she and the cat went into the den, and we went ahead with our game. Then Rina came home, and she said hello and went to talk to Ginny."

Trainer's light, shrewd eyes moved to Rina, who nodded, trying not to glare at her mother. Didn't she realize that it wasn't going to help poor Mr. Spencer to tell all their private problems to the police? Well, try to get past this part. She said, "Yes, I talked to her. She was in the den with Kakiy. The cat. She was—upset."

"Upset." Carmody wrote it down.

Clint's hand on her arm helped Rina. She went on levelly, "We talked for a minute, and she decided to go out for a while. She took the cat with her."

"Before Mr. Spencer left?"

"Oh, yes. It was barely four-thirty. She said she was going to the library."

Carmody glanced at Trainer, whose gaze sharpened as he said, "I see. With the cat, you said?"

"She's made a sort of carrier for him, from her backpack. With the flap down no one can see him."

"Okay. And when did she return?"

"Well, she's not back yet," admitted Rina.

"In fact, when we arrived, you were afraid something had happened to her?"

"I was getting worried. I expected her back an hour ago."

"Does she often return later than expected?"

"Not often. Sometimes."

"Well, we would like to talk to your daughter when she gets back." He turned back to Mamma. "You mentioned Miss Marshall's boyfriend."

Mamma's nostrils flared. "Boyfriend! He's more of an animal than that cat! That girl's life is going right down the toilet because of him!"

"Now, Mamma, don't exaggerate," said Rina. "He's just a high-spirited boy." Not strictly true. Hadn't she been upset enough herself today to vow that he wouldn't set foot in this house again?

"Buck is rude," said Mamma bluntly. "And he was drunk. And he bumped into Mr. Spencer. I don't know what Ginny sees in him! Not that she wasn't yelling at Mr. Spencer too. Poor man. What a visit!"

"This boy had an argument with Mr. Spencer too?"

Rina said hastily, "Buck came to see Ginny. I told him she'd gone to the library, and he left right away to look for her."

"Buck. Last name?"

"Landon. He lives over on Monroe Boulevard. Dr. Landon's son."

"What happened between him and Mr. Spencer?"

Rina noticed that her hands were clenched together. She relaxed them and said, "It was just an accident."

"Accident!" snorted Mamma. "Being drunk is an accident?"

"Rina, is that right? Buck was drunk?" Clint demanded.

"He didn't mean to bump him!" Rina said, evading his question. "Mamma's friends were all down in the entry hall, saying good-bye, when he got here. Mamma opened the door.

She told him Ginny was gone, but he wanted to see for himself, and went to look in Ginny's room."

"Pushed right in like I was the doormat!" said Mamma.

"He forced his way in?" asked Clint.

"Sir, please let us ask the questions," said Sergeant Trainer mildly. Clint nodded and subsided into a glower. The sergeant turned back to Rina. "You saw him, then, Mrs. Marshall?"

"Yes, I'd come into the bedroom hall when the doorbell rang."

"And he was drunk?"

"Definitely!" said Mamma, and Rina nodded slowly. Better for Ginny if her boyfriend was reported drunk instead of high on ludes. So high he couldn't walk straight, or talk without slurring his words. Seeing him, Rina had resolved not to let the boy in the house again. There was no way to stop Ginny from seeing him at school, and she certainly didn't want to turn him into some kind of romantic martyr in her daughter's eyes. But it was important to underline her disapproval, somehow. Not that Buck had been unpleasant. He had smiled good-naturedly at Ginny's empty room, then turned back and launched himself toward the front door. He would have gotten there all right, lurching a little maybe, if Mr. Spencer hadn't inadvertently stepped into his way.

Clint was still frowning.

Rina said, "He was a little unsteady, and he did bump into Mr. Spencer. But he was perfectly friendly."

"There was no argument?" Trainer pursued.

"Well, Mamma and Mr. Spencer both spoke to him sharply. As though he was a little boy. At that age, you know, it can be very irritating."

"Well, he was acting like a little boy!" exclaimed Mamma indignantly. "What do you expect me to do, compliment him? He was the one bumping into people! And his big mouth! He told us to watch *our* step! Well, Mr. Spencer naturally told him to mind his tongue. Wouldn't you, Sergeant Trainer?"

Trainer didn't respond except to ask, "Were those Mr. Spencer's exact words? 'Mind your tongue?' "

"Pretty much."

Rina nodded agreement. "He said, 'They tell me your father is Dr. Landon. Fine man. I'm sure he wouldn't want you behaving this way. You must mind your tongue.' "

"And what did this Buck Landon say?"

Rina remembered the flicker of unease that disrupted Buck's happy expression, but before she could comment, her mother was answering the sergeant. "He said, 'I'll mind mine and you mind yours,' and then threw back his head and laughed as though he thought he was the world's biggest comedian." Mamma sniffed. "He's the world's biggest mouth, that's what he is."

"Is he a violent boy? Impulsive?" asked Trainer.

"No," said Rina hastily, before Mamma could answer. "He's active. On the football team, that sort of thing. But just a normal boisterous boy, not violent. And he was very— drunk." She heard an almost inaudible snort from Clint beside her.

"Okay. And after his joke about minding his tongue, he left to look for your daughter in the library?"

"That was my impression, yes," said Rina.

"Do you know if he found her?"

"I don't know. But his mother called here an hour ago asking for him. Maybe she saw them together."

Sergeant Trainer rubbed his burlappy chin. "But your daughter isn't back yet."

"Not yet," said Rina. She tried to stop squeezing the arms of her chair.

"Did Mr. Spencer say anything about his plans for the evening?"

Mamma said, "Delores and I were talking about a movie

that's going to be on TV tonight. He said he might watch it too."

"That's right, I remember," said Rina. "And Mrs. Deaver said she wanted to watch it too, but she'd have to hurry because she had to go to Eastland to pick up some groceries first. And then they all left."

"Did Mrs. Gallagher drive Mr. Spencer home?"

"Yes. Her apartment isn't far from his street."

"And after that? What did you all do?"

"Us?" Rina was surprised at the question. "We straightened up. Put away the card table. Then Mamma went out to buy dinner."

"That's right," said Mamma. "And some tuna for tomorrow." Mamma still observed meatless Fridays, no matter what the Vatican said. "I got back about six-thirty, and Clint a couple of minutes later."

Clint, still leaning back in his chair, said, "Sergeant Trainer, you're very interested in where we were. Was Mr. Spencer killed near here?"

Trainer hesitated, then said, "Well, I suppose you'll see it on TV tonight. The body was found three blocks away. Just outside the public library."

"Library!" The word rang like a gong in Rina's frightened ears. "But that's where Ginny was!"

"Yes, ma'am. A lot of people were there," said Trainer soothingly.

"But she might have—" She stopped, half out of her chair. Clint's hand was on her arm, restraining her.

"A lot of people were there, Rina," he said gently. "But you can see why Sergeant Trainer wants to talk to her."

Mamma's forehead was pleated in confusion. "But John Spencer went home with Delores!"

"Yes, ma'am. Now, can you think of anything else that might tell us something about his death?"

They all looked at each other. Rina remained silent, and

Mamma said, "I can't think of anything else. I can't believe this!"

"Well, call us if anything occurs to you." Trainer stood, and Carmody followed suit, pocketing his little notebook. "Please tell your daughter to contact us when she gets back."

"All right, Sergeant Trainer." Clint showed them to the door.

Mamma hurried downstairs to her own telephone to tell Marie and Delores the incredible news, but Rina remained in her chair, leaning forward, hands clasped, studying the shaggy hearth rug without seeing it. A killer at the library! Oh, God, Ginny, please be all right!

Buck had gone to the library too. Maybe she'd left with him and would be back soon. He was a strapping boy, he'd protect her.

If he wasn't stoned.

Clint came striding back up the stairs. "That does it, Rina! She's got to stop seeing that Landon kid!"

"Clint! Her life is in danger, and you're worried about Buck?"

"Her life?" He looked at her in astonishment, then picked up her hand in his and gave it a comforting squeeze. "Oh, God, Rina, don't frighten yourself! There were a lot of people there when Ginny was. Muggers look for people who are alone. That poor old man! No, I agree with your mother. Ginny's problem is that no-good boyfriend of hers."

Rina held his hand gratefully. Maybe Clint was right, maybe Ginny wasn't alone at the library. Buck had been looking for her. Though that was a problem too. "About Buck. We can keep him out of the house, Clint, and I will. But we can't stop her from seeing him."

"Why not? We could take away—oh, hell." Clint ran a hand angrily through his hair. "You're right, Rina, we can't lock her up. But it's so damn frustrating! We can't let her throw away her life like this. There must be an answer some-where!"

"I guess we could change her to another school."

"Oh, they'd defy us." Clint gloomed. "Meet in secret."

"I know." Rina was glad he understood. "They'd think they were Romeo and Juliet."

"Anyway, we've already got her in the so-called best school in the area! Well, she's not stupid. We'll just have to hope she comes to her senses." Clint stamped across to his chair and hid behind the *Washington Post.*

"Yes, she'll settle down soon," Rina murmured to the news-paper.

Still, she worried. Poor Mr. Spencer. She knew him so slightly. His death shocked her without quite seeming real. Ginny's problems, on the other hand, were vivid. She'd been at the library with a killer loose! And Buck, on drugs, what kind of company did he keep? Her daughter was not a drug user, not really, not often. Ginny was confused right now, maybe, but weren't most teenagers confused?

But then Rina hurried to the phone to try to call Buck and Ginny's other friends. She had to find her. Because another frightening thought had suddenly surfaced. Muggers wanted money. And Ginny might have some. Rina had glanced through their strongbox as she put it away. The papers were there, the wills, the medical records from Dr. Panolous, the agency letter from Mrs. Farnham, the passports they'd used for the Mexican vacation, the insurance.

But Ginny's bankbook, the one she could sign for herself, was gone.

Friday, September 14, 1979

III

Nick O'Connor's shoes gurgled as he crossed Flatbush Avenue. The rain had begun in earnest before he'd caught the bus at La Guardia, and by now was streaming down here in Brooklyn. You cataracts and hurricanoes, spout till you have drench'd our steeples. He hoped Julia's flight wouldn't be delayed. His neighbor was on her way to Seattle to take part in a children's book conference at the University of Washington, and to see her daughter. It would be a shame if the weather interfered. Well, Julia could take it, she was as tough as they came. It had been all he could do to get her to consent to his help getting her suitcases to the airport.

Horrendous rain. He adjusted the cap on his bald head and huddled into his raincoat, turning from Flatbush to hurry down Eighth Avenue to Garfield. The young trees on his block shimmered behind gauzy veils of rain. Nick ran up the steps of the brownstone to his front door, fumbling for his keys. The rain was relentless, and the stoop offered little shelter from the wind-driven gusts. Poor Nick's a-cold.

He had the key in the lock when he became aware that someone had been waiting, had climbed the steps behind him. He glanced around in mild surprise and found himself gazing into a pair of blue eyes.

It was like being slammed by a baseball bat.

She was young, still in her teens, and very wet. Rain dribbled off her black fedora, down long strands of black hair, down the folds of a poncho. She stood stiffly, almost belligerently, and he realized she was frightened and struggling to be dignified. She said, "Please, does Margaret Mary Ryan live here?"

For a wild instant Nick wanted to say no, to send her away, to banish this disturbing person from his life before the inevitable trouble followed. But he knew that the forces at work here could not be denied. He said politely, "She should be back soon. Would you like to come in and wait?"

She leaned dizzily against the stone balustrade, blinking, as though she hadn't really expected this answer. She said, "Yes, please."

They went together into the hall, and he took her streaming hat and poncho and hung them with his raincoat on the brass coat tree. She was wearing jeans, a flame-red cabled sweater, a man's black vest, and she held a backpack in her arms. There was a faint stench about her, as though she'd been sick, but she looked healthy enough, surveying every detail of the hall with fascination. He rubbed his wet hands on his jeans and said, "I'm Nick O'Connor."

Those amazing eyes settled on him again, checking his black turtleneck, his bulky frame, his bald head and homely face. "My business is with Margaret Mary Ryan."

"Okay. Maggie will be here soon. Why don't you sit down in here a moment and dry off? I'll go get us both some coffee, if you want some too."

"Yes, please."

He indicated the door at the back of the hall and they went into the big dining room. Again, she looked hungrily around the room, wordlessly inspecting the round oak table, the baby grand piano, the fireplace, the French windows, the little cocker spaniel that Nick had scooped up at the door. "Have a seat. I'll put the dog out in our backyard and be right back," he said. "It's a raw day, isn't it?"

"For sure." She chose a chair that faced out into the room and put the backpack carefully under it.

Nick carried the spaniel to the back door. "It's all right, Zelle," he murmured to her as he put her on the porch; then, with a deep breath, "at least I hope so." He fixed the coffee, trying to get his dismay under control. This was not the way it was supposed to happen. Look, Nick old man, he told himself, you've weathered tougher storms than this. But he wasn't sure that it was true.

She was up looking at the framed theatrical posters on the wall when he pushed open the swinging door to bring in the coffee. "Cream and sugar?" he asked.

She jerked around, that frightened look again, that endearing struggle for dignity. "Yes, please." She sat down.

He handed her a mug and placed the cream and sugar before her. "There you are."

"Thank you, Mr. O'Connor."

"You're welcome." How inanely mannerly they were. Practically Victorian. Diplomacy across an unbridgeable gulf. He sipped his coffee black while she carefully measured the cream and sugar and stirred her mug. Then he said, "I'm afraid I don't know your name."

But the busy young mind was pursuing its own concerns. She asked, "Is Margaret Mary Ryan your—" Then she stopped, confused.

He smiled. "We're married, yes. She kept her own name."

"I see." He could almost see the chaotic thoughts tumbling after each other behind her guarded face. She drank some more coffee, hiding behind the mug just as he was doing, then began, "How long—"

There was a noise. "What was that?" asked Nick, grateful for the distraction.

"Just Kakiy. My cat." Nonchalantly, she reached down and flipped open the top of the backpack. Golden eyes looked out at them.

Nick squatted on the floor. "Does she want to come out?"

"He's been out. He's okay."

"But maybe he'd like to look around. It's okay, I put our dog outside."

She shrugged. "Okay." She opened the top. A beautiful orange cat hopped out and strolled over to Nick.

"Hello, fellow," he said, and tickled him behind the ears. In a minute the cat decided to tour the room and ambled away toward the piano.

"He's nice," said Nick, returning to his chair. "You said his name was Cocky?"

"Spelled K-A-K-I-Y. Short for Akakiy Akakiyevich."

Nick laughed. "Because his overcoat is cat fur!"

Her astounded eyes fastened on Nick again. "You know Gogol?" she blurted.

"Sure. I like him." He would have gone on, but realized suddenly how upset she was. Until now he'd been only a means to an end, like a gatekeeper or porter. Suddenly she had seen him as a person too, and was rethinking her position.

She was very young.

She lurched to her feet, looking queasy. "Maybe I'd better come back later."

He wanted to say, yes, it would be better. But he knew he couldn't let this beautiful, wet, smelly child get away now. "No, no," he said, "it won't be long. Finish your coffee, at least. Maybe the rain will let up."

Still clutching the back of her chair, she looked down at her mug. "No, really, I just wanted to sell her a magazine subscription. I'd better—"

"Just a minute." Nick had heard the scrape of a key in the door. He bolted for the hall before she could stop him.

Maggie left her cardinal-red umbrella open in the tiled vestibule and breezed in, still dripping. "Hello, love. Horrendous storm! I feel like a—"

"Maggie, you've got a visitor."

Her vivid energy condensed, focussed on him, and she paused halfway out of her raincoat. "Who is it?"

"She hasn't told me her name."

He took her raincoat and hung it up, then followed her into the dining room. Just inside the door Maggie halted, one hand gripping the door frame for support.

The two stared at each other. Maggie was taller and more angular than the girl, with heavier bones, a blue plaid suit instead of damp jeans, black curls instead of straight wet hair. But the two pleasant squared faces were similar, and the two pairs of intense blue eyes locked on each other now were identical.

There was no question of magazine subscriptions.

They gazed at each other for a long moment. Then the girl blurted, "Is it naturally curly?"

"Yes."

"Shit."

Laughter flickered in Maggie's eyes. She asked, "What's your name?"

"They call me Ginny."

"Virginia?"

"Yes."

"Shit."

The girl looked startled, then grinned as she took Maggie's meaning. "Oh, God. Well, their cover story is that they thought it was a pretty name."

"It is. What's your whole name?"

"They say it's Virginia Alice Marshall."

Maggie gave a quick nod of approval and relief. She walked over to the girl and picked up both her hands. "Hey," she said, "I'm glad you came, Ginny. Happy birthday." Then she slipped a blue plaid arm companionably around the suddenly rigid young shoulders and turned back to face Nick, who was still waiting in the doorway. "Nick, love," she said, "I'd like you to meet Ginny. My daughter."

He'd known, of course; but it didn't make it any easier. Nick closed a mental door on the pleasant chaos of his life to date and bowed his head politely. "Pleased to meet you," he lied.

IV

The three of them looked at each other. Nick wondered if the girl's emotions were churning as much as his and Maggie's were. She was holding herself very stiffly under Maggie's friendly arm, and Maggie withdrew it as she said, "We've got a lot to talk about, Ginny. You can stay a while?"

"Yeah. I guess."

"Great. Then maybe you want some dry clothes. Do you have a change in your backpack?"

"No." She was in full retreat, Nick saw, flinging up defenses, pulling into herself. Not surprising. Even Maggie, who had longed for this encounter for years, was looking damn shaky.

"I'll loan you a pair of jeans, then, until yours dry," Maggie suggested.

Ginny said coolly, "Mr. O'Connor gave me coffee. I'm fine. Thank you."

God, this was going to be as difficult as he'd feared. Maybe they'd do better without him. Nick said, "I'll get you a cup too, Maggie."

"Thanks."

Nick went into the kitchen and let the little spaniel in from the porch, where she was huddling damply. "Welcome to the great reunion," he muttered to her. He got out a mug and put it on the round oak table by the window.

"Who brought you here, Ginny?" he could hear Maggie asking in the dining room. Changing the subject.

"Nobody."

"You came by yourself?"

"Yes."

Nick finished pouring the coffee and sidled through the swinging door so the dog couldn't follow. Maggie took the mug without looking at it. He could sense the strain in her, the storm of emotion held under tight control. But her voice was pleasant and friendly. "Did you get my letters, Ginny?"

"Letters?"

"She didn't give you the letters?"

"Who?"

"The caseworker. Mrs. Farnham. I wrote you a letter every year for your birthday. Just took one over Tuesday, in fact. The letters were supposed to go in the file, and then if you ever asked about me, you were supposed to get them."

Ginny looked stunned and shook her head wordlessly. Then she frowned. "Maybe I saw one. Did it have this address?"

"No. It had to be nonidentifying. Very general. They all did."

"I mean on the envelope. The return address."

"Yes." Maggie was puzzled now too. "But Mrs. Farnham wouldn't have given that to you. Only nonidentifying stuff. And I thought she was going to wait until you were of age even for that."

"I sort of jumped the gun." Ginny looked down at her cat, who was nuzzling her ankles. "Actually, Mrs. Farnham didn't tell me anything."

"Your mother, then? Did she find out somehow?"

"Her! She doesn't know. Doesn't want to know."

"You found out by yourself?"

"Yes."

"Hey! How?" Maggie's delighted approval was apparent. Nick could see that Ginny was caught off balance again.

Whatever she'd expected, Maggie wasn't it. The girl picked up her big cat and held him across her chest, a furry shield. They could hurt each other, she and Maggie. Nick, a helpless bystander, pulled out a chair from the table and sat down.

"Cream, Maggie?" He reached for the little pitcher.

"Oh. Thanks," she said absently, holding her mug down so he could add it. She took a few sips, a little frown on her face, measuring the warring emotions in the girl's silence. Finally she said, "Ginny, look. I'm glad you're here. Incredibly glad. Let me tell you what I'm thinking, and you can just say if I'm right or wrong, okay?"

"Yeah. Maybe." Her nose was still buried in the cat's gingery fur.

"Okay. I think you've been curious about me for a long time, because that's natural."

"Gram doesn't think so."

"Well, I hate to disagree with Gram, but I think it's natural. Because I've been curious as hell about you."

"Yeah." There was a warm instant of fellow-feeling in the girl's wary blue eyes.

Maggie continued, "And you came today because it was your birthday."

"Partly. Yeah."

"And your parents don't know you're here."

She groped for an answer, then seemed to realize that her silence had already said it. "No, they don't know," she admitted. "They couldn't handle it."

Maggie exchanged a quick glance with Nick. Bad news. But he knew already they could not send her back. He nodded briefly. Ginny caught the look and frowned angrily down at the cat in her arms. "Maybe I should call Mom."

"Okay," said Maggie.

Nick said, "The phone is in the kitchen."

"I'll pay you back for it," she said belligerently. Carrying Kakiy, she followed them into the kitchen. Zelle leaped up, interested, and Nick picked her up to avoid problems. But the cat merely blinked disdainfully at the little spaniel and set out on a tour of the countertop as soon as Ginny put him down. Nick sat by the oak table, Zelle in his lap.

Maggie indicated the wall at the end of the counter. "It's right there."

The girl stared down at her wet shoes, as though trying to think of what to say. Finally she dialed, stabbing her finger savagely at the phone. Someone answered almost immediately. Ginny said, "Hello, Mom. . . . Yeah, I'm fine. I just wanted to tell you not to worry. . . . I'm in Philadelphia. It's okay, I'm with friends. . . . Just friends, okay? Don't worry about it. . . . Mom, for Chrissake, don't flake out! I'm not dead, I'm not raped, I'm not kidnapped, I'm not mugged. I'm not even high. Everything's mellow, okay? So just relax! I'll call you later."

She slammed the receiver down and stood glaring at it, jaw clenched. Then she looked over her shoulder at Maggie, who was standing near Nick by the oak table.

"Philadelphia," said Maggie. "Okay."

"I lie a lot," said Ginny defiantly.

Maggie shrugged. "Sometimes necessary."

Ginny whirled on her, anger flaming. "Listen! I'm trying to be up-front with you, okay? I lie a lot. And I sleep around some. So I'm not what you wanted either, am I? So all right, just say the word again and I'll leave!"

"Is this a contest?" asked Maggie mildly.

"What do you mean?"

"I mean, hell, I've done all that stuff too."

Disbelief gleamed in the young eyes. Ginny waved her arm at the rows of spices, shiny pots and pans, bentwood chairs, Maggie in her trim blue plaid suit. "Uh-uh. This whole place is pure bourgeois respectability!"

"Well, sure. If I feel like it, I'm respectable too."

"Well, I'm not!" Ginny flung her words like darts at Mag-

gie. "I do drugs. I hang out with the so-called wrong crowd. I
break rules."

"So do I."

"Oh? Like what? Parked too long at some meter?"

"Well, for example, when you were born, there was a rule
that I couldn't see you."

Nick looked up sharply at his wife, the knot of worry within
him tightening. She shouldn't expose her tenderest feelings to
this angry young stranger! But then he saw that Ginny's eyes
had jerked up too and locked again with Maggie's. His wife's
clear voice continued, "Back in 1963, they wouldn't let mothers see babies who were going to be adopted. The idea was to
erase the whole relationship. They took you away while I was
still groggy from all the sedatives they used to give. But I'd
checked out the hospital earlier, so I knew where the nursery
was. They gave me sleeping pills, but I hid them instead of
taking them. I didn't want to be dopey. I was thinking of a
plan."

All the defiance had drained from Ginny. Nick could see
her voracious hunger to learn about her birth. She asked
breathlessly, "A plan?"

"Yes." Maggie leaned back, hips propped against the table.
"The problem was that only nurses were allowed in the nursery, and the entrance was next to the head nurse's desk. A
tough, really sharp-eyed woman. Sort of the *Monitor* and the
Merrimac rolled into one. I thought I'd have to bash her with
a bedpan." A grin flickered across Ginny's face. Maggie went
on, "But luckily I overheard one of the younger nurses brag-
ging that she'd brought her dress to work because her boyfriend was going to pick her up right after her shift ended. So
I stole a sheet."

Nick stroked the little dog in his lap. He knew the story but
had never heard these details before. Across the room Ginny
was listening ravenously. She'd been there too, he realized. It
hit him suddenly how excluded he was from what these two

shared. Barred irrevocably. Nick the outsider. Ishmael O'Connor.

Come off it, Nick old man, he scolded himself. Jealous pangs were pointless. Besides, Maggie might need him. Ginny was a live bomb, unpredictable, and able to wound Maggie as no one else in the world could.

But at the moment, the live bomb was intent on Maggie's story. "You stole a sheet?"

"From the laundry cart. And just before the shift ended I sneaked into the nurse's restroom and hid in a stall. Just as she'd said, the nurse who had the boyfriend came in to change. Took her dress out of a little suitcase and put her uniform in it. And while she was trying to pull her dress over her puffy sixties hairdo, I tiptoed out and whisked her uniform from the suitcase and substituted the sheet."

Engrossed by the story, her young face rapt, Ginny was lovely even with damp stringy hair and spattered clothes. That enthusiasm, those eyes, so like Maggie's when he'd first seen her a dozen years ago. Ginny exclaimed, "God! Didn't she notice you?"

"Her dress was over her head. I dodged back into the stall like a flash. Hurt like hell, I remember. My stitches were brand new, and I wasn't supposed to move fast. Anyway, I waited till she was gone, and then sneaked the uniform back to my bed and under my pillow. They'd left me another pain-killer pill. I saved it too, and waited for the night shift."

"Not so many people?"

"Right. After dinner my roommate went to the john, and I put three pills on her table. When she came back I told her they'd left us more pills, and she took them all like a little lamb. And—" Maggie glanced at them both apologetically— "well, you bleed a lot after you've had a baby, you know."

They both nodded.

"Well, I'd taken off my sanitary pad before dinner and I'd been carefully puddling onto my sheet."

"Gross!" Ginny was fascinated.

"Okay, here's the picture: Everybody goes home, and the night shift comes on. My lamb of a roommate is in a deep, deep sleep. I take my bloody sheet and arrange it around my poor roommate's hips, then pour a glass of water on it so the stain becomes enormous and drippy."

"Ugh!" Ginny sounded delighted. Her mother's daughter, Nick realized, sharing that irreverent glee in the unexpected that had drawn him to Maggie years ago.

"Ugh isn't the half of it," Maggie admitted. "Next I pull on my nurse's uniform and my bathrobe over it. I shuffle out to Nurse Merrimac and whine that I can't sleep because my roommate is moaning wildly."

"And?"

"She's suspicious. Pops into my room, sees my roommate almost comatose with a tankful of blood dripping from the bed, and hits the alarm button. All the nurses, even the nursery attendant, come galloping to help her. Except one. She takes off her bathrobe and goes in to check the babies in the nursery."

"God!" Ginny was enchanted.

"Most of the babies were asleep. I just poked along, reading the names on their little plastic bracelets." Maggie's voice had become softer. "Finally I hit Ryan. And I picked you up and held you. And it was the most wonderful thing in the world."

Ginny's young face was taut, fighting tears. Then she seemed to notice the wetness in Maggie's eyes too, and she hurled herself across the kitchen into Maggie's arms. They clung to each other fiercely, as they hadn't for sixteen years. Maggie murmured, "Oh, God. Oh, God."

Nick studied the swirling grain of the oak table.

After a moment Ginny pushed herself away and asked rather gruffly, "Did they catch you?"

"Not just then." Maggie brushed a hand past her eyes and reluctantly let her arm drop from Ginny's shoulder. "I wrapped my bathrobe in your baby blanket and left it in your crib, and took you into the supply closet and undressed you, very carefully, to see how you really looked."

"And how did I look?"

"Terrific! Very tiny and very perfect. Except that you'd crapped all over your diaper."

Ginny giggled.

"So I got a clean one from the shelf and changed you. You still had a big bandage over your navel. And then you woke up and started whimpering, so I nursed you a few minutes. You weren't really very hungry. I think you just wanted attention."

"Probably."

"Hey, let's go sit down." They walked back into the dining room, smiling at each other, and sat down at the table. Nick decided that the first hurdle was safely crossed. Time to face the second. He eased Zelle to the floor and went into the front hall to put on his raincoat again.

"Did they catch you?" Ginny was asking again.

"Sure, they weren't that dumb! One of the nurses came back," Maggie said. "I guess they'd decided my poor old roommate wasn't going to die after all. They gave me a real fire-and-brimstone scolding and hustled us both into our respective beds." She looked at Ginny. "I thought about you all night long."

Nick could see the question trembling on Ginny's lips, but she didn't seem to be able to get it out directly. Instead she scowled at the bowl of apples on the dining room table and asked, "Why did you do all that if you were—if I was going to be adopted?"

Buckling his trench coat, Nick felt his hands tense. How could you explain to a child? Especially to a child as angry as Ginny seemed to be? Nick wanted to enclose Maggie in his arms, to protect her from the hurt that was sure to come.

But she was braver than he. She tried to explain. "I did it because I loved you very much. We'd already been together for nine months. A tough nine months. God, there were days when I thought you were my only friend." Blinking, Maggie ran a finger along the edge of the table, then looked back at the girl. "I mean, I knew babies need families, and I was determined that you'd have the best. But you were my responsibility until I left the hospital and signed the relinquishment and release, so your real mom could take you home."

"But then—" Ginny stopped. It was hopeless, Nick saw; this was too much for one so young to absorb. Too much, and too subtle. She had not expected Maggie. And she could neither ask the question that burned in her nor understand the answers Maggie was struggling to give. Ginny grabbed an apple from the bowl and bit into it ferociously. "Hey," she said, noticing Nick at the door and grasping wildly for a new subject, "where are you going, Mr. O'Connor?"

Maggie said, "Ginny, do you think you could call us Nick and Maggie?"

"Nick and Maggie?" The girl looked inquiringly at Nick.

"I'd like that," he agreed.

"Okay. How come?"

Maggie explained, "Well, it helps me to call you Ginny. I always thought of you as Alice when I made up stories about how you were doing. But you aren't Alice, you're yourself. It'll be better if we don't mix up our real selves with our imagination."

"You made up stories too?" she asked eagerly.

"Of course. I thought about you a lot."

"Why Alice?"

"My dad and I always liked the Carroll books."

"*Alice in Wonderland?* Crap!"

Maggie grinned. "Reread it in a couple of years. It's not bad."

"Maybe," she said dubiously. The amazing blue eyes flashed back to Nick. "Anyway, where are you going, Mr.— um, Nick?"

"I'm going to get some kitty litter," said Nick, and waited for Maggie's slight nod before he added, "and to pick up the children at playschool."

"Children!" Ginny's spine jerked straight, and she stared at him.

"Yes," said Nick. "Your half-sister and half-brother."

"Oh, my God! I never thought of that!"

"Never?" asked Maggie.

Ginny shrugged. "Maybe sometimes." She glanced at Nick. "I never thought of anyone like Nick. But sometimes I imagined my mother was very poor and had lots of children, and smiled and hugged them a lot."

"And made soup, probably," added Maggie.

"Yes."

"From old shoelaces."

"Something like that." They smiled at each other.

"A noble mother indeed," said Nick.

Maggie nodded. "Yes. But what the real Maggie actually has is a daughter going on seven and a son who's three and a half. And generally I use noodles."

Ginny took a nervous bite of the apple. "A sister and brother. Just little kids."

"That's all. Nobody in between." Maggie answered the unspoken question.

"I was your only mistake." Ginny tried to sound flippant.

But Maggie was shaking her head firmly. "No," she said. "I was mistaken, a little bit, about your father. And a little bit about myself. But you were not a mistake, love. You're one of the best things ever."

Ginny twirled the apple core in her fingers. A whirl of emotions played through her flickering expressions. She said shakily, "I guess maybe I do want to take that shower."

"I'll show you." Maggie stood up and led her to the staircase. Her eyes met Nick's at the foot of the steps, and she gave his hand a squeeze before she started up. "We'll find something dry, okay?"

"Thanks. I didn't know the weather would be such a bummer," said Ginny.

"Yeah, that happens. Reality never quite fits our dreams." Ginny slowed on the bottom steps, and Maggie turned back inquiringly. Ginny asked, "Are you disappointed?"

"I'm delighted. I think you're terrific. Are you disappointed?"

The girl's gaze didn't drop. "I don't know yet."

Nick saw relief in the slight softening of Maggie's posture. Maybe she was right. If the girl was honest, there was a chance. Maggie said, "Yeah, it's confusing," and started up again. "See you soon, Nick."

"Right." He went out into the storm again, into the blasts of wind and icy rain.

It seemed balmy compared to the forecast indoors.

V

Dizzy with relief, Rina was still touching the telephone, as
though she could will it to life again, could bring back Ginny's
brusque young voice. Not kidnapped, she had said; not even
high; everything's mellow. She was all right! Half of Rina felt
like whooping with joy at the news that Ginny had not been
hurt, or worse, by the killer at the library. But the rest of her
still wanted to scream in frustration at the remaining questions. Where was Ginny? Why had she run away? Not drugs,
surely. Not the other—Rina refused to think about that. Was
it something Rina had done, or failed to do? Ginny hadn't
seemed angry at her when she left—but had Rina missed
something?

And who were these friends she was visiting? Last night
after the police had left, Rina had phoned every one of Ginny's friends she knew. All had denied seeing her after school.
She'd thought for a while that Ginny was with Buck, because
even at eleven he wasn't home. His annoyed mother was not
helpful, blaming Rina for the police visit and for worrying her.
But then a call to Chip's house had located Buck. He'd
sounded astonished in a muzzy way. "Ginny's not home?
No'm, I didn't see her at the library. Chip said she was there
and left before I got there." But how had Ginny gotten to
Philadelphia? And why wasn't she coming home now? If only
she hadn't hung up so soon!

Rina looked up from the phone. Mamma and Delores Gal-

lagher and Marie Deaver had just spread both newspapers
onto the dining room table to compare the brief accounts of
Mr. Spencer's death, but right now all three pairs of eyes were
turned to Rina. They reminded Rina of stuffed toys: Mamma
a terrier in off-white with black accents, Delores Gallagher a
plush turtle in bright-green with yellow stripes, Marie Deaver
a squirrel, perhaps, in gray mohair. "Was that Ginny, Rina?"
asked Mamma.

"Yes. Yes, she's all right, Mamma." She felt like a Raggedy
Ann herself, limp with relief, flopping about between joy and
frustration.

"Thank God! When will she be back?"

"She didn't say. She seemed in a rush, said she'd call back."
That was a consolation. Add hope to Raggedy Ann's stew of
emotions. "But she's all right. That's the important thing."

Mamma bounced into the kitchen to hug Rina, who was
still standing with her fingertips against the phone. "*Cara,* sit
down, then. Relax! She's all right! The biggest worry is over!"

"Yes." Rina was touched by her mother's concern. "Yes, I
know. But—"

"She didn't tell you when she'd be home?"

"No."

"Oh, she's too young to understand how we worry, *cara.*
But she did call, finally. She's not heartless. She's learning."

Rina sighed. "Not enough! She wouldn't listen, wouldn't
answer my questions!"

"Did I hear you say she was in Philadelphia?" asked Mrs.
Deaver.

"Yes, you're right. She did answer that one," Rina admitted. "She's with friends."

"Who?" asked Mamma.

"I don't know, Mamma. She was in such a rush, I didn't
even have a chance to tell her the police want her to come
back too." *Don't flake out,* Ginny had admonished her, as
though she could help it. "She just said she was all right."

"She'll be back, *cara.*" Her mother stroked Rina's hair as though she were nine again. "We have to have patience with youngsters. God knows, it's hard, no one knows that better than I do! But what can we do?"

"Well," said Rina, trying to be practical, "we should call that detective and tell him she's in Philadelphia." Maybe the police could find her there, talk to her. Rina turned back to the phone and dialed the number Sergeant Trainer had left them. He wasn't available, but the officer on the line promised to pass on the message that Ginny had called from Philadelphia. "Do you think you can find her?" Rina asked him anxiously.

"Well, ma'am, Philadelphia is a pretty big city," said the officer cautiously.

"But can you alert the police department there?"

"Ma'am, I'm sure Sergeant Trainer will do everything necessary."

"Thank you."

But Rina was not satisfied. She called Clint at work. "Philadelphia?" he asked when she'd explained. "Who does she know there?"

"I don't know, Clint. I'll ask her friends," she said with sudden decision. Her spine was back. No more Raggedy Ann. "As soon as they get home from school."

"Good idea. And listen, Paul Buchanan works in the DA's office in Philly." His voice was bright with eagerness. Ginny's problems usually required measured responses, gentleness, restraint, but Clint's instincts and lawyerly training were for action, confrontation. Now he was clearly grateful for something concrete to do at last. "I'll call him, we went to law school together. And as soon as we get a name or address, we'll drive up there and get her."

"Wonderful! Oh, Clint, I just know we'll get her back soon!"

"You're sounding better, honey." He'd called her twice today already.

"Of course! She's all right!"

"Yes, honey. I'll call Paul right away. You stay near the phone for now."

She hung up, then joined the others in the dining room. "The police say they'll do everything necessary, whatever that means," she reported. "And Clint will be calling a friend of his in Philadelphia, at the district attorney's office."

"Oh, Rina, but she's all right! That's wonderful!" exclaimed Delores Gallagher, her smile as bright as her clothes. Then she sobered. "It's been terrible for all of us, first poor John and then your daughter disappearing. I remember when my Berta was fourteen, she went to visit a friend, and they decided to stay in a tent in the backyard overnight. And she didn't even call me! I was terrified! Her friend's parents didn't get back until midnight, and meanwhile no one was answering the phone—oh, I was just terrified!"

"Children are so thoughtless," said Marie Deaver. She looked haggard today. Rina felt a pang, thinking of Marie's autistic son. Bobby's profound inability to connect with other humans made thoughtlessness seem a virtue. But the older woman continued, "It's such a relief to hear that she's okay!"

"Yes, that's the important thing," Delores Gallagher agreed. "My Berta is doing fine now. Her husband is principal, did I tell you?"

"Several times," said Marie Deaver.

"She says the only problem is the school board always looking over her shoulder."

"Did Ginny take clothes? Books?" asked Marie Deaver.

"No. Only the cat and her rain cape. She likes to take the cat with her." Especially if Mamma has been raging at him.

"Mm, yes. She does love that cat. Did she take food for him?" Mrs. Deaver asked.

"No. A box of treats, as usual."

"Well, then, she isn't planning a long stay."

"Yes, I keep telling myself that." Rina was cheered, though. Before Ginny's call, the fact that she hadn't packed books or a change of clothes was evidence that pointed to kidnapping or worse. But now that she'd called to say she was all right, it meant that she'd probably be back soon. If only she had explained what her problem was! Or if only Rina had kept her wits about her instead of stammering in her joy and relief. A good mother would have been calm, explained about Mr. Spencer and how important it was for Ginny to hurry back. Well, Ginny had said she'd call again. When she did, Rina would just have to forget all her questions, blurt out the fact of the murder, and get her to come back and explain so the police wouldn't be suspicious of her.

She wondered again if she should—but no, that couldn't be useful, could it? She'd wait till Ginny was back.

She looked down at the newspapers on the table. She really hadn't thought much about poor John Spencer, she realized guiltily; fear for Ginny had wiped concern for the old man from her mind. But her mother and the others had been his friends, or at least his acquaintances. "Is there anything new about poor Mr. Spencer?" she asked politely.

"Oh, nothing much we didn't know," said Delores Gallagher. "Except he never told me he had a married cousin in Florida."

"Did he?"

"A woman, with a family of her own. His only relative, poor fellow. John's wife died ten years ago, he told me once."

"A lot of us are pretty much alone in the world these days," observed Marie Deaver. She had nephews and nieces, Rina remembered, but her only close relative was the helpless, unresponsive Bobby. Life took courage. She resolved to be a little braver about Ginny.

Mamma said, "The other thing in the papers that I didn't know was that he died around five-thirty or six. How terrible to think we were all calmly fixing dinner and poor John was dying!"

Delores Gallagher snuffled. "Oh, Leonora, I know! It's terrible! And I had just let him off at home, and he was so friendly and curious in the car—" She paused for a moment, sobbing into a tissue. Marie Deaver patted her heaving grass-green shoulders consolingly until she could continue. "We were talking just a few minutes before! But he didn't say a thing about going to the library. Oh, it's terrible!"

Marie Deaver said, "They still haven't found the weapon either."

"I suppose the mugger just walked off with it." Mamma shivered. "He's probably stabbed somebody else by now."

"I wonder why he was at the library." Delores Gallagher's sobs had stopped, although she still clutched the tissue. "And why didn't anyone see him there?"

"This branch closes at six on weekdays," said Mamma. "After that it's pretty deserted."

"That's right," said Rina. "Clint used to take Ginny to the parking lot there right before dinner, when she was learning to ride a ten-speed. It's very quiet, he said. Every now and then someone would drive by the night book drop, but otherwise they were all alone."

"Well, why was John there, then?" asked Marie Deaver logically.

"Maybe he wasn't!" A new thought had occurred to Delores. "The police talked to me a long time because I was the last person who saw him before it happened. And you know, they kept asking about other places he might have gone. Not the library. So I wonder if he was killed somewhere else and moved to the library later."

Rina made a decision. If the police knew the time, and knew that John Spencer might have been someplace besides the library, then they already knew more than she could tell them. Her job was to find Ginny and get her home to explain things properly. No need for Rina to increase their suspicions by reporting that Mr. Spencer had telephoned yesterday a few minutes before six. Had telephoned, and had asked about Ginny.

Clean and dry again, Ginny brushed out her hair before the bathroom mirror and considered her new mother. She was baffled. She had a vivid image now of Maggie, young and stubborn, fighting with all her ingenuity to see and hold her child despite the hospital regulations. Scheming. Breaking rules. Stealing the uniform. Running painfully with her fresh stitches. All for love of a baby.

And then calmly signing the relinquishment papers, so that very same baby could be taken away forever by someone else.

Shit. It just couldn't be that way. It just couldn't.

The jeans and sweater Maggie had loaned her fit okay, though she had to roll up the cuffs. She swabbed out the tub carefully, transferred Buck's envelope to the clean jeans, and gathered up her bundle of dirty clothes.

There were four rooms on this floor besides the bathroom. Two children's rooms, bright with posters, books, dinosaurs. Through one window she saw a maple branch with a hook-on ladder. Next was the big blue-and-white bedroom where Maggie had handed her the clean clothes, then a small study that looked out over the front door. Ginny glimpsed a calculator, a sofa, lots of math books. Maybe Nick was an engineer, she thought as she went down the stairs.

There were voices in the kitchen. She opened the door and found herself in a crowd of people and animals. The small black spaniel barked once and then wriggled feverishly in greeting. Maggie, in sky-blue sweater and jeans now, was making peanut butter sandwiches at the counter, observed closely by Kakiy. Nick sat at the table by the window, a small boy on his lap and a little girl next to him. The children both had curly black hair and brown eyes, and both looked up, interested, as Ginny entered. The little girl asked, "Are you the new sister?"

The boy whooped with laughter. "That's not a sister," he said scornfully. "That's a lady."

"Why do you say that, Will?" asked Nick, smiling at Ginny.

"She's grown up!"

"Sisters grow up, silly," said the little girl. "She's a grown-up sister. Silly Willy."

"Silly Sarah!"

"Here, all you silly people, have a sandwich," said Maggie, deftly inserting one in each quarrelsome mouth. "Ginny, this silly person is Sarah, and this silly person is Will. The silly dog is named Zelle. And you can dump your laundry in the corner by the washer there."

Ginny dropped her bundle and patted Zelle. "Hi," she said to the children.

Both small mouths were full. They mumbled, "Hi." Then Sarah swallowed and said clearly, "Actually, Ginny, I'm not silly. I was just acting silly. Like Daddy."

"Hey! *I* wasn't acting silly!" protested Nick, laughter glinting in his brown eyes.

"But sometimes you do," explained Sarah patiently. "At work."

Maggie said, "Nick is an actor, Ginny. Do you want a sandwich?"

"Yes, thank you." Not an engineer, then. An actor. He didn't look much like an actor. Ginny eyed him surreptitiously as she sat down at the table.

Maggie said, "Well, Will. Did anything interesting happen today?"

"We made leaves," said Will. "Red and orange and purple."

"That sounds pretty. What about you, Sarah?"

"We learned a song."

"What song?"

Sarah sang seriously, "Five fools in a barrow drove into Harrow, tra la, tra la, tra la!"

"Good song," said Nick. "Later we'll do it on the piano, okay?"

"Okay."

"Something interesting happened to Kakiy and me today," Ginny told the children as she bit into her sandwich. "We rode on the subway for the very first time."

"Oh, yes!" said Sarah excitedly. "You know what's scary? The noise. When the train comes. Were you scared?"

"Yes, a little," Ginny agreed. "Even Kakiy was a little scared, and he's a tough cat."

"I'm not scared anymore. But it's pretty loud," said Sarah sympathetically.

"I gotta pee," announced Will.

"Okay, fella, let's go." Nick took Will's hand, and they went out.

"Are you finished with your sandwich, Sarah?" asked Maggie.

"Yes. Can I have an apple?"

"Sure. You can get it from the dining room yourself and take it up to your room."

"Okay." Sarah skipped away too.

Ginny and Maggie looked at each other. Finally Ginny said, "There were four people in my house. Three grown-ups and me."

"You seem to count as a grown-up here," Maggie said, smiling.

"Not there. Never with Gram. Not even Mom really counts as grown-up with her."

"I think it's hard for some people to accept it when kids grow up."

Or when kids are born? Ginny quashed her bitterness and asked, "Maggie, how old were you when I was born?"

"Sixteen."

Sixteen. Jesus. Ginny was suddenly enraged, as though being sixteen were an unforgivable familiarity from the calm woman sitting across the table from her. "Well," she said coolly, aiming to shock, "my boyfriend and I will really have to move to even get a tie in that round of the contest."

Maggie's blue eyes didn't flicker. "Sixteen years and seven months," she said evenly.

Damn unshockable woman! Ginny muffled her rage; she didn't want to lose it. She leaned back in her chair and snapped her fingers nonchalantly. "Shucks! No sense even trying to compete, then."

"Oh, no need to bow out of the contest," said Maggie, nonchalant too. "You could shoot up a lot and eat junk food, and try for a preemie."

So Ginny was the one who was shocked. She gaped a minute, looking into those cool, challenging eyes, and suddenly understood. A baby was a person. Not a trophy, not a proof that its mother was daring, or grown up, or bad. A person. As she, of all people, should know. And this woman knew, and would not let her forget it, even in jest.

She grinned grudgingly. "Ouch. You sure don't argue the way Mom does."

"Maybe not." Maggie was friendly again. "Maybe I argue the way you do."

"Maybe." It was true, Ginny sensed an agile mind that could keep step with her own. She changed the subject. "Listen, did you go back to school afterward?"

"Yes. It was my senior year in high school. I only missed a couple of weeks at the beginning."

"Did you tell anybody about me?"

"My parents knew, of course. But it wasn't anyone else's business. Later there was a guy I almost married. I told him, and of course I told Nick."

So he'd known all along, even at the front door. Ginny

remembered her talk about magazine subscriptions and felt foolish. She asked, "Is Nick the only husband you've had?"

"Yes." Maggie frowned a little, leaning forward, both forearms on the table. "Ginny, I don't understand. Why don't you ask about your father?"

"But you don't know who he is, do you? The certificate at the agency says 'Unknown.' "

"Oh, Christ, of course!" Maggie thumped the heel of her hand against her forehead. "So you thought I slept around or something, not knowing which of a hundred guys did it. A prostitute, maybe."

"Yeah. Either that or I was Jesus Christ the Second, right?" Maggie laughed.

Ginny said, "Or I thought maybe it was rape. Was it?"

"No. That was my story to the agency, but it was love, Ginny. Unsuitable but genuine. He was a wonderful man. I spent my junior year in France, you see. Exchange student. And at a gym I met a bright French engineering student, a gymnast, a cousin of my coach."

"My father was French?" asked Ginny in disbelief.

"Yes, French. We liked each other right away. I was living with a very strict French family, and at school, a girls' school, we were very proper. Uniforms and everything. But Alain and I managed to meet a couple of times a week. At the library, the park, eventually at his friend's apartment. Thursdays especially. I had Thursday afternoons off from school. I'd say I was going to the library or something, and meet him instead. We talked about poets, and gymnastics, and Piaf, and the Beatles. He showed me Paris. He was a very exciting friend to have."

"So I'm part French!" Ginny was still astonished.

"Yes. That was the problem, you see." Maggie was sitting very quietly, hands folded on the table before her, trying to read Ginny's reactions. "I didn't want to give his name on the agency certificate, because I didn't know what kind of international complications might result. I wanted you to have a home right away because it's important for a baby. And he was Catholic. That might have limited the choice of parents. So I made up the rape story, pretended I didn't know."

"What was his name?"

"Alain Picaud."

"Peeko?"

"Yes. P-I-C-A-U-D."

"Alice Picaud Ryan!" Ginny bounced on the chair in her excitement. "My name! I mean, on that certificate."

"Yes. Your baby name."

"Why—I mean, how did I happen?"

"We were in love. It never occurred to me that we might not be spending the rest of our lives together. And I don't know if you'll understand, but I was so far from home, and very much in love, and suddenly the Americans and Russians were getting ready to blow up the world. The Cuban missile crisis, that time. And I wanted so desperately to live, and to live with Alain."

"Well, they didn't blow up the world."

Maggie grinned. "True. We lucked out that time."

Ginny licked her dry lips. "Why didn't you use the pill?"

"Ginny, it was scarcely invented yet. This was 1962. You know, back when the dinosaurs lived? Even married women weren't using it much yet. And I was fifteen, unmarried, a stranger in a Catholic country."

"Oh."

"Alain said he'd take care of it, but sometimes he forgot. And I was young enough to think it was romantic, you know, carried away by true love. God, I was such a kid! I was in love, so all natural laws were suspended, right?" She pushed her black curls back from her forehead. "Besides, I really thought we'd be together forever, or at least until the end of the world. Even when I started missing my periods, I thought, well, it's a little early but we'll want children eventually if we don't get nuked. I assumed it would be okay."

"But it wasn't okay."

"No." Maggie fiddled with the children's plates on the table. "I found out the rough way. It was in April, I was three or four months along by then, and I'd realized it wasn't just irregular cycles. So I finally told him. And he disappeared."

"Disappeared?"

"Yes. Poof. His friend with the apartment claimed he had no idea where. I couldn't believe he'd gone. I went to my gymnastics coach, his cousin. But we'd been so clever, you see, she had no idea how involved we'd gotten. I asked her where he was and she said, 'Who knows?' And then she must have seen that it mattered, because told me I shouldn't be looking in that direction."

"He disappeared. Because of me?"

"No, no, no! It would have ended anyway. It was the old trite sad story. He was married already."

"Oh."

"The year before, my coach said, he got a girl pregnant, and the family demanded marriage. And they were Catholic, of course. No divorce."

"Oh."

"So there we were, you and I. And for the first time I let my brain in on the action and really thought about your life and my life and what I should do. It dawned on me that marrying Alain might not have worked anyway. I'd had a vague idea of bringing him to the U.S., but he probably wouldn't have wanted to go. I certainly didn't want to stay in France forever. And of course, as it turned out, there was his wife and kid. It really hit me how much everyone would have to sacrifice if I did track him down somehow and marry him. And I realized that the concerts and gymnastics and happy afternoons were not quite enough for a whole life together." She looked anxiously at Ginny. "Do you understand what I mean?"

Ginny thought about Buck, about actually being married to him. What a drag. She said, "Yeah, maybe."

"Yeah. Anyway, a couple of days after he disappeared the friend with the apartment caught me after school and handed me an envelope from Alain. It had a thousand francs in it. That was worth a couple of hundred dollars then. I was furious that he'd try to buy me off."

"Boy, me too!" Ginny straightened in her chair, indignant. "What did you do?"

For the first time, Maggie seemed a little discomfited. She adjusted the stacked plates again. "You might not like it."

"Listen, I can handle anything! Anything except not knowing."

Their eyes met. Maggie gave a brief nod. "You're right. Okay. I pulled out all my emergency money. Every penny, so I could send him back two thousand francs. With a polite little note."

"Saying what?"

Maggie looked away. " '*Pour la saillie.*' "

"What does that mean?"

Maggie hid her eyes with one bony hand. "God, Ginny."

"What?"

" 'For the stud fee.' "

"Oh, my God. Like a horse?"

"Or a dog."

"Oh, my God."

"Yeah. After that I cried for three days." She peeked back at Ginny and lowered her hand. "But you know, later I got to thinking that maybe the money wasn't really to buy me off. Maybe in his way he was trying to do the right thing for you. Because it was true, getting married was not such a hot idea."

"So you think he felt responsible for me?"

"Now I do. Now I think that according to his own standards, he was trying to be reasonable. Of course, he should have told me about his wife. I might have done exactly the same things, but I should have known the truth. Still, he was basically a good man, bright and lots of fun. Also young and hot-blooded and impulsive, just like me."

Ginny looked down at her hands on the oak table. She decided she needed more time to think about all that. She tucked the new information into a back corner of her mind and said, "I was born here. In New York."

"Yes. I thought things over and wrote my family and friends that I wouldn't be back in Ohio till September. But I flew back in June. I called my mother from New York, and she and Dad both came. They checked out homes for me, and hospitals. Got me a summer job. They were very understanding about the whole thing."

"Sorry to be so inconvenient!" blurted Ginny. And before Maggie could object, she added hastily, "Do I look like my father at all?"

"Your bone structure is about halfway between us. And you have the Picaud hair." Maggie reached across the table and gently lifted a strand of Ginny's new-brushed hair, then let it fall. "He had splendid shiny black hair, perfectly straight."

"I always sort of wanted curly," Ginny admitted. "Were his eyes blue?"

"Yes. Not as dark as ours."

"Was he like Nick?"

"In some ways. Not in looks. But they're both musical. Both athletic too. Nick does dance and fencing and mime instead of gymnastics. And they both have a sense of humor."

"Were you sad when my father disappeared?"

"Very sad."

Ginny rubbed her eyes, overwhelmed, and tried for a lighter topic. She said, "I danced until a couple of years ago. Ballet."

"Did you like it?"

"At first. Then I got sick of it. I got sick of everything. They say I'm an underachiever," she added defiantly.

"They think you should be making better grades, or something?" There was no disappointment in Maggie's voice, just curiosity.

"Oh, I made good grades when I was a kid. But why bother? If I'm really just a—" Shut up, Ginny, she told herself.

But Maggie had heard the unspoken thought. She asked, "Did you always think your birth mother was a prostitute?"

"Oh, God, no! She could have been anything!" Ginny welcomed the change of subject and waved her hand at airy forms. "Sometimes I'd think she was a beautiful ballerina who couldn't keep me because of her career. Or sometimes she was a murderer who killed all my brothers and sisters. Or I'd think she was very rich, a Rockefeller or something, and her family wanted to keep everything quiet. Or sometimes my father was the rich one, and my mother was poor but too proud to approach him for money."

"God. So it must be hard to adjust to someone with an ordinary story and an ordinary house and family."

"And even peanut butter sandwiches." Ginny grinned suddenly. "But hey, at least you sent back the stud fee!"

Maggie laughed. "God, Ginny, what standards you set!"

"Didn't you set standards for me?"

"For Alice? Not really, not like that. It was much more fragmentary. I kept thinking about my daughter, hoping she was happy and learning all the wonderful things in life. I'd see a little girl somewhere having fun, hearing a bedtime story, maybe, or reading about the hobbit, or learning to turn a cartwheel, and I'd think, 'Oh, I hope they've taught Alice to turn a cartwheel!' You know."

"But I mean like grades and things. Didn't you worry about that?"

Maggie shrugged. "Not really. Alain and I are both bright, so I figured our daughter would be too. I didn't worry because I've had too much education myself to be all that impressed by grades. Good grades just mean somebody has used her intelligence to fulfill the requirements. I figured you'd be smart enough to tell if they were worth fulfilling."

One phrase stood out. "Too much education? You mean you went to college too?" Ginny was excited. Few of her imaginary mothers had gone to college.

Maggie pulled a blue-jeaned knee up from under the table and propped her elbow on it, regarding Ginny with mild surprise. "Yes, of course," she said. "I went to college. I was Phi Beta Kappa. I went to graduate school and got a Ph.D. in statistics. Right now I'm partner in a statistical consulting firm."

Ginny stared at her. "Jesus Christ!" she said. Then a bark of laughter escaped her, and she put her head down and pounded her fist on the table in helpless mirth. "Oh, Jesus!" she gasped. "There's one in the eye for Gram!"

"What do you mean?" Maggie asked, smiling, wanting to share the joke.

"Oh, Jesus!" giggled Ginny. "When I brought home those D's, you know what she told Mom? She said it was my bad blood!"

Suddenly Maggie was around the table, holding her tightly, fiercely, and saying over and over in a cold furious voice, "Goddamn her! Goddamn her!" Ginny's gasps of laughter suddenly turned into sobs. She wrenched herself away from Maggie's grasp and ran, blindly, all the long way through the house and out the front door. A cold, wet gust of wind stopped her, and she stood on the little porch sobbing, blinking at the dismal soaked September street, darkening now. It was a long time before her plunging emotions settled enough to let her go back inside.

VI

Rina pulled into the Selkirks' drive, cut the lights, and sat in the afternoon gloom a moment gathering her thoughts. Of course kidnapping was still a possibility. But there had been no ransom demands. That was good, Clint had decided, maybe Ginny really was with friends. Rina herself put her faith in the way Ginny sounded: no fear, no caution in her voice this afternoon, just the usual impatience with a mother who fussed about her. So to find the Philadelphia friends, Rina would build on what Ginny had told her. Jan Selkirk had been Ginny's best friend ever since they'd arrived in this Washington suburb. She hadn't visited much recently, Buck had monopolized Ginny's attention. But Jan might still know something. Rina walked to the front door, flanked by holly bushes, and knocked.

Jan answered: curly brown hair, jeans and lime-green T-shirt, textbook in her hand, her finger hooked in the edge to mark the place. "Oh!" Her hazel eyes widened in surprise. "Hi, Mrs. Marshall. Come in. I'll get my mom."

"Well, it's you I'd like to talk to," Rina said, stepping into the hall. It was Early American, with maple side table, hobnail milk glass shades, pineapple patterned wallpaper. A television stuttered in some distant room, alternating speech and snips of lush music. "About Ginny."

"Is she sick? I didn't see her in English class today."

"Well, no. She's fine." Rina clenched her hands around the

strap of her leather shoulder bag. This was hard to admit, especially to Jan, the good student, the talented dancer. Everything that Ginny had once been. But Rina had to tell her something, or she'd never learn a thing. She mustn't let her own embarrassment at being less than perfect hinder the search. So she wasn't Donna Reed, so what? She raised her head and met Jan's puzzled gaze. "She's left home."

"God! She just left?" Scandalized, Jan stared at Rina. "I remember you called about her yesterday, but I never thought —I mean, why would she leave?"

"I don't know. And I don't know where she is, Jan. A couple of hours ago she called and said she was in Philadelphia. I wanted to ask you if you had any idea why she'd go there."

"Me?" The brown head shook, and Jan looked at the braid rug, embarrassed. "No. I, um, don't really see her a lot these days."

"I know. Jan, please don't try to spare my feelings. I know she's friendly with a bunch of kids you don't like much. Frankly, I agree with you. But if they've gotten her into some kind of trouble I have to know all I can."

"Yeah, but I don't know anything."

"Can you tell me what she was doing yesterday? Who she was with? Anything she said to you. You did see her yesterday, in English class, at least?"

"Yeah." Jan turned her head to frown at the maple console table and run a finger of her free hand along it. "But we didn't talk much then. Hi at the beginning, you know. She came in a minute late."

"I see."

"She, um, hadn't done the homework." A furtive glance at Rina.

"Yes, sometimes she doesn't." Rina nodded encouragingly. "I appreciate your telling me."

"Well, it doesn't matter a lot really." Reassured, Jan looked at her more confidently. "Hunt never asks anything that's not in the book, and Ginny doesn't have to write out the homework, she knows the answers. Anyway, he doesn't take off much if you don't hand in written homework."

"Yes. I wish she had a different philosophy, but you're right, somehow she scrapes through."

"Well, she's right, it's a bore. Of course I do the stuff because I have to get into college. But she doesn't seem to care." Again that furtive glance to see if she had offended.

Rina tried to keep the pain from her expression. "Yes, I know. So there wasn't any problem yesterday?"

"Not really. She was daydreaming and Hunt asked her a question. He does that sometimes to catch people. So I sort of nudged her and told her the number of the question. She knew the answer."

"Good." Rina was perversely pleased, maybe at this proof of Ginny's intelligence, maybe at Jan's loyalty to her friend.

"But that was all. Then I saw her again, in the bus."

"Oh? Did you sit with her?"

Jan glanced over her shoulder toward the source of the television noise and nodded. Rina realized with a pang that the girl's parents had told her to avoid Ginny. Jan said, "Yeah, she wanted to thank me for the hint."

"Good. Did you talk at all?"

"Just stuff. You know. Nothing about Philadelphia, if that's what you mean. Nothing about going away."

"Did she mention any friends?"

"No. She was talking to Linda Lang just before she got on the bus. And of course Buck."

"Linda and Buck. That's helpful to know, Jan. I'll check with them again too. But did she mention anyone else? Anyone who might be in Philadelphia now?"

"Oh, I see what you mean. No. We just joked around a little."

"What do you mean?"

"Well, she asked me what I was doing these days, and I complained about the College Board tests. I'm taking them this year. I asked her if she was taking them, and she said no. So I asked her what she was going to do." Jan ran her finger along the edge of the table again.

"What did she say?"

Jan grinned. "She said she was going to be the Wicked Witch of the West."

"I see." Rina was disappointed.

"And I said, no, really. So then she said she was going to be Baryshnikov's mistress."

"I see. Teasing you." Rina remembered that Ginny and Jan had shared a crush on the Russian dancer when they were in ballet classes together.

"Yeah, we were joking around. And she said he would teach her Russian and she would become a famous spy. And she said she was going to be a cat breeder." She looked at Rina, a little frown in her eyes. "She said, in America she could be anything. As though it meant something."

"Mm." Rina tried to think what it might mean. One of her mother's pet phrases. But Ginny had repeated it to her yesterday too. What was its significance? Could it have anything to do with this trip to Philadelphia? She'd think about that. "Did she say anything else?"

"No. About then she got off the bus."

"And she didn't mention anyone? These Philadelphia friends she has?"

Jan shook her head definitely. "No. We were just joking around, honest."

"Well—" Rina adjusted the strap of her handbag. "Thanks so much, Jan. I'll see if I can get in touch with Linda and Buck. On the phone last night Buck said he had no idea where she was, but maybe she said something about Philadelphia to him. Anyway, I'll try him. Linda too."

"Yeah. They'll know more than I will."

"Thanks so much."

"Sure." Jan started to close the door, then blurted, "I really hope she's okay."

"Jan, you're very special to her. I hope, someday—well, you know."

"Yeah. I hope so too."

Rina returned to the car. Jan's affection for Ginny, even in the face of parental disapproval, was heartwarming. Rina was glad she had decided to come in person instead of just phoning again. In fact she had learned little here. But somewhere, Ginny must have left a clue to the address or name of those friends in Philadelphia. Rina headed for Monroe Boulevard.

It was a neighborhood of broad lawns, huge houses, burglar alarms. She drove up the arc of a driveway and walked to the trellissed porch, feeling small and dowdy. A Burberry was all very well, but this front door demanded mink. She firmed her jaw and punched the doorbell. No one answered. She punched it again.

There was a clatter of locks, and the massive door was eased open. A broad, brown woman with incurious eyes gazed at Rina. "Yes, ma'am?"

"It's all right, Maria, I'll get it!" sang out a voice from within. Maria withdrew silently, and the voice hurried closer. "Coming, com—why, Rina Marshall!" Rosamond Landon of the champagne-colored hair blinked at her in surprise. "I thought you were the paper boy! See, I had the money all ready!" She laughed and waved a couple of dollars. "Here, come in. But you know, Rina, we have a bone to pick with you!"

Rosamond's cashmere sweater and slacks matched her hair but couldn't hide the fortyish droop of a once Barbie-like figure. Rina followed her into the living room. Maria was nowhere to be seen. Rina said, "I'm sorry to bother you again. I wanted to talk to Buck, if he's here."

"Oh, well, he has football practice on Fridays," said Rosamond. She had opened a teak cabinet at the end of the long room and extracted two glasses. "Sherry?"

"Thank you, no, I'll come back later when Buck is home," Rina said, halting in the middle of the room. "Unless you can tell me, does he have friends in Philadelphia?" She couldn't help glancing around the room, at the Italian leather sofas and Breuer chairs, at what looked like a genuine Braque over the fireplace.

"Philadelphia? Not that I know of." Rosamond turned back to her, sipping at her sherry. "You know, Rina, it wasn't very kind to mention Buck to the police," she said reproachfully.

"They asked us who had been at the house yesterday, and Buck had stopped by for a moment."

"But that was all he did! Just stopped by!" Rosamond waved her sherry glass, already empty. "He doesn't deserve to be grilled by the police just because he stopped by! Rina, I don't know what kind of trouble your daughter has gotten herself into. But we really don't appreciate having Buck dragged in too."

"We didn't drag—" Rina began hotly, then caught herself. Ginny's trouble was Buck's fault, probably, but this was not the time for a scene. "I'm sorry this happened, Rosamond, but it's none of our doing either. It's just that a man we'd never met before happened to visit our house, and later a mugger killed him. So the police are asking questions. They want to talk to everyone."

"Sure you won't have a sherry?" Without waiting for an answer Rosamond refilled her glass. She hadn't even asked Rina to take off her coat. "You just have the one girl, Rina. I have three boys, and believe me, it's much harder. Much." She turned back, propping herself against the darkly gleaming teak cabinet. "Well, John Jr., he's the oldest, you know, he wasn't such a problem. But Drew and now Buck, it's just so difficult with athletes, you know. John tells me it's natural.

Healthy high-energy kids, he says. I mean, John's hours are terrible, of course, a doctor's hours are always terrible. Not much time at home. But he played touch football with them, did all he could. We've sent them to the best summer camps, got the best equipment. And they're good boys, you know that."

"Yes, Rosamond, but—" Rina looked down at the champagne-beige carpet, unable to confess that Ginny had left home, not to this woman.

"Of course you know it. But boys don't grow up as fast as girls, I mean mentally. They're so easy for a smart girl to lead, you know that. So what can a mother do? When Drew smashed up his Porsche—well, of course the girl denied it, but it was clear that she was distracting him. Young men find it hard to resist. And then they said he'd been taking drugs, can you imagine? A boy from a good family? Oh, Rina, you can't imagine how hard it is to cope with boys. Everyone always wants to blame them."

"Do you know when Buck will be home?" Rina broke in.

"Home? Oh, late. He's usually invited to a friend's house afterward. He's very popular, you know that. Sure I can't pour you a sherry while I'm at it? But what I wanted to say, Rina, is that you mustn't mention Buck to the police again. His father gets very upset. And it's bad for the boy to think people blame him."

That was bad for any child. But what if the child deserved the blame? Rina said, "Yes, you're right, Rosamond. Well, I'll be going now. I'll try to catch Buck later." She backed toward the door, almost bumping the leather sofa.

"Good. I knew you'd understand. It's so difficult with boys, really! Well, thanks for stopping by." Rosamond opened the door for Rina and waved her out with her third sherry.

Rina shivered as she drove down Dr. Landon's long drive to the boulevard. Rosamond was blinding herself, clearly, to a lot of problems. A lot. But what frightened Rina was her own instinctive sympathy for Rosamond, her own sense that Rosamond's defense of Buck was heroic and motherly.

Was she too blinding herself about her child?

Nick was frowning at some small pimples on Will's tummy when he heard the rapid steps downstairs and the slam of the front door. Damn. He pulled up Will's clothes, lifted the little boy to a firm seat on his shoulders, and trotted downstairs.

He didn't see Maggie at first. She wasn't in the dining room, and when he went through the swinging door into the kitchen and unloaded his giggling, ear-pulling burden, she wasn't there either. Kakiy was on the refrigerator. Nick picked him up. There was a half-healed scratch on the cat's side, and he wondered again about how Ginny had come here. He showed Will how to tickle Kakiy behind the ears, and left the cat to the attentions of his son and of curious Zelle. Nick hurried to the living room with the big shuttered bay window. Maggie was there, forehead bowed against the side window frame. He put his hand on her shoulder and felt her shaking.

Damn that girl. Didn't she have any sense at all? Any feeling for her own mother?

He looked through the louvered part of the shutters and saw Ginny on the stoop, face hidden in her hands. Well. Damage on both sides. He squeezed Maggie's shoulder. "What have you two done to each other?"

"Oh, Nick, those assholes! God, if I'd known—" She turned to him, thumped her fists against his chest harder than she knew. He put both arms tight around her until she relaxed, if that was the word for a shift from shaking to mere trembling.

"Is there anything we can do to help?"

"The damage is done," she sobbed into his shoulder. "Assholes! How could they tell a helpless kid she has bad blood?"

"Mm, I see." Nick was angered too. Naked infants spitted upon pikes, while the mad mothers with their howls do break the clouds. . . . But anger wouldn't help now. He said, "When I was a kid it was Uncle Hal. He was a drunk, never could hold a job. So every time I had a beer, or complained about my boss on a summer job, my mother got upset and told me how important it was not to turn out like Uncle Hal."

"Yeah, but Nick, for you there were other choices! You knew other people in your family. You knew you were a lot like the good guys too. But Ginny is defenseless! How could they say that to her?"

"Yeah. Although it seems to me she's not defenseless anymore."

"What do you mean?"

"She's met you, Maggie."

"But Nick, she doesn't understand! She thinks they're right about me! I just don't know how to explain." Grief pooled in her eyes.

"You'll find a way. She's bright. It's just that she's young, Maggie, it may take her a few years." Damn kid, why was she in such a hurry? Why hadn't she waited until she could hear and comprehend the truth? Deaf as the sea, hasty as fire.

Maggie nodded. "Yeah. You're right, I've got to be patient. And honest with her, no matter what." She straightened.

"That'll help." He kissed her nose. "Are you up to hearing some more bad news?"

"Oh, God. What?"

"News fitting to the night, black, fearful, comfortless, and horrible. Will has some pimples on his tummy."

"Oh, God," Maggie groaned. "This is, what, two weeks plus a couple of days? Yeah, that's about right. Chicken pox. And you going to St. Louis Sunday. And everyone coming for brunch tomorrow! Well, let's go have a look."

At least it distracted her to another child's needs. Over the next hour Nick collected what he needed for tonight's new play reading, put in a load of laundry, played "Five Fools in a Barrow" on the piano for Sarah. Maggie worked beside him, sympathizing with Will, picking up toys, starting a pot of soup, singing along with them, but always Nick was aware that a piece of her attention was still at the front door. Two or three times she slipped away to peek through the louvered shutter at the stoop.

Was Ginny trying to torture her? Why the hell couldn't the girl at least come inside to sulk?

But nothing happened until after he'd had his soup and was ready to leave for the reading. He was in the hall buckling his trench coat when there was a knock on the door. He opened it for her and said, "Hi."

"Hi. Um, is there a tissue around somewhere?"

Her face was red and streaky. Nick was jolted back to his own teenage years, to his father's death. His youthful grief had been tainted by rage that in death his father had abandoned him, totally, unfairly. Not true, he knew with his head, but the heart had its own logic. Nick's anger toward Ginny dissolved. He fished in his pocket and pulled out a little cellophane packet of tissues. "Take it. I've got more at the theatre."

"The theatre? Oh, yeah, you work there, right!"

"Acting silly," he said solemnly.

She tried gamely to grin, blowing her nose and eyeing him over the white tissue. "What a funny family you turned out to be."

"Yeah. We like it."

"Yeah, I like it too," she said, and seemed astonished at her own words.

Nick grinned. "I'm glad. Even Kakiy has made a great hit with the kids."

"He's a good cat."

"Question. He looks very healthy. But he's got a scratch on his side that looks fresh."

"Yeah, that's Gram. Kicked him. She's always hated cats."

"She kicked him?"

"Yeah, he wasn't supposed to be in that room." Her lip quivered. "But it's impossible to keep him away from her a hundred percent of the time! I mean, he's curious."

"Yes, he'd be hard to keep in line," Nick agreed, relieved at her defensiveness. It showed a sense of responsibility and laid to rest the nagging worry that this angry youngster tortured pets. "Listen, I think there's soup in the kitchen for you."

"Okay. Hey, Nick, thanks."

"Sure." He saluted and went out to simpler tasks.

Ginny watched him lumber down the stoop steps. A big, comfortable man. She was sorry he was entangled in this mess. But she could not spare a lot of pity for him just now. Other questions came first. She squared her shoulders and headed back to the kitchen.

The other three with their black curly heads were sitting around the oak table with soup, salad, a crusty round loaf of bread. Kakiy rubbed against her ankles.

"Hurray!" said Will when he saw her.

"Hurray yourself!" She smiled at him. Her brother. Her brother! It hit her suddenly that all of them here in this room were blood relatives. Biologically related. What Gram called *famiglia*, what Grandma Marshall called kin. Until today she had never ever seen her own kin. A rush of joy she'd never known overwhelmed her. She sagged against the wall and blew her nose noisily, too high for a minute to even look at them.

Maggie said cautiously, "There's soup on the stove. Help yourself."

"Thanks." She gathered her forces, thrust the tissue into her jeans, and ladled herself a bowlful. "My favorite kind," she said as she sat down. "Made out of old shoelaces."

Will crowed with delight. "Old shoelaces!"

Sarah was laughing too. She hauled a bit of noodle from her

bowl with thumb and forefinger, and displayed it proudly. "Hey! Where's the shoe?"

Maggie gave her a rather misty smile, and Ginny bowed her head and applied herself to the soup, trying to disguise the singing in her blood. *Famiglia.* Kin. She felt herself suddenly connected, part of an organic whole. A family tree. Stretching back in time, reaching forward into the future. And she was part of it. Forever linked. No judge could destroy this cellular cement. The legal papers in Mrs. Farnham's file were lies, helpless against the infinite power and connectedness of their microscopic genes. Suddenly it came clear to her how Mom could put up with Gram. *Famiglia.* Kin.

"Gin-nee!" Sarah was insistent, exasperated.

"I'm sorry. I was thinking. What do you want?"

Sarah looked wicked. "Do you like worm soup?"

"Worm soup? Yuck!" She made a face. The children giggled.

"What about bug soup?" Will offered with evil anticipation.

"Yuck!"

Each reaction sent them into fresh spasms of laughter. Ginny suggested, "Eye of newt and toe of frog soup!"

"Yuck!" chorused Will and Sarah gleefully. From the corner of her eye Ginny caught a look of delight on Maggie's face.

"Tongue of dog soup!" Ginny continued.

"Yuck!"

"Finger of—"

"Cool it," said Maggie sharply. Ginny, horrified at what her mind had selected from all those Shakespearean ingredients, glanced at her in panic. "Cool it with a baboon's blood," Maggie finished quoting smoothly. Will laughed again dutifully, but Sarah's wise brown eyes were on her mother, troubled.

"I think that's enough of that game," said Ginny shakily. "What do we do next?"

"Dessert," announced Maggie briskly. "You can have some cheesecake now with Will and Sarah, or wait till Nick gets back and have some with us."

"I'll wait."

"Okay. Now, our big news is that Will is getting chicken pox."

"See?" Will pulled up his shirt proudly. Ginny could see pimples coming on his face too.

"Mine are gone." Sarah held out an arm.

"Hope you've had it," Maggie said to Ginny.

"Yeah. Long ago."

"Good. Anyway, after dessert we usually turn a few somersaults on the top floor, and have a bath, and read a story, and go to bed. Will you be staying the night?" She was cutting cheesecake, her back to them.

"Oh, Jesus. I'm sorry. I haven't thought."

"It's okay. Nobody expects anyone to think much today. You have a choice between the sofa in the study or a mat on the top floor. If you decide to stay."

Ginny laid down her spoon slowly. "Yes, please, if it's okay. But maybe we shouldn't, um—"

Maggie plunked the cheesecake in front of the two children, then straightened to look full at Ginny. "Me too," she said. "I want to tell you everything you need to know, Ginny. But all these revelations are damn hard on us both. Maybe tomorrow."

"You too?" Ginny was a little surprised, but only because she hadn't thought. She'd done a hell of a lot of not thinking today.

"Yes, of course me too." Maggie struck a gallant pose, fist on chest, for the benefit of the children. "Beneath this calm exterior lies total emotional devastation."

"Me too. Obviously. Okay, nothing new tonight."

"It's a deal."

"What's motional?" asked Sarah. Will was methodically stuffing cheesecake into his mouth.

"Emotional?" Maggie sat down next to Sarah and put her arm around her. The way Mom used to do with Ginny. "That has to do with your feelings. Loving and hating and being happy and so forth."

"What's that other word?" Sarah took another bite.

Maggie rolled her eyes helplessly at Ginny. "Devastation?"

"Yes. That one," mumbled Sarah.

"That's when things are all mixed up. Wrecked."

Sarah, troubled, inspected Ginny. "But it's good to have a sister."

"Of course it's good!" Maggie squeezed the small shoulders. "It's wonderful! But when you're grown up, you have a lot of feelings, and most of them are mixed up with other feelings. So even when you're very very happy, the way I am about Ginny, you'll probably have a very very large number of other feelings mixed in."

Sarah nodded, satisfied. Will said unexpectedly, "A googol."

Maggie laughed. "That's right. I have a googol of feelings about Ginny."

As soon as she saw it, Ginny decided to sleep in the big room on the top floor. It occupied the entire floor, fifty or sixty feet long and twenty wide, and was clear except for a couple of structural columns. Nick and Maggie had outfitted it for exercise space. The wall opposite the stairs was mirrored for most of its length, with a barre; nearer the stairs there were stacks of tumbling mats, a set of child-height parallel bars, and a low balance beam. The ceiling was too low for rings or high bars, Maggie explained. "The kids like to climb in the maple tree outside when it's nice," she went on. "We hook on a ladder so we can climb up from the back porch roof. But most of the time we're in here. It's great for tumbling and dance."

"Mom said they told her you liked sports," Ginny remembered.

"Gymnastics?"

"No. Guess they weren't very specific. I sort of had the idea you watched baseball on TV."

"Goddamn nonidentifying buggers."

"Yeah. Do you dance too?"

"Not much. Nick is better trained than I am. I just know a few basic ballet things for floor exercise and beam. Do you want to work out with us?"

"I'm out of shape," Ginny demurred. "Also tired. Kakiy and I'll just watch."

Maggie had changed to a black leotard. The children, in their underclothes, began some simple tumbling exercises. Maggie, keeping a sharp eye on Will for signs of fatigue, switched on a little tape recorder, and Ginny held Kakiy and watched contentedly as her little relatives were guided through the exercises. Will was getting grumpy but insisted on pulling himself sturdily along the parallel bars with his short arms. He was still very chubby, baby fat, but Sarah was lengthening out, her knobby-kneed frail child's body surprisingly wiry and well coordinated.

When they had finished the short workout, Maggie said, "Bath time," and sent them downstairs to get ready. She paused at the head of the stairs. Ginny was still sitting on the floor, leaning against the wall near the stairs, hands resting limply on Kakiy in her lap.

"You look exhausted, love," said Maggie.

"Yeah. Maybe I'll skip dessert and just sack out."

"Okay."

"But listen, I did want to say one thing."

"What?"

"Mom always said you were good. Gram is the only one who said that other stuff."

"Yeah, but—well, thank you, that does help, Ginny."

"Yeah." She looked up into the eyes like hers, and wondered if her own were as full of pain. "Hey! I almost forgot!" She put Kakiy down and scrambled to her feet.

"What?"

"Look!" Ginny ran to the middle of the floor and quickly turned a neat cartwheel.

"Hey! All right!" Maggie clapped her hands in delight, and for a moment they smiled across the room at each other, still linked somehow by an unbreakable umbilical of love. But then suddenly there was nothing to say, or rather too much to say. That rush of joy brought angry questions in its wake. Crap, she was too tired to get into all that now. It was a relief when Sarah yelled, "Hey, Mommy!" from the foot of the stairs.

"Coming, love." Maggie hurried down, calling over her shoulder, "I'll bring up some sheets for you when the two bozos are tucked away."

"Thanks."

The door at the foot of the stairs closed, and Ginny hauled one of the thick mats to the narrower back part of the room. Yes, she was exhausted. She lay down, and Kakiy curled against her hip. She could look out the window at maple leaves and, behind them, the line of brownstone roofs against the hazy glow of city sky.

Hazy darkening sky . . .

Saturday, September 15, 1979

....

VII

Saturday morning there was still no Ginny.

Rina woke early, having slept little. Rain spattered the windows. She hadn't realistically expected Ginny home yet; but she couldn't help hoping, and feeling disappointed. The only good news was that there had been no ransom demand either. So she wasn't kidnapped, she really was with friends. Once again, Rina's mind combed through that brief telephone conversation. Ginny had said that she was fine. But Philadelphia! Why Philadelphia? Who could she know in Philadelphia? Jan hadn't known, nor Buck's mother Rosamond, nor Linda Lang. The police hadn't called either. As Rina sat up in bed, the cheerfulness of the birthday presents heaped in the corner of the bedroom mocked her.

Clint had had a restless night too, but now he dozed beside her. Without his glasses, his lined face looked vulnerable. Rina felt a sudden return of the old grief, the old sense of worthlessness. Two ordinary people, daring to hope that the usual miracle would occur for them, that they would conceive and bear a child as others conceived and bore children, that their love too would bear fruit. Two ordinary people discovering that they were wrong. Incapable. Unworthy. Cut off from the future. Two ordinary people slowly realizing that they were not ordinary at all, but far inferior. Realizing that ordinariness was a goal much too lofty for them ever to achieve.

Rina dragged herself away from the ugly thoughts. She rose

and put on her blouse and slacks, pulled on a blue Fair Isle sweater she had knitted herself, and went to the kitchen. She made coffee, and heard the shower running in her mother's rooms as she poured herself a cup. She hoped Ginny was not out in the rain somewhere, alone. No, she had said she was with friends. It would be okay. At eight o'clock, unable to wait another agonizing moment, she called Buck Landon.

"Sorry," said Rosamond groggily, "he's still asleep."

Clint was standing behind her when she hung up. He gave her a hug, and they clung to each other a moment, as they had on those terrible recurrent days twenty years ago when her period returned and they knew that once again the dream was smashed. He said gently, "She'll be back soon, honey. Let's go get something at the bakery."

"What if she calls?"

"She won't this early. Besides, your mother is here."

He was right, of course. But at the bakery she was so distracted that she could hardly focus on the breakfast rolls. She shouldn't have come. A good mother wouldn't have come. Clint finally made a selection, then took her arm tenderly and guided her out to the car again. The trees and the sidewalk were drenched, but the rain had finally stopped.

Rina asked, "Sergeant Trainer would know to tell the Philadelphia police about Kakiy, wouldn't he?" Ginny would never be separated from her cat.

"Yes, of course, honey. And I told Paul Buchanan, so his office has passed on the word to the police there too." Clint looked so old in the watery morning light, his hair faded, his wrinkled fair skin sagging. We're too old, thought Rina despairingly. We should never have tried to take on a child in our thirties. No wonder she rejects us. We're over fifty. What could we possibly have in common with a teenager?

"She said she was fine," said Rina, reminding herself as much as Clint.

"I know. Damn it, Rina, we're doing what we can!" He was

blustering a little, as he always did when she was upset and he couldn't help. He added, "I'll check back after breakfast and see if Paul has found anything."

"Good," she said, trying to sound hopeful.

He put a gentle hand on her arm. "We've got to trust her not to do anything stupid. She's bright, damn it. She won't go far wrong."

Rina wanted to believe it too. But the wild lurchings of her emotions, from hope to despair, were out of her control. She clutched the plastic armrest of the car as they turned toward home. The houses, hedges, lampposts, trees, utility poles were a blur outside, passing the window in fuzzy rhythm.

Her daughter was gone. Her darling. How had she failed her? She had tried so hard.

They had followed the agency's advice and told Ginny she was adopted as soon as she had shown any interest in birth. The interest came when the guinea pig at nursery school had babies, and in the beginning Ginny had been much more intrigued by the tiny guinea pigs than by any implications for herself. But over the next year she had asked Rina about it from time to time.

"Susan was inside her own mommy," she had said once.

"Yes. That happens a lot, Ginny. Usually."

"But I wasn't inside you. I was inside somebody else."

"That's right. But she wanted you to live with us, and be part of our family."

"Where is she now?"

"I don't know, Ginny."

"Why didn't she want me in *her* family?"

"She did want you, honey. But you see, she didn't have a family when you were born. And she wanted you to have a family, so she let you live with us."

A year later it was Cinderella that caused the trouble. Clint's sister had sent a book for Christmas, a beautifully illustrated book of fairy tales. Ginny had been fascinated by the story. She had also started having nightmares, screaming at night, wetting the bed. Rina hid the book, but the nightmares continued, and during the day Ginny asked oblique questions about it, and hunted for it almost furtively. Finally Rina collected her courage, pulled out the book again, and went to her little daughter's room. Ginny was sitting on the floor, a sneaker in her lap. Her black hair had been pulled back in two little ponytails that bobbed as she very somberly laced the sneaker with some bright red yarn.

Rina said, "Look, Ginny. I found your book."

"Oh!" The little face looked up quickly, the huge eyes filled with more fear than pleasure.

"Do you want me to read Cinderella?"

She looked back down at the sneaker and carefully began poking the fuzzy red end of the yarn through the next hole. "Yes," she mumbled.

Rina sat down in the rocking chair. Back then they were still on Long Island. Ginny's room had had a birch tree outside, and on bright days the light bouncing through the delicate trembling leaves had a shimmery, watered-silk feel. Rina opened the book and began to read, glancing at her daughter from time to time. After a few paragraphs she stopped. Ginny was sitting rigidly, staring at the sneaker.

"She certainly is a bad, cruel stepmother, isn't she, Ginny?" Rina said conversationally. Her heart was pounding.

"Yes." Ginny glanced up at her quickly, then began lacing the sneaker again.

"But you know, most stepmothers are good," Rina said. "They love their children very much. I'm a little bit like a stepmother, Ginny. But I'm not like Cinderella's stepmother. I love you very much, so I'll never be cruel to you."

Ginny stabbed at the metaled hole with the frayed red end of the yarn and drew it through carefully.

Rina licked her lips and said, "Cinderella's stepmother was cruel because she didn't love Cinderella. That was the problem. But I love you very much. Daddy does too. We'll always love you very much."

Ginny still didn't reply. She finished lacing her sneaker thoughtfully and put it on her little foot. "Look!" she demanded of Rina at last. "Isn't that pretty?"

But Rina knew soon that she had guessed correctly, because the nightmares and wet beds stopped, and the Cinderella book was left on the shelf more and more often.

But maybe she hadn't been able to show her love enough . . .

"Are you all right, Rina?" Clint asked as he helped her from the car. She was staring numbly at the garage wall, at Ginny's bike, a geometry of dark rubber circles and metallic blue angles.

"Maybe Mamma was right," she whispered. "Maybe God didn't mean for us to have children, Clint."

"Rina, Rina!" He shook his head, his dear old silvery head. "Don't start that, please!"

"But maybe we're not up to it, Clint."

"Of course we are! We're fine, Rina. Everyone has problems sometimes!"

But the old, old wound was throbbing again. I'd rather be blind, thought Rina, or in a wheelchair. Not barren, no, not a foolish old barren woman, playing at motherhood and revealed at last to be nothing but a wicked stepmother, sobbing to the unhearing heavens.

"Rina!" He was shaking her by the shoulders. She took a deep breath, and the sobbing stopped.

"What's wrong?" Her mother's voice was sharp, reverberating in the hollowness of the garage.

"Nothing," said Clint, his own voice strained. Rina bowed her head onto Clint's shoulder and took another deep breath. Mamma had never really understood. Mamma was not barren. Not handicapped.

"What's wrong, Caterina?"

"Mamma, it's all right." Rina fumbled in her bag for a handkerchief. "I'm just so worried."

"I know, *cara*. Here, come have some coffee." The dark eyes were soft, solicitous.

"Yes. Yes, let's have some breakfast," Clint agreed. Rina let him lead her into the house, across the dining room and living room to the sofa. In a moment Mamma brought them coffee. "No calls yet. Not even the police," she said as she handed Rina a cup.

She's anxious too, thought Rina. She had herself under control again. "They're doing everything they can, I'm sure."

"She'll be back. You know she will."

Clint patted Rina's hand. "Yes. She knows."

Mamma settled into her rocking chair across from the sofa and said, "Ginny takes things so much to heart. She's like me, you know."

Rina paused in astonishment, her cup halfway to her mouth. "Like you?"

"But she'll get over it too. You have to ignore us a little, Rina. You're even-tempered like your father. But Ginny and I are too dramatic about things. We don't really mean it."

"Oh, Mamma, bless you!"

"She'll be back."

"I know. But I worry, I can't help it."

"I know." Mamma gazed past Rina, out the glass doors toward the garden. "Do you remember when you were in high school? That church trip you took to the beach?"

"The beach?" Rina frowned.

"St. Francis church. Remember? They chartered a bus, and you were going with the Giordano boy."

"Pete Giordano? Mamma, that was so long ago!"

"Well, I remember it well enough!" said Mamma tartly. "Don't you remember? The bus broke down on the way back."

"That's right. Oh, we were all furious!"

"Furious! And how do you think we parents felt? It killed me, Rina! You were supposed to be back at nine. It was four in the morning!"

"Oh, Mamma, surely not that late."

"Four in the morning. And you with that terrible Giordano boy, all pimples and loud voice. He was terrible, Clint. I was dreading the worst. It was like a knife in my heart."

Rina put down her coffee cup on the end table. "But I got back all right, Mamma! You know what I did on that bus? I slept! Some people sang, but we'd been swimming and playing volleyball on the beach all day, and I just went to sleep."

"Yes," said Mamma gently. "But in those days, Rina, girls weren't so knowledgeable. We tried to protect you so much. I told your father that night, no more! If Caterina gets back, I'm telling her about the world."

"What do you mean?"

"There you were, Rina, with that idiot boy all night, with your beautiful woman's body and the wisdom of a four-year-old."

Clint said, "She means it's good that you've talked to Ginny about things, Rina. She'll recognize trouble, maybe avoid it. She can take care of herself pretty well."

"But she's still so young! There's so much I should have warned her about!"

"Nonsense!" said Mamma briskly, fetching the coffeepot and pouring Rina another cup. "You're a good mother, *cara.* You've done everything possible. And that girl is older than you in some ways, you know." She nodded wisely. "I've been thinking about it. She's not such a baby. She's ready to look life in the eye."

Maybe Mamma was right. Rina drank her coffee and ate the Danish that Clint had chosen for her. Not comforted, because no one but Ginny could do that now, but ready to settle in to wait again, or to fight, whatever turned out to be necessary.

Clint left the room, and she heard him talking on the phone. He returned after a moment shaking his head. "Paul Buchanan says they don't have any news in the DA's office, but they're working on it. I offered to drive up, but he says it wouldn't help. He's got the photo of her we sent with our last Christmas card, so he says they're in good shape."

"I wish she'd call again!"

"Why don't you bring your work out near one of the phones?"

"Yes. That's a good idea, Clint."

She called again, but Buck still wasn't awake, and the local police said there was no news.

Over the course of the morning, the phone rang several times, friends of hers and Clint's, friends of Mamma's. Every time, she trembled as she reached for the receiver, and then, like a stone, disappointment weighted her down again when it was not Ginny, not even the police.

She stitched carefully on her quilt. Soft bulging tan hills, long dark appliquéd strips for the tree trunks, the ridges of bark carefully corded. There were people in the design, fat hearty farm people, parents and children. But today she could not do children. She worked on the ancient trees, the eternal hills.

VIII

"St. Louis doesn't sound all that exciting," said Ellen Win-field-Greer as she speared a sausage. Her shrewd hazel eyes frowned doubtfully at Nick.

Nick smiled at her. From upstairs wafted the lively voices of Sarah, Will, and their little friend Alison Greer. Nick said, "I get to sing, dance, and twirl my mustache. And it's only for a few days."

Jim Greer put down his coffee mug. "A mustache. Are you playing the heavy again?"

"Right. It's a dealers' convention, and the show helps intro-duce a new line of electronic appliances. My character is sort of a Simon Legree who wants to enslave people to old-fash-ioned appliances."

They had loaded their brunch plates at the dining room sideboard and had settled here in the living room to eat: Nick and Maggie, Jim and Ellen, and Nick's friend and agent George. The agent, bright-eyed and knobby-nosed, was al-ready halfway through his plateful. "Mays goon oo," he mum-bled.

"What?" asked Jim.

George swallowed and repeated, "Pay's good too. It's legit, the producer's good, and you get paid a lot. What more could an actor want?"

Jim and Nick grinned at each other. "Shakespeare!" they chorused.

"Chekhov!" added Nick.

"Hellman!"

"O'Neill!"

"Mmpf-mmpf!" George waved his hand for silence while he swallowed. "Let me rephrase the question. What more could an actor reasonably ask for?"

"Shucks. Got me there," Jim said. "And it's over soon. You get back Thursday, Nick?"

"Right. Fly out tomorrow, set up Monday, shows Tuesday and Wednesday, fly back Thursday. Not a bad gig."

"Except for the chicken pox," said Ellen. She nudged Maggie, who had been silently munching her muffin.

"Oh, we'll survive." Maggie, not as far away as Nick had feared, smiled at her friend. "Alison had it last year, right? It's obviously not the end of the world."

"Well, Jim had to take three days off to watch her because the au pair had that weekend off," Ellen said. "And Alison was grouchy as a horned toad."

"So was Sarah," admitted Maggie. "But we have to get these diseases out of the way sometime. And I can reshuffle my work until Nick gets back. See, I have a very understanding boss."

"Boy, I wish I worked for myself!" said Ellen fervently. She was a rising star at a respected Manhattan law firm. "What about your downstairs neighbor? Julia? Didn't she give you a hand when Sarah was sick?"

"Julia's on tour," said Nick proudly. "She's doing a workshop on children's books at the University of Washington. Also visiting family that lives in Seattle."

"She claims she's in the jet set now," Maggie added.

George had taken his empty plate back to the dining room for a refill. Nick, his nerves tuned to sounds from above, heard the steps on the stairs. He flashed a glance at Maggie. She too had tensed, but with a microscopic shrug at him she lounged back in the chair and returned her attention to Ellen.

George's voice was jolly and appreciative. "Well, what have we here?" The approaching footsteps paused as he continued, "You are a vision, ma'am. Will you marry me?"

"Sure, if you'll get me some coffee," said Ginny's bright young voice. As unabashed as her mother.

"An offer I can't refuse!" They came into view through the arch: George holding her elbow, Ginny back in her own laundered clothes, the long straight hair gleaming. George's gnomelike face was beaming at her. "I'm George," he said. "And you must be related to our beauteous blue-eyed Maggie. Her little sister?"

"No," said Ginny cheerfully. "Her little bastard."

George dropped her elbow, speechless. Nick couldn't quite muffle his chuckle, and George turned to him in mute inquiry. Nick nodded in confirmation. Ginny darted a glance at Maggie and started pouring her own mug of coffee.

Maggie had bounced up and was going to Ginny. "Ginny, meet George," she said, laughter in her voice. "Our favorite aging juvenile."

George rallied a little. "Dear me, you've got your own coffee. Let me serve your plate. What do you want?"

Ginny surveyed the sideboard: plates of sliced meats, hot sausages, a bowl of fresh fruit, muffins, croissants. "Everything," she declared.

"Fine! You're related to our Maggie, all right." George busied himself filling her plate.

Maggie caught the girl's free hand and drew her to the living room. She announced, "Hey, everybody, this is my daughter. Ginny Marshall. Ginny, meet Ellen Winfield and Jim Greer."

"Pleased to meet you," said Ginny. Nick watched her inspect them—their faces, their jeans, their running shoes. Probably comparing them to her parents' friends. He wondered how they measured up.

"Come sit down," said Maggie. "George will bring your

food." She led her to one of the shabby comfortable chairs by the fireplace, then sat on the end of the sofa near her.

They were all looking at the girl uncertainly. With dignity, Ginny said to Jim, "I met another Greer upstairs. Alison."

"Yes, our daughter," said Jim. "Ellen's and mine."

"Was she behaving herself?" asked Ellen.

"Oh, yes," Ginny said. "She and Sarah were full of social graces. Commented with admiration on how grown-up I was."

"It is the striking thing about you." Maggie, shameless, sounded amused.

"Voilà!" said George, arriving with a heaped plate. He leaned over the back of the chair to hand it to Ginny, then rejoined Nick at the other end of the sofa.

George began to talk about the producer of the industrial show, but half of Nick's attention remained on the girl sitting at the other side of the mantel. She seemed content to listen quietly and eat the plateful of food, those astonishing eyes busy, filing everything. From time to time Nick felt himself observed. Finally Maggie leaned over and asked her quietly, "Want any more?"

"No, thanks. I'm fine. It's very good. Especially the sausage."

"Thanks. It's homemade." Maggie hesitated, looking at Ginny, before she added, "A Picaud recipe."

"Oh." A spasm of pain in Ginny's eyes.

Ellen must have been listening too. She leaned suddenly toward Maggie and exclaimed, "Alain!"

"Yes," said Maggie evenly.

"You never said a thing to me about this, Maggie!" Ellen was clearly flabbergasted.

"Ellen, I had no right to say anything. Still don't. The records are sealed."

Ellen looked sharply at Ginny. "How old are you?"

"Sixteen." The word was accompanied by a suspicious glare.

"Adopted?"

"What if I am?"

"Do your adoptive parents know you're here?"

Ginny's lips tightened. Maggie put a hand on Ellen's arm and said, "Cool it, Ellen. Some things are more important than the law."

"Not when you're in court," said Ellen tartly.

"I followed the rules. She found me."

"Well, that may help a little. But if the parents find out—" Ellen's hazel eyes, troubled, shifted to Ginny. "Oh, hell, you're right, Maggie. I wouldn't have resisted either."

"With this one you wouldn't have had much choice," said Maggie. She turned to Ginny, whose hands were clenched beside her plate. "Ellen's an attorney, Ginny. She thinks she's giving good advice, and—"

"All for my own good, right?" Nick recognized the blaze of fury veiled behind Ginny's crisp words. "The goddamn best interests of the goddamn child! Well, Ms. Esquire, do you know how long your law will consider me a child? How many years your law gets to tell me what my best interests are?" She thumped her empty plate onto the end table and ran from the room. They heard her rapid steps all the way to the third floor.

Maggie was on her feet too. Ellen said, "God, Maggie, I'm sorry!"

"Not your fault. You were honest. If only we could have had a little more honesty, a little earlier. Damn agency!" Maggie took a step toward the stairs.

Nick said uneasily, "Shouldn't you let her settle down a little?"

"She'll be thinking I asked Ellen here as a lawyer," Maggie said. "I've got to explain." She hurried out.

"So who the hell is this kid?" George demanded. "Nick, your wife is barely out of the cradle herself!"

"Yeah, precocious, isn't she?" snapped Nick, and George shut up.

"God!" Ellen was still frowning in the direction Maggie had disappeared. "What a hell of a thing! The kid's right, you know. I never thought of it that way. Sealing the records to keep her away from her biological mother is supposed to be in the best interests of the child. Maybe for a while it is. But the records are never unsealed. She'll never be of age in the eyes of the law. Never be able to find out legally about her own background."

"Isn't it to protect the mother too?" asked Jim.

Ellen snorted. "You know Maggie. She sure as hell doesn't want protecting. I'm surprised she stayed quiet this long. God, sometimes it really hits home what a clumsy instrument the law can be!"

Ginny threw herself onto her mat. Best interest of the child. What a laugh. What a goddamn laugh.

She'd awakened slowly that morning, to one of those eerie moments of complete disorientation, floating nowhere, no meaning available to her groping mind. She'd seen her backpack, floating with her in the void. A cat's litter box. A window, gray light on maple leaves. Oh. Everything had shifted into place, like a kaleidoscope falling into a new pattern. A pattern of kinship and confusion.

She dimly remembered dreams of running, trying to catch people who grew wings and flew away as she reached for them. Her fingers had been the fingers of a birth-strangled babe.

Her own clothes, washed and dried, had been next to her backpack. And a brown bag with a note: *Ginny—Some friends are coming for brunch Saturday. You're welcome to join*

*us if you want. If not, that's fine too. There's an orange and a
bagel in the brown bag for you, but the real food is downstairs.*

She had puzzled over the note, trying to decipher whether
it was secretly urging her to come down or to stay away. It was
impossible to tell. She was of two minds herself, curious about
what kind of friends her surprising new mother might have,
but not eager to suffer any more shocks to her shattered sense
of self. In the end it had been the scent of coffee that had led
her downstairs. Straight into the trap.

There was a knock on the door at the foot of the stairs.
Maggie called, "May I come up?"

"It's your own damn house, isn't it?"

She came upstairs slowly. Ginny sat up on the mat and
turned to face her.

"God, Ginny, this is hard."

"Well, you don't have to call in the lawyers again, you
know! I'll go quietly. You don't have to sign any more papers,
just say the word."

"Not my decision."

"Oh, you're going to force me to stay this time?"

Maggie pushed her fingers back through her dark curls.
"Ginny, I'll try to answer your questions. You may not like the
answers, but they'll be honest. But you'll have to ask the questions straight. If you really want to know."

If you really want to know. God, it was all she wanted. To
know. To understand. And she couldn't say the words. She
rubbed her forehead with her fist and finally asked instead,
"Ms. Esquire is a friend of yours?"

"I've known Ellen since college. We were roommates. She's
a wonderful woman, much more sensible than I am. Last
week I invited them for brunch today. She happens to be a
lawyer now."

"Coincidence. I see." Ginny leaned back against the wall
next to the window and closed her eyes. She sensed Maggie's
light tread crossing the room, stopping not far in front of her.

Without opening her eyes Ginny said, "Shouldn't you be with your honored guests?"

"They're friends, they'll understand. And no doubt Ellen is right now impressing on them all how important it is not to breathe a word of your existence to anyone until you're at least twenty-one."

"Goody for her." Ginny shifted a little on the mat, eyes still closed. She suddenly wanted very much to leave, to return to the warm familiarity of Mom and Dad. She needed time to think, to absorb the self-inflicted blow of this mother, this family. She said, "Don't you want me to go away?"

"Only if you want to go."

"God!" Ginny opened her eyes. Maggie was sitting cross-legged on the floor a few feet in front of her, leaning back against the frame of the parallel bars. Ginny said, "You don't make things easy for me."

"I think too many decisions have been made for you by other people already. Including me. Especially me. It's time for you to control your own life. You're adult, intelligent."

"Oh, yeah, sure, I'm just about perfect. Because you say so. You!"

Maggie shrugged. "Well, I believe it."

Ginny leaned forward. "But there's got to be something wrong! Because—" She rammed her fist into her own mouth, stopping the words. Maggie's hand moved toward her instinctively, then checked. Strong bones in that hand; but graceful in motion. Ginny pulled out her fist and stared at her damp knuckles a moment. Her own bones suddenly had a location in the universe: halfway between Ryan and Picaud. She said roughly, "Listen, how come I'm always asking the questions? Don't you want to know anything about your dear little goddamn Alice?" When she glanced up she was surprised to see tears standing in the other blue eyes.

"Sure," said Maggie steadily. "Is it my turn?"

"Yeah."

"Well, I admit I'm curious about how the hell you found me."

"You thought you were safe, huh?"

"Safe! I left you every clue I legally could! Damn it, Ginny, be fair!" Maggie pulled out a tissue and swiped angrily at her nose.

Ginny stared down at her knuckles again. "I don't know what fair is," she said.

"Okay, I understand. But just accept for a minute that, whether you like it or not, I love you. I'm delighted you're here. I've wanted to be with you all your life."

"Oh, Jesus! How can you say that? How?" Ginny squeezed her eyes closed again, shutting her out, shutting out her lies.

There was no answer for a minute. Then Maggie said, "Okay, then, don't accept it. But you still haven't answered my question, and you said it was my turn."

Ignore the festering boil. Back off, talk about other things. "Okay," said Ginny. "Well, begin at the beginning. The fake beginning. Mom and Dad always said I was adopted. They said I was special, I was chosen."

"Yes."

"And they gave me some line about how you loved me so much, you let them have me, because they could love me so much. Nifty logic."

"It's hard to explain to a child."

"It's hard to explain, period. Right? Because if you're chosen—" Oh, crap, she was poking at the sore again. Couldn't stay away from it.

Maggie said thoughtfully, "If you're chosen, you can also be rejected. And if someone loves you so much they give you away, you can never trust anyone else who loves you."

Ginny flinched as the words jabbed into the heart of her pain. But she struggled back to a fighting stance and said, "Right-oh. Bang on the button."

"Okay, go on," said Maggie brusquely. "You knew you were

adopted. That somewhere in the great world there was an-other mother. A dancer, or a murderer, or a princess, or a prostitute."

"And what I drew was a fucking statistician!"

Their nerves were too raw for much control. Their eyes met, Ginny's mouth twitched, and suddenly they both ex-ploded into laughter. Maggie gasped, "What a blood-curdling discovery!"

"Hey, gimme a chance!" cried Ginny hysterically. "Maybe in a few years I'll curdle your blood too. I'll be a—a podiatrist! Or maybe even a notary public!"

Maggie had collapsed against the bars, laughing helplessly.

"Order, order!" commanded Ginny, gulping back her gig-gles as best she could. "The tale proceeds! Now of course when I learned all this, I started reading about adoption. I mean, Mom is a dear, but she got so nervous when she talked about it, I quit asking." Maggie nodded, attentive again. Ginny went on, "And Mom didn't know much anyway. There was more in the library. I learned about agencies, and homes for unwed mothers, and all that stuff. And I learned that there were real records somewhere. Not like my so-called birth certificate at home."

"Right."

"But there were also books that other adopted people had written, about how hard it was to find the information."

"You read Fisher? And Lifton?" asked Maggie eagerly.

"All those dudes. And it was clear that nobody tells us adopted so-called children anything, not if they can help it. A few people found out a little bit if they got a judge or a doctor to ask for them. But they were of legal age, and they didn't find out very much. It took them years and years. And if they did find anything, it was because they tricked someone into making a mistake."

"Right."

"So I knew Ms. Esquire's law was no help to me. And then, Thursday afternoon, I broke into Dad's strongbox."

"You broke in?"

"Oh, well, he didn't make any big secret of the combination. I remembered it from watching him one day. Just lucky. Anyway, down there amongst all the insurance papers was one that said McKinley Agency. And Mom had written 'Farnham' on it."

"I see." Maggie was leaning forward now, following the account eagerly, fascinated by each step.

"So I went to the library and looked in the Manhattan phone book. The agency was still there. Fantastic good luck again."

"Right."

"And I got some money, and off we went on the five-thirty bus, Kakiy and I, to the big city to seek our fortune. We were waiting at the agency door when they opened Friday."

"Mm-hmm." Maggie leaned back against the bars, eyes fixed on Ginny. "And when you stepped into the McKinley Agency, they said, 'Oh, you sweet child, we're overcome by your cleverness! Here's everything you want to know!' "

"You've been there too," Ginny deduced.

"Often."

"Yeah, they were just as stuffy and cagey as the books said. Farnham wasn't there, but a Mrs. Elkin was. They made me wait a long time. Finally she said she had a moment. So I went into her office and explained to her that I was developing a horrible digestive disease, and I had to know if there was a history of malabsorption or anything. She asked how old I was. I said twenty-two."

"Oh?"

"Yeah. She said, 'You don't look it,' and went across the hall and got out a file and brought it back behind the desk to look at it. Still cagey, though. I was sitting right on the other side of the desk, but she was still standing up, holding it up straight, so I couldn't see. I was furious. Just a few feet away! And she was allowed to see it and I wasn't, and it was my life in there!" Ginny unclenched her hands and took a deep breath. "Then she got very schoolteacherish and scolded me. She told me I was sixteen and I should be ashamed of myself, because my parents were such good people, and if it was important, they'd ask for the medical information. She was really upset."

"It wasn't exactly a situation to win her confidence."

"Right. So then I burst into tears and told her it was all because of Mom. She was the most terrific mother in the entire world, I said, and I didn't want to worry her needlessly, but I really was sick with this digestive thing. And Mrs. Elkin tried to soothe me. And while I was pretending to blow my nose I covered my hand with a tissue and ran a couple of fingers down my throat, and threw up all over her carpet."

"Jesus, Ginny!" Maggie was delighted.

"She leaped up and said, 'Oh, golly gee,' or whatever caseworkers say, and ran to the door to call for help. And I grabbed the folder, and there was a certificate. Alice Picaud Ryan, born September 14, 1963, father unknown, mother Margaret Mary Ryan. And there was an envelope with a return address. Ryan, right here. But of course Elkin was back before I could see any more. She snatched it away, swearing." Ginny grinned, remembering. "Not like a caseworker this time."

"I'll bet!" Maggie beamed.

"She said—" Ginny glanced at her cautiously. "She said I was just as bad as my mother."

Maggie studied her own crossed ankles. "Did she now."

The suspicions that had been growing ever since Ginny had seen Mrs. Elkin suddenly coalesced. She said, "So. The security of that sacred file has been violated before?"

"Once," admitted Maggie. She played with her damp tissue a moment before continuing. "I went in every year to leave you a birthday letter, you see. I went to college in New York State so I could stay in touch more easily. And most of the time I was very good, but on your third birthday Mrs. Farnham happened to get the file out when I asked if there was any news from your family. She said no, she always said no, but this time she put the file down on the desk instead of reading it over by the file cabinets and putting it away before she came back. And when I reached in my notebook to pull out the letter to you, somehow my papers spilled all over the desk. And grabbing at them, somehow I picked up the file."

"Clumsy of you."

"Oh, yes, I apologized lavishly. Didn't tell her that I'd caught a glimpse of your new family name."

"I see."

"But it looks as though I didn't fool her. And I'm still not back in her good graces, if Elkin had heard about me too. Farnham herself would never have put that file within your reach, I bet."

"We're a couple of bad 'uns, all right." Ginny felt herself sliding into a murky depression. She said, "My third birthday."

"Well, it took me a couple of weeks to find your house on Long Island."

"You *found* me?" Ginny stiffened. Despair switched to outrage.

"Just a quick peek. I didn't want to lurk. You were getting into the car with your mom. Little ponytail, little sneakers, a Band-Aid on your knee—God, you were so real! And she gave you a hug. You both looked happy."

"You found me!"

"Yes. I've been keeping track for thirteen years. I got a

glimpse of you several times while your family was still on Long Island. It was harder after you moved to Washington."

"Damn you, Maggie! You never told me!"

"Ginny, I had no right! Your parents were doing this wonderful thing for us. I was afraid they'd feel threatened, maybe think I wanted to take you away. You looked happy and healthy, and you got hugged a lot. When you were little I thought it would just confuse you. And later I didn't know how you'd feel. Whether you'd feel betrayed, and hate me, or romanticize me, or maybe be completely indifferent."

"Indifferent! My God!"

"Well, that's what the agency told me. You and your child are now nothing to each other, they said. They'd ordered up fresh new lives all around. I guess—oh, hell, you're right, Ginny. I never believed it in my heart. I'd held you in my arms, and I knew. The papers took away my legal rights, but not biology. Not love. Still, I didn't want to worry your parents."

"Yeah. Elkin gave me that line too. She said it would be cruel and ungrateful to my sterling parents. It would make them think that they weren't enough. And she said you'd made a new life, and not to bother you. Not to ask. You didn't want to be reminded of the ghastly fact that I exist."

"Damn her! My waiver of confidentiality has been in that file from the beginning!"

Ginny's anger had ebbed again into despair. "Well, it doesn't matter anymore. What with your clumsiness and my stomach trouble."

"Yeah, that agency nauseates me too."

"Must be genetic," said Ginny. They nodded at each other gravely, collaborators; and again there was that obscure family magnetism, and the crushing sense of loss. Her third birthday. Ginny turned away abruptly to stare out the window. The tree was still green, the leaves barely edged with gold. Two floors below she could see the roof of the back porch. A googol of feelings. She no longer knew how she felt about anything. The more she saw of this strange new mother, the more confusing things became. Friendship and anger, fascination and repulsion, hatred and something akin to love, all seethed together in her heart.

And finally she asked it. "Would you do it again?" She was still staring at the tree.

"Today? 1979? There are other options today. A few, anyway. For one thing, they'd let me go back to high school. Or do you mean if it was 1963 again? If everything was the same except for knowing how much we hurt?"

"Yes. If everything was the same." Ginny didn't look around, just studied the tree, until finally the low voice answered.

"Yes. I'd do it again."

Ginny jerked around then in her agony to glare at her. "Well, then, the problem is with you, isn't it? Because I sure as hell wouldn't give away my own little baby! Not for anything! There's nothing wrong with me!"

"Of course not."

"Well, then. It's you!"

Maggie bowed her head onto her hand. "I'm sorry, Ginny. But I won't lie to you."

Ginny punched the mattress beside her, but when she spoke she was surprised at her own voice. It sounded like a plea. "Aren't you going to throw me out?"

"Ginny, it's your decision."

"Damn you!"

"Yep." Maggie stood up. "Listen, I think what you did at the agency was terrific. But right now I'm going down to see the others." She disappeared down the stairs again.

Ginny threw herself full length on the mat and drummed her toes on it in childish frustration. Abandoned child. Forever a child. She rolled over and blinked back the tears. Outside, a sturdy branch of the maple tree brushed against the window. The gold-edged leaves were complex, fantastic in outline and patterned veining. Yet each one was exactly like the others. The mystic tyranny of genes.

There was no escape.

IX

"Mrs. Marshall, is it true? Ginny's still gone?"

His curly blond hair smoothed down, the teenager stood a little awkwardly at the front door, worried and on his best behavior. Rina said, "Come on in, Buck. We've been trying to reach you."

"Yeah, the guys said Mr. Marshall was asking at football practice. And somebody said you'd told Jan Selkirk that Ginny was gone!" He followed her up the stairs.

"Yes." So it wasn't Rosamond's urging that got him here, it was the efficient high school news network. Rina resumed her seat and picked up her quilt. Only a few inches of border to go. She motioned Buck to the sofa nearby. He sat on the edge, uneasy in this adult world. God, I'm so old to him, thought Rina. Older than his own parents. But she smiled and said, "Ginny called yesterday, but she didn't say much, really. Just that she was in Philadelphia with friends."

"What friends?"

"Buck, that's exactly what I wanted to ask you. They aren't friends of the family. I hoped you could tell me if anyone she knew at school has moved to Philadelphia."

He smoothed back his hair, thoughtfully. "No. A couple of guys moved to Pennsylvania. One to Harrisburg, one to some other place up north. But I don't think Ginny knew them. I mean, not very well."

"Who were they?"

"Andy Akers, he was a senior last year. And Chuck Rule, he's the one in Harrisburg."

"Ginny hasn't mentioned either one of them," said Rina doubtfully. "Is there anyone else? Maybe someone who would meet her there for some reason?"

"Heck, Mrs. Marshall, I thought maybe you could tell me."

"One of your friends saw her at the library, you said. Did she say anything to him?"

"No, he didn't talk to her."

"He didn't?" Rina paused, needle halfway through the quilt.

He scowled and shifted his weight on the sofa. "One of the guys was there and said he'd seen her on the other side of the library, over in the reference section. But she wasn't anywhere around when I was there. I looked all over."

"And didn't find her."

"No. God, I wish I knew where she was! Because then I'd jump right in my car and go up there and find her!" He smacked his fist down on the sofa arm. Rina was touched by the boy's youthful longing for action, his frustration at finding there was nothing a strong young athlete could do. He added miserably, "I keep thinking she might be in some kind of trouble."

"What kind of trouble?"

But Buck only shrugged unhappily. "You know. Just trouble. I don't know what. She seemed fine at school."

"Yes. She said on the phone she was fine. But even so, I worry a little." Rina was stitching steadily again, her eyes on her work. "She said she wasn't even high."

"Yeah, she hardly ever gets high." But when she glanced at him, a guarded look had come into his eyes.

"Buck, if she went there for pot or ludes or something, how much money would she need?" Rina jabbed the question at him, and the flutter of alarm before he lowered his eyes told her that she was on the track.

But he said, "I don't know about that kind of thing, Mrs. Marshall. And like I said, she doesn't do that much."

"I know she doesn't." Rina knotted the thread and clipped it. How could she get him to help? "Look, Buck, all I want is for her to come back. If you can think of anything that might help, I can keep it confidential."

"No. No, Mrs. Marshall, I can't think of anything." He stood up uneasily, eager to leave now. "Well, let me know what you hear."

"I will, Buck." Rina followed him down to the entry hall. "And you'll tell me what you learn too, okay?"

"Sure." But his answer held little conviction. He added, "Oh, hello, Mrs. Rossi!"

Mamma nodded at him and kissed Rina hello, then turned to take Delores Gallagher's coat. Marie Deaver was parking her car in the crowded driveway. Today Buck was deferential and stood aside while they hung up their raincoats. He held the door while Mrs. Deaver made her way toward them, peering at Buck's red sports car as she passed it.

She nodded at Buck as she came up the flagstones. "Hello, Buck."

"Hi, Mrs. Deaver, how're you doing?" He nodded back, then hurried to his car and backed it carefully around the other cars.

"Well, he's driving all right today," Marie said to Rina in relief.

"Yes."

"Here, Marie, let me take your coat. You must be hot in that wool," Mamma offered, opening the closet door again.

"Thanks, but I'm leaving right away. I just stopped by to pick up the shopping bag I left."

Rina went up the steps with them. "Tell me, what did you find out?" The three of them had been to the public library to look at the scene of Mr. Spencer's death.

"Not much. It's just what we remembered," said Mamma.

"There's the parking lot, and that separate driveway at the end closest to the building, for people who want to use the book drop. You remember those big yew bushes on both sides of that drive?"

"Yes." A massive hedge, broken only by the library entrance itself.

"Well, there was still police tape around those bushes, and a policeman keeping people away, so I guess that's where they found him," said Marie Deaver.

"On the book drop side?" asked Rina, trying to visualize it.

"No, across the drive."

"But you didn't get any more ideas about how it could have happened?"

"No, not really. Does everyone want a cup of coffee?" asked Mamma.

"Love one!" said Delores.

But Marie Deaver said, "Thank you, Leonora, but I really can't stay. Today is the day I have dinner with Bobby."

"Oh, that's right, it takes a couple of hours to drive to the Shadyland Home, doesn't it?"

"Yes. We talk and have dinner. I think he enjoys that."

There was an edge of uncertainty in her voice, and Rina realized she didn't know if he enjoyed it or not. Marie seemed suddenly small and frail and brave to Rina. For forty-some years, she had had to cope with the profound rejection of her autistic son, and yet she never gave up hope, never stopped visiting, never stopped searching for ways to bridge the chasm. In contrast Rina's past problems with Ginny seemed small, ripples on the surface of a deep pool of affection and loyalty. Maybe at the moment Ginny was confused, secretive, reckless; but there were years of love, years of happy moments as they'd read books together, or sewed, or enjoyed music. A million moments that Marie Deaver would never know. But Rina knew, and Ginny knew; and Ginny would come back.

While Mamma and Mrs. Gallagher saw Marie Deaver to

the door, Rina moved back to her workbasket and pulled out some scraps to check color for her next project. There had been some bad moments too, of course. Not as bad as Marie's, but bad all the same. She remembered Long Island, before they had moved to Washington. Back then they had been open with their friends. Most of the hurts had been little unthinking cruelties and condescensions. My, Rina, she looks like your real daughter! *She is my real daughter,* Rina wanted to scream. My, weren't you lucky not to have to go through all the bother of giving birth! *I would have sold my soul to give birth!* Or, worse, the questions their children asked Ginny: Why didn't your real mother want you? Were you left in a basket? When Ginny asked what fathers had to do with babies, she listened soberly to Rina's nervous explanation, and had only one question. "Did I have another father too?" She accepted the answer stoically.

When she was nine, though, she'd come running home one day, her face cut and bruised, and demanded of Rina, "What's a bastard?"

Rina's skin went clammy. She stammered, "Ginny, my Lord, what's happened to you?"

"What's a bastard?"

"Did you fall down? You're bleeding!"

"Mom, I asked you a question! What's a bastard?" Her child's lovely blue eyes were coldly insistent.

Rina could still remember the sickening rush of realization that from now on she was on her own. The agency had prepared her for the earlier questions. Tell the child he is chosen, they said. Tell him his mother gave him up because she loved him. Tell him you love him. Your family will be a real family, just like every other mother's family.

But other mothers didn't have to face a bruised and angry child and force themselves to say, "A bastard is someone whose parents aren't married."

"I'm not a bastard! You're married!"

"Yes, we are."

There was a terrible throbbing pause.

"It's that other woman, isn't it? That first mother?"

Rina was silent.

"Was she married, Mom?"

"I don't think so, Ginny. I think that's why she didn't have a family for you. She loved you, and wanted you to have a family, and so she asked the agency to pick one for you. And they picked us."

This was mostly old information, and Ginny ignored it. She said, "Jean said I was a bastard. It's a bad word, isn't it? She said my mother was a tramp. Was that first mother a tramp?"

"No, Ginny! Of course not! She was just a very young woman, a girl really, and she couldn't take care of you the way she wanted you to be taken care of."

"She wasn't a tramp?"

"No. They told us that. Jean is completely wrong."

"Well, I flattened her," said Ginny with some satisfaction.

"Are you hurt?" Rina tried again to inspect the cut cheek.

"No. Not much. She's hurt more."

Rina, head reeling, said automatically, "You really should try to talk your way through these problems if you can, Ginny."

Ginny's look dripped contempt. "Talk? Oh, sure. What kind of talk? What do I call her? *She's* not the bastard, Mom. *I'm* the bastard." She stalked off down the hall, filled with nine-year-old huffiness, refusing all offers of help as she went to clean her bruises. Rina, the bathroom door shut in her face, found her own heart still galloping, her jaw still clenched to keep herself from shaking. Mrs. Farnham hadn't told her how to handle this.

Later that night, at dinner, Ginny said to Clint and Rina with too much casualness, "I think we should stop telling everybody I'm adopted."

A year or so later, when they told her they were moving to

the Washington area, Ginny had been miserable at the thought of leaving her friends. But one day she had asked, "Will anyone down there know I'm adopted?"

"No, I suppose not. Unless we tell them."

"Good. We won't."

And for years now Ginny had hardly mentioned the subject. Rina worried sometimes, because she suspected that it was still important to her daughter, but she was relieved too. Talking about it always frightened Rina. Always ripped open the old wounds, the old cycle of bereavement as, month after month, she had failed to conceive. "Well, *cara,*" her mother had said from across a great gulf, trying to comfort her, "perhaps God doesn't mean for you to be a mother. He has another plan." And slowly, weeping, she had accepted it. But there were children, she knew, who needed love and guidance as much as she needed to love and guide. Surely God wanted her at least to love and guide a child?

But often she still feared that He didn't.

And Ginny's questions were hard to answer in another way. Be positive about the first mother, the agency had decreed. Raise the child to be moral and sensible. But how? How could you tell a daughter that sex and children belonged in a context of love and commitment, not casual lust, and at the same time maintain that her unmarried young mother had been a good person? How could you explain that you rejoiced at the happenstance that had brought her to you, and at the same time denounce irresponsible sex? Rina found her own feelings so mixed and confused that she despaired of ever being able to explain them to Ginny. She did the necessary: bought books on the facts of life, even got birth control pills for her. But she seldom brought up the subject of Ginny's birth mother, and was relieved that Ginny did not.

But the rebellions became more vigorous, and then Mamma had lost her house and moved in with them. Ginny's grades had fallen, her dance lessons had been abandoned, friends like Jan neglected. Before long Buck, and drugs, had entered her life.

And now she had run away.

Rina picked up a sample of blue calico. Too purple. She put it aside.

But running away couldn't be connected to the adoption. Because where could she run? She didn't have that young mother's name, and could never get it. No one could. It was sealed away. Ginny might know she had been adopted in New York City, but there was no way to get more specific information there either. Rina had contacted the agency two or three times herself, asking timidly for more information about the mother's talents and interests, but her questions had been politely rebuffed. Besides, Ginny had gone to Philadelphia, not New York. So it couldn't be connected to the adoption.

And it wasn't connected to Buck, not directly at least.

Did that mean it was drugs?

Rina had pored over pamphlets and books, and had concluded that Ginny had experimented, as most kids had. But could it be more serious than she thought?

Or could it be a kidnapping, after all?

But then why no ransom note? Why no fear in Ginny's voice on the phone?

Clint came in, and Rina put down the scraps of calico she had been testing for color. "What did they say at the bank?" she asked.

"She withdrew eighty dollars." He hugged her and took off his trench coat.

"That's not a lot, is it?"

"No. Bus ticket to Philadelphia. Food."

"She would have taken more if it was for drugs, don't you think?"

"Rina, I don't know. It wouldn't pay for a lot, anyway."

"Okay, I understand what you mean. I won't get my hopes up."

"Well, there's got to be a reason she won't tell us her friends' names!" he exploded. "If I could just give Paul Buchanan's office a name, they could look!"

"I know, Clint. But she didn't know how serious it is. She hung up before I could tell her anything about it. When she knows the police want to talk to her, she'll tell us where we can find her, I'm sure."

"I know, honey, but it's so damn frustrating!"

"Yes. We'll just have to tell her first thing, so she can't hang up the way she did before. I shouldn't have—"

"Hush, honey, you did what any good mother would have done, you asked about her first."

Rina squeezed his hand gratefully.

"And you know," he continued, frowning down at the floor a moment, "she's obviously got troubles, but somehow—well, I guess I just have faith in her not to do anything absolutely stupid."

"Yes," said Rina eagerly. "I feel that too."

The police came two hours later. Detectives Trainer and Carmody again, a fingerprint man, and a photographer. This time they wanted to search Ginny's room and look around the rest of the house.

"Okay," said Rina, "but I already hunted, and there's nothing. No note, or anything."

"We'll just take a quick look, Mrs. Marshall."

They were very thorough. After the fingerprint man had finished, Carmody and Trainer examined Ginny's schoolbooks and notebooks, her sewing table, the closet and bookshelves. They looked behind the books, Tolstoy and Haley and Dickens and Blume; they looked under the bed. Every little stuffed animal or doll was frisked; every magazine, even the *Playgirl,* riffled with care. Trainer replaced it quietly, without comment, just as he later replaced the birth control pills in the drawer. Rina, although hopeful that they would notice something she had missed, nevertheless felt that she was allowing Ginny to be violated.

Clint was standing behind Rina in the hall outside the bedroom door, frowning. "Sergeant Trainer, what is all this about?"

"We're trying to find your daughter, Mr. Marshall."

"Yes, I appreciate that. But she left Thursday night. This is Saturday afternoon, and suddenly you start working on the case!"

"We've been working on it, sir." Trainer came into the hall. "We're about finished in there now. May we look around the rest of the house?"

"Of course," said Rina.

"But what's the purpose of this?" Clint demanded.

"They're trying to find Ginny!" Rina said.

"I know, honey. But this doesn't feel right." Clint's jaw was jutting, the way it did when he was working on a hotly contested legal case.

The police searched all the drawers and closets, even in the garage and the laundry area and in Mamma's room. Politely, they opened Ginny's brightly wrapped birthday presents, trying not to rip the paper. Finally they were finished and Trainer came to see Clint and Rina, who were sitting in the living room.

"Thank you, Mr. and Mrs. Marshall," he said. Detective Carmody waited partway down the half-flight of steps by the front door.

"Sergeant, can't you tell us what this is all about?" asked Clint. "Maybe we can help."

"Yes, sir, perhaps you can. We appreciate your cooperation." Sergeant Trainer's light-blue eyes were wary. "You see, we've found the weapon that killed Mr. Spencer."

"The weapon?"

"Yes, sir. In Buck Landon's car."

X

"But I want to go to the park!" Sarah pouted at Nick.

"Will is too sick to go." And Ginny is too upset, and your mother is too worried, and your old dad here is not exactly a model of cheeriness either. More like the "before" pictures in an Alka-Seltzer ad. Nick jammed the last of the forks into the dishwasher, sprinkled detergent into the cup, and tried to comfort his daughter. "You helped me walk Zelle this morning, remember? So you did get to go for a while."

"Sometimes Alison gets to go twice." She dug her toe at the floor tiles. Zelle sniffed the spot hopefully, hunting for crumbs left behind by the departing guests.

"Sometimes you get to go twice too. But not today," said Nick firmly. He latched the dishwasher door and started the machine. "Look," he suggested over the throb of the pump, "why don't we go up to the exercise room? We can dance or do some gymnastics and still be around here if Will needs us."

"Well—" This was clearly second-best to the park.

"But maybe you'd better run up and see if Ginny wants to dance with us," he added. "Make sure she's not taking a nap in there."

"Okay." The idea that Ginny might participate cheered her. She trotted upstairs while Nick let Zelle out into the little backyard and then wiped the last of the brunch crumbs from the dining room sideboard.

Sarah's invitation must have been persuasive. Ginny agreed

to borrow one of Maggie's leotards, and Maggie herself decided to join them. She'd been reading to Will, but the fretful little boy now seemed more interested in napping than anything else. The four of them changed and trooped up to the top floor. Kakiy, who had been supervising Will's storytime, streaked upstairs past them and leaped to the sunny windowsill, where he settled calmly to observe them with inscrutable golden eyes.

They all started with warm-up stretches at the barre. Although he kept himself in shape, no waste on his burly body, Nick felt massive, almost Falstaffian, next to the three female forms. A tun of man. Maggie was linear, long strong bones, a womanly lightness softening the lean stretch of muscle. Sarah, fawnlike, had no bulk at all, just springiness, as though she worked by rubber bands. Ginny's newly ripe young figure was slender, not as rangy as Maggie's, not as flexible at first. But as she warmed up she seemed to relax, letting herself respond to the music of the little tape recorder, dreamily. The long black hair, caught in a ponytail, swayed with her movements. Nick saw Maggie watching the girl, delight in her gaze, and had to agree. There was strength and grace there, and not just from Maggie. Ginny's father had also been a gymnast.

Nick was still angry with that father, with Alain Picaud.

With his head he knew that without Alain, without Ginny, Maggie would probably not have become the woman he loved. She would not have the depths of vulnerability and empathy that answered his soul's needs. That was what he knew with his head.

But in his heart he was angry. And jealous, okay, that too. Young Maggie must have been bursting with life and defiance and joy. She still was. But she'd only been fifteen. How could that slimeball have taken advantage of a fifteen-year-old?

"Hey, look," Maggie had said once, "you weren't exactly a virgin either when I married you. Haven't you ever thought there might be a kid out there somewhere that's yours?"

No, he'd never thought that. Not seriously. Not Casanova O'Connor. And anyway, it wasn't the same. He'd used protection. Well, usually. And Carmen and the others had been adults, not girls. And if one of them had told him she was pregnant, he would have—well, okay, he wouldn't have married her. But he would have been responsible about it.

Alain had tried to give Maggie money, he knew. And she'd flung it back in his face.

Would Carmen have flung it in his face? Would Carmen even have told him?

So in theory, maybe, Maggie could be right. But only in theory. It hadn't happened, damn it. And Alain disgusted him, whatever Maggie said.

Je ne regrette rien, was what she said.

After a few minutes Maggie changed the tape and started rearranging the mats. Nick warned, "Ginny, better come down to this end of the barre, or those two will run over you like trucks." Sarah giggled at the thought. Ginny moved closer to the corner so that Maggie and Sarah could have the entire length of the room for their tumbling runs. Nick watched as the little girl tried to copy her mother's combination: handspring to aerial somersault. The first time Sarah managed the handspring, but then something went wrong and she fell, eased to the mat by Maggie's waiting hands.

"Think about the somie before you start the handspring," Maggie suggested.

"Okay." Undaunted, Sarah skipped back and started the run again. This time she bounced from the handspring high into the air, a little tennis ball, and Maggie, her hand ready to guide her daughter's hips, helped her through the aerial lightly. Sarah landed beaming.

"Terrific!" said Maggie, ruffling her hair.

Ginny, beaming too, turned to Nick. "Hurray for Sarah!"

"Yes. An okay kid." He was grinning also, proud of his insubstantial bouncy daughter. A daughter of most rare note.

"Hey, we're done with the floor," called Maggie, getting Sarah launched on the low beam. "All yours, Nick."

"Okay, but I'll need some help, Maggie. I've been having problems with one of the dances for the St. Louis show." He shoved a mat aside and changed the tape. "Look, this is your part." He demonstrated a simple sequence. "One two three four, turn jump three four, I lift you here, four, one two three four. Okay?"

She frowned, concentrating, and mimicked him. Sarah, practicing splits, was watching them closely.

"Okay. Now this time I'll try my part too. I have to fall to my knees and then snap back up and around in time to do the lift. I couldn't quite get it in rehearsal."

He couldn't quite get it here either. The fall to the knees left him facing awkwardly away from his partner, and he was not in position to swing her up easily.

"I think she'll have to slow after the jump, just a little," suggested Ginny from the sidelines. "You'll pull something for sure, twisting and lifting like that."

"Show us," said Maggie. She stepped back to the barre, and Ginny joined Nick. When the count started she went through the steps neatly, and when he turned for the lift she was exactly right, ready to move with him as he swung her up and around.

"Great!" He was impressed; there were sound instincts here, sound training. "That felt a lot better. We'll make that adjustment in St. Louis. Thanks."

"That was wonderful, Ginny!" Maggie was glowing with pride.

"Yeah, well, thanks." Her rubber band had slipped, and she pulled it off, shaking her hair free.

"Look," Nick suggested. "While we've got you here, let's put on some ballet music, okay?"

"Yeah! That'd be fun," Ginny agreed.

Will's crusted face appeared in the stairwell. "Mommy," he whined, "it's itching again."

"Okay, just a minute, Will. I want to watch Ginny dance."

"But it's *itching!*" The whine escalated to a whimper.

"Don't you want to—oh, hell." Maggie started toward her miserable son. "I'll come give you a soda bath, that'll help. And I guess it's time to start the biscuits too."

"I'll make biscuits!" exclaimed Sarah, rising from her split.

"Okay. Will, go on down to the bathroom and start the water, okay?" Maggie smiled regretfully at Ginny, and paused at the top of the stairs. "Come on, Sarah."

"Bye, Kakiy!" Sarah ran to the windowsill and lugged the big orange cat to the middle of the floor, kissing him good-bye and then handing him solemnly to Ginny.

Amused, Ginny accepted the furry bundle. "See you later, Sarah."

"Okay." Sarah grinned at her, waved at Nick, then hurled herself at her mother. Maggie, laughing, caught her and hoisted her onto one hip, carrying her down the stairs, the little girl's thin legs wound around her. Nick felt a rush of warmth, of delight at the happy fate that had connected him to this family. But when he glanced at Ginny, whose blue eyes were also following her mother and sister, he surprised a look of the rawest loss. The young hands holding the cat were tensed into claws. Nick was chilled. Thou hid'st a thousand daggers in thy thoughts.

He turned away hurriedly to pull out a couple of tapes. Best to get her dancing, hard body exercise to burn off that inner poison. "So, let's see what we've got here. What do you want?" he babbled cheerfully, Nick the chucklehead. "How about an old chestnut, *Swan Lake,* maybe?"

"Fine."

His back was to her, but he could hear jealousy and hatred thickening her voice. He inserted the new tape quickly and said, "Here we go!" He punched the button, turned back to her, and froze.

In the seconds it had taken him to change the tape, she had stripped off her leotard, tossed back her hair, and picked up Kakiy. For a throbbing moment nothing seemed real to Nick: the lush strains of Tchaikovsky filling the big room, the beautiful young woman facing him boldly, the hum of his own responding blood. She was holding Kakiy upright against her belly, his head between her breasts, his orange fur shaggy against silky skin. The slanting late light glossed them with a warm apricot glow. They were motionless, all three, except for the golden brush of Kakiy's tail, flicking back and forth, back and forth, alternately concealing and disclosing the dusky pubic triangle. In that instant of ambiguity, the world teetered between reality and make-believe: the lovely body was forbidden, yet beckoning; it was his wife, yet not his wife; it was incest, yet not incest.

Nick shook his head, and the frozen moment shattered, reassembled itself into reality. What faced him here was a wily, lost, infinitely fragile human creature, foolish in her despair. "No, Ginny," he said hoarsely, and cleared his throat.

She coaxed, "C'mon, it won't mean anything. Just for fun."

He wanted to escape downstairs, to jump out the window, to evaporate into the air, anything. He was also profoundly sad for her. "Be honest, Ginny. It won't work."

"Hey, c'mon, don't be old-fashioned. Why shouldn't it work?"

She was forcing him to be the one to summon up truth. Okay, so be it. "Two reasons," he said brutally. "The big one is, she'll never relinquish you again. Never. No matter what you do."

He saw her reel as his words thrust aside the golden show of skin to display her true nakedness: the motive that she herself could not quite face. Nick the hatchet man. He went on relentlessly, "There's nothing you can do, absolutely nothing, that would ever lead her to give you up again. If *you* want to leave, okay, she'll accept that. But she won't ever turn you out, Ginny, no matter what. She's grieved for you too long."

"Grieved?"

"You think it's easy to give up the person you love most in the world? Even when you think it's best for her?"

Ginny fought back, dizzily, brandishing Maggie's words at him like a sword. "She said she'd do it again!"

"She thinks it was best for you. Even so, she's mourned for you every day for sixteen years."

"Some mourning! She's known where I was since my third birthday. My third birthday! And she never did a thing!" Her voice had a shrill edge, and he could see her fighting it, trying to regain her casual tone. "Anyway, she didn't even meet you till I was three!"

"Okay." He grinned a little, letting her deflect the attack a moment. "You're right, I can only vouch personally for the last dozen years."

"Yeah. Well."

"But I've seen her writing letters to you, visiting your neighborhood every year, ignoring friends to sing 'Eentsy Weentsy Spider' to a four-year-old girl when you were four, or discussing Tolkien with a twelve-year-old when you were twelve. Because of you, Ginny. When Sarah was born she clobbered the poor nurse who tried to take her away to be weighed. Because of you. You've been in her heart and mind every single day."

She looked at the floor then, and turned her back on him awkwardly. He pulled the sheet from her mat and tossed it to her, and she set Kakiy down and shrugged it around her shoulders. Roughly, trying to hide her confusion, she said, "There were two reasons, you said."

"Well, the second is probably insignificant in comparison. It has to do with me."

"You don't like straight hair," she suggested in a brittle voice.

He didn't smile. "Ginny, I love Maggie. And I won't let myself be used to hurt her."

She looked down at the mat again. She seemed nunlike: the smooth, severe drape of the sheet like a white habit, her black hair fanning back from her brow like a veil. A pilgrim, searching for grace. "Okay, I apologize," she said with obvious effort. "You're right, I shouldn't try to drag you in. It's nothing to do with you. Except, you make her happy."

"I wish I could help, Ginny, but I don't know how."

"I don't either." The blue eyes flicked up at him, clouded with confusion. "I thought if I found her it would straighten everything out. But it's worse, it's all worse!"

"You thought you could forgive her."

"Yes." Slowly, the nun shook her head. "But she doesn't want my forgiveness. She's not sorry. You say she grieves, but she says she'd do it again! I just don't understand."

She was so young, so very very young. Nick rubbed his hand helplessly over his head. "Yeah. Maybe I should let you think things over for a little."

"Maybe."

He hurried down the stairs. Behind him, Tchaikovsky rolled on, rich cellos and violins in melancholy harmony. Nick wondered if he would ever know harmony again.

But as he changed into his jeans he did feel a grudging flicker of empathy for that slimeball Alain.

Maggie, her hair damp from a shower, was in the kitchen helping Sarah make biscuits. "Gotta talk a minute," Nick said to her.

The quick blue eyes, so like Ginny's, checked his face and registered alarm. But she dusted off her hands and said breezily, "Back in a minute, Sarah. Just keep stirring," and followed Nick up into their bedroom.

He told her bluntly, "We just had the big seduction scene, Maggie."

"The what?"

"Ginny just invited me for a quick roll in the hay."

"What do you mean? She wouldn't—oh, God, she still thinks she's half whore, I should have—well, damn it, why didn't you shut her up? Stop her?" The blue eyes were ablaze.

"Stop her? Are you kidding? I turned . . ."

"Yeah, stop her!" She was striding angrily around the room. "You're the adult, right? You ought to be able to change the subject, something!"

"Maggie, listen, damn it! I turned my back for an instant to change the tape, and when I looked back she was naked!"

"What?" She paused, facing him. "That fast?"

"Doesn't take long to get out of a leotard. You've been known to be pretty nimble that way yourself, lady." On much happier occasions.

"Yeah." She raked her hand through her black curls.

"Believe me, there was no way to change the subject. The subject was all too obvious."

"What did you do?"

"Nothing to do but try to patch things up."

"You really didn't see it coming?" The question was almost wistful.

"Maggie, you know I would have been away in a flash."

She touched his arm. "Yeah, okay. I know."

"Although there was something—well, here's the sequence: you go downstairs hugging Sarah, Ginny looks daggers at you, I try to make conversation while I'm changing the tape, I turn around, and there she is."

"I see. Of course. Goddamn it." She sat down limply on the big blue-and-white bedspread. "I'm the one who should have warned you, after what I had to tell her today. Shot down her pet illusion. No wonder she's furious at me."

"Loves you too."

"Yeah, I know. And thinks she's like me. Teenage whore. Thinks I seduced a married man, so it's in her blood, right?"

"I see how she might have thought so before. But she's met you now."

"She's been dealing with ugly possibilities all her life. It'll take a while to shake them off. Rape, incest, prostitution—she doesn't know who she is, doesn't know where she came from . . ." She shook her head.

"Yeah. It's hard for a kid to figure out." Nick half-sat, propping himself against the dresser near her.

"Yeah." She leaned forward, her elbows on her knees, her forehead on her hands. "I mean, to a little kid mothers are mythic for a while. Perfect. All-powerful, all-loving, all-protective, all-giving. It's hard to grasp that mothers are regular human beings, just bumbling along as best we can in a very unyielding and unfair world. When I was Ginny's age I was only just beginning to understand that. The myth tells us that a woman who relinquishes her child is the ultimate Bad Mother. The ultimate evil." She looked up at him mournfully. "It must be a real smack in the face when the all-powerful doesn't keep you. When the all-giving doesn't give to you."

"But you *did!*"

"Yeah. More than any human should ever be asked to give. But she's not thinking of human realities, she's thinking about that perfect mythic mother we all wish we'd had, and that evil mythic mother she thinks she got. Nick, she's still so young! Of course she can't understand. May not understand for years."

"Probably not."

"If only . . ." She frowned down at the design of the spread, tracing it with her finger, then glanced up at him again. "I'm sorry you have to put up with us, Nick. Do you think she'll be after you again?"

"Not that way. I gave it to her straight. Said I wouldn't be used to hurt you, and that you'd never reject her anyway, no matter what."

"Good. What did she say?"

"Well, she'd been pretending to be, I don't know, the thorougly modern young woman. So what if it wrecks people's lives? If it feels good, do it. Even had herself half convinced. But when I hit her with the truth she was honest enough. Admitted I really wasn't part of it. Admitted it was more a test for you."

"Yeah. She's honest at the core, Nick. Even when it's painful."

"I know." Nick hesitated; he didn't want to hurt Maggie further, but something else had to be said. He began cautiously, "Maggie, I value her imagination and mind too. She's bright, and talented, and beautiful, and she'll be a terrific woman."

Maggie smiled at him, her eyes shining. "Oh, Nick, I know! She's wonderful! I'm so grateful to those people for doing all the things I couldn't do for her!"

"Yeah, right. But she still has a lot of demons to wrestle down. And I'm worried about our kids."

Maggie shook her head, so promptly that he knew she had already considered this problem. "No. She won't hurt the kids. She'll find ways to test me again, sure. She's angry because I'm not the perfect mythic mother. But even if she's furious and full of hate for me, she'll see them as fellow victims."

This was a lost cause, he could see. She was as fiercely committed to Ginny as she was to Sarah and Will, as she was to him. He sighed. "Maybe. She sure didn't see me as a fellow victim."

"Nah, you're a big guy, you can take care of yourself. And she's more likely to try to rescue the kids than hurt them." Maggie stood up again and touched his arm lightly. "But I am sorry it's turned out to be so difficult."

"Yeah. Wish she'd waited a few years before she came looking for you."

"We Ryans aren't very good at waiting. But I am sorry."

"Oh, hell." He took her gently by the shoulders to kiss her. "You told me this came with the package. And I wouldn't change the package for anything in the world."

She squeezed him gratefully. "Yeah."

"Let's check on Will while we're up here, okay?"

He was asleep but restless. Maggie tested his rosy forehead with a gentle bony hand. "A little feverish. Just like Sarah two weeks ago," she said sadly. "We're in for it again."

Kakiy was sitting now on Will's windowsill, an icon of serenity among the toys and tumbled sheets. Nick and Maggie went down the stairs, hand in hand.

Sarah's biscuits had been thoroughly mixed. They got them into the oven and sent her upstairs to wash her hands and face. Nick lifted a lid and saw creamed chicken simmering in the pan.

In a moment Ginny appeared at the kitchen door, dropped her backpack to the floor, and leaned wearily against the door frame. "I give up," she said.

"Give up?" Wary, Maggie perched on the oak table.

The girl looked exhausted, but she was watching them both closely. "Yes. You win. I can't take it. I have to go back home and think about things a while."

Nick could see that it was a blow to Maggie, but she said steadily enough, "You'll come back?"

"Maybe. Not soon." She waved her hand airily. "I might set fire to your house."

Nick and Maggie exchanged a quick glance, just a fleeting flicker of shared amusement and pain, but Ginny caught it. "Shit, you tell her everything!" she burst out.

"We're partners," said Nick.

"Yeah. I know. Wedlock," said the girl bitterly. "And I'm out of wedlock. Locked out. Right?"

"I'm afraid not," said Maggie. "You and I are bound together too, Ginny. Like it or not, it's forever."

Their gaze held for a moment, then the girl looked down and nudged her backpack with her toe. "Yeah. That's what I have to go home to figure out. I seem to be freaking out here."

"Okay. But I hope you'll come back when you can."

"Yeah. Listen, I'd better call Mom and tell her."

"Sure." Maggie moved aside readily so Ginny could reach the phone, but Nick could see that she was lanced with the pain of this second parting. She was right, of course, there were problems aplenty that still needed to be worked out. But as he opened the cabinet to get out the plates, he had to admit that he, like Ginny, could use an intermission. No one spoke while the girl dialed.

Someone answered immediately.

"Hi, Mom," said Ginny with forced cheerfulness; then her hand clenched on the receiver. "A murder? The day I left? Are you kidding? . . . Mom, that's impossible!" Ginny licked her lips. "My friends here won't want to talk to the police! And why should the police care where I am anyway? And what do . . ." She halted, staring in bewilderment at the silent receiver. Maggie had pressed down the cradle to cut the connection.

"Hey!" Ginny said furiously. "What the shit are you doing, Maggie? I've got to talk to her! She says there's been a murder!"

"So I gathered. But I thought you didn't want your parents to know you'd searched for me. Therefore, you get off this phone."

"But—" Realization dawned. "You mean they're tracing the call?"

"They might be. For murder they might be. For someone the police want to talk to. And so you and I are going to find a

public phone booth right now, a little closer to Philadelphia."
She bounded toward the front door.

"Oh, God. I see. Okay." Frightened into docility, Ginny
dashed after.

Maggie, at the coatrack, called over her shoulder, "Nick?"

"I know." He stood abandoned, holding a plate at the
kitchen door. "If anyone asks, I've never heard of Ginny. And
I'll keep an eye on poor old Will."

"And the biscuits come out in three minutes. Thanks, love.
See you in a couple of hours."

Then they were gone.

XI

The car was a black Camaro, quicker and smoother than Buck's car. Ginny was astonished at how skillfully Maggie wove through the city expressways, across the bridges, and down the New Jersey Turnpike, slackening speed only when a police car was near. Maggie made her repeat the fragment of conversation with Mom, then fell silent, except to say as she missed a pickup by inches, "Pardon the recklessness, but if they were tracing that call we have to move fast to the phone we're going to let them trace. Make them think there was a mistake on that one. Though I think we hung up soon enough."

"God, I hope so." The traffic came in knots, and right now they were slipping around vehicles of every shape, cutting through split-second gaps between cars, weaving among the trucks and semis to the next open stretch. The sky was darkening. It's all a dream, thought Ginny, it can't be real.

But she knew it wasn't a dream. In her dreams the people ran from her, flew away. They didn't claim to love her, or grieve for her. They didn't confuse her so much. Damn.

In about an hour they pulled into a shopping mall near the Trenton exit. "This should be close enough. Philadelphia's just across the river," said Maggie, cruising past the plastic-roofed walkway until she spotted some phone booths. She parked nearby. "Call collect."

Ginny did. The air was cold in her nostrils, smelling of

exhaust and a nearby hamburger place. She found she was hungry.

"Will you pay for the call?" The operator sounded sleepy.

"Yes. Oh, yes!" Mom's eager voice.

"Go ahead."

Ginny took a deep breath. "Hi, Mom. Sorry about the interruption. Ran out of change."

"Ginny, please, come home. I've been crazy—wait, don't hang up, please!"

Ginny felt a pang. Mom didn't deserve this pain. She was loving and accepting. Everything Maggie only claimed to be.

"Hey, Mom, I didn't mean to scare you. I told you I was okay."

"I know, I'm sorry. I just naturally worry when you're away."

Ginny repeated, "I didn't mean to scare you. But please, tell me about this murder!"

"It's serious, Ginny. We think your Philadelphia friends should be willing to sign a statement, you see, for evidence that you were there."

"Mom, they just can't. I won't drag them into this. I mean, why is it so important? Who was killed?"

"Mr. Spencer. Do you remember him?"

"Spencer?"

"He was playing bridge the day you left."

"Oh, Gram's friend! Sure, I remember him."

"Well, he was murdered, Ginny."

"God, that's spooky! I just saw him, Thursday afternoon!"

"Where?"

"At the bridge party. Where else?"

"Yes. Well, he was killed not long after he left this house."

"What happened?"

"They don't know, exactly. Mrs. Gallagher took him home, and he was fine then. But he was found around seven-thirty or eight that night. In the bushes by the library. He'd been stabbed, Ginny."

Ginny shivered. "God! Poor old guy."

"Yes."

"But Mom, I still don't understand. Why do they want to talk to me about it? I didn't know him, Gram did. And he was still in the house when I left for, um, Philadelphia."

"Well, the police are very thorough, Ginny."

"Sure, I know. But there has to be more to it than that, Mom. Come on, tell me."

Mom said carefully, "Well, you see, Ginny, the problem is, he was stabbed with a pair of scissors. They found them in Buck's car."

"Buck's! My God!" A whisper of cold was running down behind Ginny's breastbone.

"Yes, but that's not the worst thing."

"What do you mean? What could be worse?"

"Ginny, they were your scissors."

"And that's all she knew?" Maggie asked.

They were sitting at a table made of wood-grained plastic in the mall hamburger shop, eating hamburgers and fries from yellow foam trays that impersonated plates. Maggie had taken one look at Ginny's bloodless face when she emerged from the phone booth and had steered her to the nearest source of food. Ginny didn't feel so dizzy anymore, but the shock had given way to a growing panic. She shook her head violently.

"That's all! Somebody got my scissors out of my room and stabbed that poor old guy! The body ended up at the library, but he could have been killed anywhere, she says. The scissors were in Buck's car. But Buck was with a couple of friends at the time of the stabbing."

"How do they know they're your scissors?"

"Easy. My name is scratched onto the blade, so they won't get mixed up with Mom's."

"I see."

"And the police think that's why I disappeared! Jesus, why did I ever come here?"

The other blue eyes widened innocently. "Hey, wow, that's it, all right! That's our major problem! Figuring out why you came!"

"Lay off, Maggie! They want me for murder! Murder! Don't you understand?" She looked wildly around the green-and-yellow restaurant. "And here I am, miles from everyone, and I can't defend myself!"

"That's better." Maggie's voice was cool, tugging her back from the edge of panic. "Now we're zeroing in on the problem. But you might keep your voice down. Remember, you're half French."

"What does that have to do with it?" asked Ginny in spite of herself, and then felt like a fool. Maggie could play her like a fish, she thought helplessly. Any reference to her origins diverted her from anything else. No matter how serious.

Maggie explained, "The French pride themselves on being able to think clearly and precisely. Descartes and all that."

Infuriating woman. Ginny had imagined a hundred possible mothers, a hundred reasons she didn't live up to Mom's dreams or her own. But she'd never imagined one who outsmarted agencies, and knew Shakespeare, and drove faster than Buck, and in a crisis told her to be more like Descartes. Infuriating! But she was right too. A bit of logic wouldn't hurt now. Ginny ate her dill pickle and tried not to sound surly. "Well?"

"We have to decide what to do. And the best way to start might be to define our goal."

"Staying out of jail! God, that's obvious! Isn't that clear enough for you? Precise enough?"

"Thank you, yes. I think jail can be avoided. He was killed while you were on the five-thirty bus, right? Who did you sit with?"

"A deaf old man who snored all the way to New York."

"Not too good. Will the driver remember you?"

"Maybe. Maybe not."

"How about once you got to the bus station? Did you meet anyone there?"

"Three nuns and a pimp."

"Lucky you. Usually the ratio is the other way around. Well, maybe the nuns will remember you, if we can find them. Know where they live?"

"No, but they took the bus on to Albany."

"Okay. And of course Mrs. Elkin at the agency can tell them about your visit."

"No!"

"Oh?"

"Look, don't be funny. That would kill Mom."

"You mean she'd prefer to see you arrested?"

"No, but—" It was unthinkable, that was all. Ginny tried to explain. "Look. She'd do anything to keep me from being arrested. But knowing I searched for you would hurt her too much, Maggie. You don't know how—how fragile she is about that. I just can't do that to her."

"She may have to know someday."

"Maybe. But with everything else—no. Right now it would be brutal. I can't do it."

"I know you want to hide it from her. That's why we changed phones. But we've got to make hard decisions now. Would you really rather be arrested? Rather than hurt her?"

Damn. Was that what it came down to? Ginny poked at her French fries, thought about Mom, and said, "Yes."

"Okay." Maggie seemed suddenly and unaccountably cheered. "We don't want to hurt your mother. So it turns out that we have two goals. Keep from being arrested. And keep your parents from discovering where you've been."

"But you just said we couldn't do both!"

"No, no, I was just asking in case we were eventually forced

to choose. Let's look for better ways first. Did Buck hate
Spencer?"

Ginny felt as though she'd been punched. Clear thinking
could hurt. Still, Mom had said he'd been in her room looking
for her, then he'd bumped into Spencer on the way out, insulted him even. But Buck wouldn't kill anyone! She said,
"No, of course not. He only met him once. Besides, he was
with friends."

"Would his friends lie for him?"

Damn. Of course they would. But what outsiders could
have been in her room? "Maybe someone from the telephone
company?" Ginny suggested desperately. "Something like
that?"

Maggie frowned. "Someone comes in to fix the telephone,
goes into your room, takes the scissors, and happens to stab
Spencer?"

"Well, it's just that it must be someone from outside, because nobody I know would do that."

"I see."

"But the outsider would have to be able to get the scissors
somehow," Ginny admitted.

"Yes. And would have to know you well enough to leave
them in Buck's car. Pretty knowledgeable for a telephone re-
pairman."

"Damn."

"The facts do narrow the field. What about you, Ginny?
Does anyone hate you enough to want to frame you? Or
frame Buck?"

"God, I don't think so." Ginny shrugged unhappily. "No
one I know of. Except maybe Debbie Macklin because she
used to go with Buck. But she wouldn't stab anybody, she's
about as tough as vanilla pudding."

"Well, think about it. Did anyone know you were leaving?"

"No."

"Sure?"

"Look, even *I* didn't know I was leaving until I saw that phone book in the library!"

"But you'd already taken your bankbook."

"Yeah. But I hadn't really decided! When I took it, it was all still fantasy, you know? Like everything else. Damn it, Maggie, you still don't seem real!"

"I know. It'll take a long time to get used to it, Ginny. For me too."

"Yeah. Well, I'll have lots of time to get used to it in jail."

"That's right. Look on the bright side."

Ginny thumped the table with her fist. "Well, what the hell do you suggest? So far we've had zero ideas!"

"We have to know a little more. Like who else was at your house Thursday afternoon. When you saw your scissors last. Where the library is. Et cetera. And you'd better tell me on the way home." She had been glancing out the window, and now quickly shoved their little plastic trays into the open mouth of a frog-shaped trash can, adjusted her red scarf, and went out the door. Ginny followed, surprised at the sudden haste.

"Whoops! Slight detour." Maggie spoke quietly but her hand on Ginny's arm was powerful. Ginny was propelled into the path of a mall employee wearing the turquoise-and-white cap of the soft-drink stand further down the mall.

"Oh, sorry!" said Ginny in confusion, staring into the young man's startled small eyes.

"It's okay," he said, and looked after them as Maggie, hiding her face from him as she studied the doors of parked cars, whisked Ginny into the seat of a metallic-blue Toyota sitting unattended and unlocked in the first rank of cars.

"Tell me when he's gone," said Maggie, head down and still hidden as she fumbled in her handbag.

"What the hell are you doing? Why are we in this car?"

"Patrol car back there. And the cops in it headed straight for the phone booths," Maggie explained.

"Oh, Jesus!" It was true. A uniformed officer, no, two of them, were inspecting the booth she had recently left, then looking around at the various shops along the mall sidewalk.

"Is your buddy in the turquoise cap gone?"

"Yes. He's just going into the soft-drink stand. And, oh God, Maggie, the cops are going into the hamburger place!"

"Good. Get out, look calm. I'll stay between you and the police." She pulled off her scarf.

They strolled in assumed placidity from the Toyota to the Camaro three ranks away. Once inside, Ginny glanced back as Maggie steered the car unhurriedly to the exit. "Uh, oh," she said. "They're coming out!"

"Get your head down. Now, it'll be okay. Nobody noticed us change cars. The cops will have to question a lot of people before they even find out we got into a blue Toyota."

"Oh. Oh, I see."

"But you'd better stay slumped down there for a few miles even so."

The ride back to Brooklyn was not so frantic, the object now being to blend into the background rather than to speed to their destination. Ginny, slouching below window level for most of the trip, watched the twilit sky redden in the west. The vast industrial fields of New Jersey stretched dead and barren to the horizon, the dusty storage tanks and steel skeletons of construction projects as grim as Ginny's mood. Under Maggie's questioning, Ginny reported what she could remember about Thursday afternoon. She described her room, her table with crafts supplies and scissors, her bed and bookcase, Kakiy's box, the layout of the house, and all the people who had been there that day. She described the argument with Gram over Kakiy, how he had been kicked and she had yelled at Gram and Mr. Spencer.

"Do you suppose she told the police about that?" Ginny asked worriedly.

"I don't know her, Ginny."

"She probably did. Because they'd want to know why I left."

"Yes."

"Damn. Why can't I keep my mouth shut?"

"Because you love Kakiy, ninny."

Ginny shot her a grateful glance. Maggie was sitting relaxed at the wheel, the western light coming from a little behind her left shoulder, glinting warm on the black curls. Ginny felt that she'd been her friend all her life, this instantly familiar woman who could appreciate her love for a cat, and laughed at her jokes, and understood her hunger to know about her birth.

And who also, she reminded herself sternly, had signed her away to other people without a backward glance.

Except to grieve, if Nick could be believed.

Damn. She could not understand.

Maggie was pursuing the problem at hand. "Okay, now. How did you leave things with your parents just now?"

"Indefinite. I said I wanted to go home, but this might delay things."

"How did they take it?"

"Dad was angry. Said my Philadelphia friends were certainly selfish to refuse to talk to the police. He said I should come home anyway."

"And your mother?"

"Mom said, 'Do what has to be done.' Which is surprising."

"Why?"

"Well, usually it's the other way around. Mom wants to protect me. Dad says, 'Use your good sense.' He's more philosophical about all my messing around."

"I see."

"I bet he's trying to protect Mom. Damn, Maggie, she

must really be worried if he's like that! I didn't mean for her to worry! I thought if I called she'd be okay."

"I know. We mothers do have an unfortunate habit of worrying. You still think it would be even worse for her if she knew you found me?"

"Well—I don't know how to explain it. She'd feel threatened, I think. I used to ask her sometimes about my first mother. She always tried to answer, but I could tell it scared her to death. As though she was supposed to be my whole world, and if I asked about you it meant she'd failed. That's why I quit asking. Read stuff at the library instead."

"She certainly didn't fail!"

"She'd think so."

"I see. So the agency is right to keep quiet?"

"Well—maybe for Mom's sake, yes."

Maggie asked wistfully, "She may understand someday, don't you think?"

"Maybe." Ginny wasn't too sure. Mom's love was so fierce. Solid. Possessive. Dependable. She wanted her, right now.

Maggie sighed and reverted to the present problem. "So, they don't know if you're coming home or not."

"They know I won't be there tonight."

"Good. That'll give us time to think."

"And maybe something will happen," said Ginny hopefully. "Maybe they'll find out who did it."

"Maybe."

They had crossed the bridge from Staten Island and were swinging north again, around the west rim of Brooklyn. Maggie left the expressway to pull up at a twenty-four-hour drugstore. "Come on in with me."

"Why? What are we doing?" Ginny followed her nervously.

"I need some shades. What model do you like?" She was taking reflective sunglasses from a big revolving display stand, plunking them onto her nose one by one and peering at herself in a mirrored column nearby.

"Jesus, the cops after me and you expect me to drop everything to help you shop?"

"Hey, come on. Which is more fashionable? Aviators or these black square jobs?"

"Aviators. Maggie, why now? It's dark already! What the hell are you doing?"

"Buying sunglasses." She paid for the glasses, dropped them into her trench coat pocket, and held the door open for Ginny.

"You're crazy."

"Yep."

They headed north again. "Okay, now," said Maggie. "How would you like to hide out at my house a few days?"

"Stay there?"

"Yes."

"Maggie, no. I mean, things have changed so I can't go home yet. But I just couldn't take that. I can't think things through when I'm with you. All these feelings keep tripping me up. I'll go to the Y or something. I've got a little money."

"Okay. If you want."

"Besides, they may figure out I'm with you."

"How would they find out?"

"Well, maybe ask at the agency."

"And if they ask at the agency, what will the answer be?"

"Well—" Ginny considered. She didn't know what the answer would be. But she knew what it wouldn't be. She giggled suddenly. "Hey, you're right. Elkin and Farnham won't ever let anyone see that file again. No matter how nicely they ask, they'll be sure they're just secret agents from one of us. And they certainly won't admit to outsiders that I saw it. Poor policemen won't have a chance!"

"Right. Farnham will be convinced it's just you or me in

disguise. They could get a court order, I suppose, but judges are pretty sticky about that. And I wouldn't be surprised if the agency fought it."

"So we've got time."

"At least a little. Yes. Anyway, the cops won't even get as far as the agency unless your parents suggest it."

"That's true!" A sudden doubt assailed her. "But you know, Mom knows I went through the strongbox that has my papers in it."

"Did you take any of the papers? Or mention them?"

"Oh, no, of course not. Only my bankbook."

"Well, Ginny," said Maggie, turning off the expressway with a worried frown, "if I know anything about parents, they're more likely to think you're after drugs."

"God!" Ginny saw that she was right. "So they won't even get as far as Elkin! Thank God!"

"Right. Not for quite a while."

"And Mom probably thinks my Philadelphia friends are pushers or something!"

"Probably. Especially since they won't cooperate with the police."

The full horror of Mom's situation was coming home to Ginny. "God, no wonder she's so worried!"

"Yep."

"But I still can't stay with you."

"Yeah, I know. Because of how you feel about me." The sad blue eyes lit on Ginny an instant, then returned to the road.

Ginny made a last desperate attempt. "I just don't see how you could still say that you—oh, never mind. I just can't stay with you."

"Yeah. Okay, two things, Ginny. Number one, you came to me for the truth. You deserve the truth. I could say what you want me to say, but I won't because it would be a lie. I hope you can believe that."

"Yeah. I guess so. But I don't understand!"

"I know. Number two, it's okay for you to stay at my place, because I won't be there."

"What?"

Maggie said patiently, "I won't be at my house. So you can stay there if you want."

"What are you talking about?"

"I've decided to take a little trip to Maryland."

Ginny's insides knotted. "What do you mean? What can you do there besides make things worse?"

"I can ask around. Find out where this fellow died, what the evidence is. Talk to people there."

"You're kidding!"

"Not at all."

"Jesus! That is probably the all-time dumbest idea I've ever heard!"

"Maybe it is. Tell me why."

"God! Where to begin!" Ginny held up a hand and began ticking off the arguments on her fingers. "Okay, first, our famous goals. Clear and precise and French. Start with staying out of jail. The minute they find out who you are, they'll find me. Two, Mom will know. Both goals shot at once!"

"Granted. *If* they find out who I am. But they won't. Next reason?"

"Of course they will! I mean, you're a statistician. Not a goddamn private eye. Why should you be asking questions? Who'd answer them?"

"I'll be a journalist. My brother's married to a reporter. Your Aunt Olivia. I'll act like her. Next question?"

Aunt Olivia. She had an Aunt Olivia! Staggered by this casual reference to connections she'd never dreamed of, Ginny needed a moment to get her reeling thoughts back on track.

Murder. Police. Keeping Maggie away from Mom. Those were the priorities.

Clearly, reasoned arguments were having no effect. Ginny switched to emotional appeals. "What about Will? Nick will be gone too, remember? Don't you want to take care of your kid?"

"Yes, I do. That's why I'm going to Maryland."

"Jesus."

"And that's why I want you to stay instead of going to a motel. You're right, Will needs attention. Sarah too, of course."

"Jesus, Maggie."

"You mean you don't know how to baby-sit? You can't?"

"Of course I can. Been doing it for years. But I won't! Because I don't want you there messing with Mom and Dad. They're not dumb. They'll spot you."

"How?"

"You look like me, damn it!"

Maggie pulled her new sunglasses from her pocket and put them on. Ginny was appalled. They worked.

"You look like the goddamn Lone Ranger," she groused. "Jesus, Maggie, this is impossible!"

"The whole situation is already impossible. We'll just join in."

"No!"

"Okay," said Maggie cheerfully, steering the Camaro along a brownstone-lined avenue. "We'll follow your plan instead."

"My plan?"

"Sure. What is it?"

"My plan?"

"Your plan. What were you thinking of doing?"

"I don't know, but not that!"

Maggie turned at the stone synagogue and found a place at the curb half a block from her door. She said nothing, but glanced at Ginny a time or two as they walked back. Ginny refused to look at her. She was trying to be clear and precise, laying out her options carefully.

If she went back, and told where she'd really been, Mom would be devastated. That one was out.

If she went back, and refused to say where she had been, the police would probably arrest her. The scissors were hers, found in Buck's car. And with such a handy and reticent suspect, would the police even try to find anyone else? Mom and Dad would be frantic. That one seemed to be out, too.

If she went somewhere, a motel or something, that just postponed the choice. And there would be no way to learn what was happening at home. She could wait forever and never hear if the police had found the real murderer. She couldn't call, they'd tapped her home phone. Maybe she could call Dad at work, or even Jan. But Jan wouldn't know much, and Ginny would be afraid to call either number more than once, or they'd tap it too. How could she find out when she could go home? If ever?

She'd be just as much a prisoner as if she'd been arrested.

And the mirrored sunglasses really did hide those eyes.

And even after she'd found Ginny, Maggie had honored those damn sealed agreements for thirteen years.

Ginny said, "When you're there, will you call and tell me what's happening?"

"Of course." Maggie, pulling out her door keys, paused at the foot of the stoop.

"The only reason I'm even considering this is Mom," Ginny said sternly. "You have to swear you won't let her find out, ever."

And under the streetlight, solemnly, Maggie raised her hand and said, "I swear, Ginny. They won't find out from me."

So Ginny, with nowhere else to turn, consented to the outrageous scheme. A scheme that would trap her in Brooklyn with her little brother and sister, and would send her new-found mother to join her real one hundreds of miles away in Maryland. Insane.

"I can't believe all this," she said grimly.

"Don't try," said Maggie, inserting the key. "Just get through one minute at a time."

Sunday, September 16, 1979

....

XII

"Nick, it won't be for long. She loves the kids, and she's responsible."

"She takes very good care of her cat, granted. But—"

"It's lots more than the cat, you know that! She's trying to take care of her mother too. Trying to shield her. Besides, we'll be checking on them."

"From hundreds of miles away, yeah. We can't get back very fast if something goes wrong."

"Look, I'm calling Ellen. She's as close as we would be if we were here, at work." Maggie's eyes, dusk-blue and intense, held him. "Nick, I've got to help her, and I just can't think of another plan."

"Neither can I," Nick admitted, resigned but unhappy still. Damn industrial show. He'd go do the private-eye gig in Washington himself if he could. But he couldn't. And Ginny's dilemma needed immediate attention.

He had packed for St. Louis last night after he got Will and Sarah settled, and had only a few toilet articles to stow this morning before Maggie drove him to his plane. Now, glumly pouring himself some orange juice, he watched Maggie dial. "Hi, Dan, it's Maggie. I can't come in for a couple of days. Family crisis. But I'll leave you the McGraw stuff, and give Rivkin a call and put him off." She listened a moment. "Oh, shit. They want to come in tomorrow? Well, you and Joel will have to manage." She laughed suddenly. "Right, that's the spirit. I'll vote you a bonus come Christmas. Thanks, Dan."

Ginny came in as she was dialing again, and she cupped her hand over the mouthpiece to say, "Scrounge your own breakfast, Ginny. Dishes there, orange juice in the—oh, hi, Ellen. Maggie. Can you walk Sarah to school for me for a couple of days? I'll be out of town. It's Claudia's week to walk the kids home, of course." She shrugged at the receiver. "Oh, he's about what you'd expect. Itchy, cranky, feverish. A delight to all around him. Ginny will baby-sit, poor thing." She shook her head. "No, I most certainly will not tell you, you don't want to know." A pause. "Listen, have I ever in my life misled you? . . . Well, except for that. . . . Yeah, that too. Okay, okay, forget I asked. Spare me your quips and quiddities. This is all in a good cause, you damn lawyer." She smiled fondly at the receiver, then dialed again.

"Annette? Maggie. Sorry to bother you Sunday morning, but I have to go out of town, and I wondered if you were going to the grocery today, by any chance." A brief pause. "Right now? Terrific! Two half-gallons of milk and some whole-wheat bread."

Nick had pulled a bag of English muffins from the bread drawer and held it up with a questioning look at Ginny. She nodded and he put two in the toaster. She poured herself some orange juice and sat down at the oak table. She looked wan and solemn today, shaken by the internal and external crises that had swept over her. Nick was not eager to leave them behind.

Maggie hung up, eyed their muffins, and said to Ginny, "Bring your fuel on upstairs. I need your advice."

A few moments later, when Nick went up to collect his jacket and overnight bag, the bedroom was a chaos of Maggie's clothes. Ginny was sitting on the edge of the rumpled bed finishing her coffee and watching the flurry of activity almost in awe.

"Oh, Nick, good, you can help too!" Maggie exclaimed. "Now, I'm a journalist, right? Eager young thing from a New York magazine. And I wear aviators"—she put on her new sunglasses—"and the question is, What goes with them?"

Nick looked at her critically. "The black cowl-neck sweater is fine. Not jeans. Something else."

"A skirt?" Maggie hauled out a navy-blue and a tweed.

"Not quite right. Though the tweed might do in a pinch."

"I've got these old gray tweed slacks. Haven't worn them for years." She held them up to herself. "God, look, I'd forgotten they flare! This journalist would never wear them. Neither would I, for that matter. Time to throw them out."

"Really?" asked Ginny, putting down her mug on the night table. "You're going to throw them out?"

"Do you want them? Take them. Hey, how about corduroy?"

"Better," said Nick. He unzipped his bag, noticed he'd forgotten his after-shave, and fetched the bottle from the bathroom.

"Got any scissors?" asked Ginny.

"Sewing kit's on the top shelf of the closet," said Maggie, pulling on the corduroy slacks. "Hey, look! How's this with the corduroys?" She pulled a long white fringed scarf from the closet.

"That's great!" said Ginny. "Do you have any knee socks?"

"Yeah, gray ones."

"Fine." Ginny was snipping industriously at her newly acquired tweed slacks. Maggie pulled on the light tan corduroy jeans and peered at herself critically in the mirror. She tied her red scarf around her head.

"How's this?"

Nick shook his head. "No. Let your hair curl. If you pull it back like that it flattens down like Ginny's."

"You're right. How about a beret, then?" She produced a

white one. "What do you think, Ginny? *Très chic, n'est-ce pas?*"

"If that's a question, it'll have to wait. You neglected to tell me I should be studying French."

"I did not! It's all in the letters the agency won't give you. Earrings, now. Your generation never wears them, right? Just safety pins through your ears?"

"Yeah, or rusty nails."

"We'll have tasteful gold circles, then. Don't want to look your age."

"Heaven forbid," said Ginny.

Will, chubby, red, and cross, appeared in the door. "Gotta pee, Mommy," he declared imperiously.

"Okay, love. Come on."

"Want me to do it?" asked Nick.

"Not if he's in this mood. We'd better not cross him." She scooped up the little boy. "Phew! You smell bad! Let's get you changed!"

Nick sat down near the window, trying to dampen his uneasiness. Ginny didn't look like a problem at the moment: young, yes, but serious and competent, stitching skillfully around the legs of the tweed pants. Maggie returned in a few minutes with a grumpy but cleaner Will. She handed him to Nick. He propped the little boy on his lap and began to murmur, "Our revels now are ended." His son, pimpled and itchy, leaned against his chest, a surly look on his face but at least listening, at least quiet. Parents had to learn to settle for less than constant joy in their children. A difficult lesson sometimes.

Ginny said to Maggie, "Get the corduroys off. Try these."

"Those old things? Really? Hey, they're different!" Maggie, intrigued, slid out of the corduroys and into the transformed tweeds. Ginny tucked pins into each leg to fasten them, and Maggie exclaimed, "My God! Tweed knickers!"

"Where are those knee socks?" asked Ginny.

"Third drawer. Ginny, they're incredible!"

Ginny found the socks and tossed them to Maggie, who was inspecting the knee pants with a rather dazed expression. She pulled on the socks, added black oxfords, and stood staring into the mirror. Nick was impressed too. Ginny's spur-of-the-moment creation fit the invented journalist's personality exactly.

"I'm perfect!" announced Maggie.

"Almost," said Ginny. "Do you have any fur? Or maybe a leather jacket?"

"Fur!" Maggie glanced swiftly at Nick. He saw her decide to go for broke. "Right. Here you are." She dove into the closet and emerged with a white rabbit-fur coat that he hadn't seen for years. She draped it around her shoulders. Nick, still murmuring to Will, felt memories crowding in. She'd worn that coat the winter he'd first met her. A bright, brash college student, determined to wring some joy from life but sometimes flung back into her grief by what he now knew were reminders of her lost child. Now, as then, she hid the pain behind a joke and a swagger. "Better than Lois Lane," she said to Ginny, preening. "I oughta be on TV."

"Yes. Now you're perfect. Take jeans and the corduroys for a change. And maybe a yellow sweater. I never wear yellow."

"God, I never do either. Makes my skin look gray. But I'll pick one up on the way down."

Ginny was stirring her finger in the little button box. "I'd better put some buttons on your knickers."

"Right. Thanks."

While Ginny fixed the buttons and buttonholes, Maggie padded storklike around the room in sweater, bikini panties, and gray knee socks, filling a flight bag with the tan corduroys, a white sweater, underwear, and notebooks. When Ginny had finished she picked up the knickers and inspected the work carefully. "Awe-inspiring," she said, handing them to Nick. She put the scissors and sewing kit away.

"I know a couple of costumers who could use your talents," Nick said.

"Say revels, Daddy!" groused Will on his knee.

The doorbell rang.

"Oh, God, Annette!" Maggie started out, then bolted back into the room to pull on her jeans before running downstairs, carrying the knee pants and her airline bag. Nick tucked Will into the crook of one arm, picked up his suitcase with the other, and followed.

"I can't get my shoelace right," complained Sarah in the hall.

"Ginny, help her, okay?" Maggie dumped her things on the hall floor and bounded out the door to talk to the driver of the car outside. Ginny knelt to untangle Sarah's shoelace.

"Get down!" demanded Will, squirming. Nick set him on the floor.

"Annette will get groceries whenever you need them, and Ellen will walk Sarah to school tomorrow, and Claudia will walk her back," said Maggie, returning with a grocery bag. "That way you won't have to worry about bundling up Will to take him out."

"Oh. Good. It all gets pretty hectic, doesn't it?" said Ginny, looking from Nick to Maggie.

"Yeah, well, this family never does things the easy way," Maggie admitted. "Sarah, you can tell her what you want for lunch tomorrow, right?"

"Yeah! Peanut butter sandwich and an apple, okay?" Sarah looked up bright-eyed at her new sister.

"Have you given Ginny the phone numbers?" asked Nick.

"Oh, right! Here's my baby-sitter's book, Ginny." Maggie led the way to the kitchen and pulled out a bright-red binder. "Schedule, phone numbers, favorite foods, et cetera. Here at the end is a special page on chicken pox. Dr. Page's number is up above the phone." She pointed out the list of emergency numbers.

"And here's my hotel in St. Louis," added Nick, tucking a scrap of paper behind the phone. "As soon as I find out my room number I'll let you know."

"Okay," said Ginny. She looked alert, healthy, competent. Nick's uneasiness abated, but only a little.

Come on, old man, he told himself, it's not the first time you've had a baby-sitter.

"The kids can explain most of their routines." Maggie picked up Will and hugged him. "Can't you, Will? While we're gone, you can tell Ginny how we do things, okay?"

Will gave a grudging nod, and she put him down again. "We'll be back in a couple of days. Ginny, I'll call tonight and tell you how to reach me in Maryland. Any questions?"

"Yeah," said Ginny. "I've got questions. Who killed Mr. Spencer? And why did he use my scissors?"

"Talk to you tonight. Come on, Nick!" Maggie kissed Will and Sarah, raced to the front hall, snatched up her things, and went flying out the door in her blue jeans, the tweed knickers and white fur coat over her arm, airline bag bouncing behind her. Nick, following at a more earthbound pace, felt a tug at his finger as he reached the door.

Will, his unhappy little face crusted with a combination of dried, broken pimples and fresh blisters, glared up at him, lips trembling. "Say revels, Daddy!"

"Hey, little guy, I can't right now. I have to go away. But I bet Ginny will read you some stories." He hugged Will and pushed him gently toward Ginny.

"Come on, little brother." She picked him up fondly.

But as Nick went down the stoop to join Maggie in the Camaro, he heard Will's whine of complaint.

Ginny was going to have a long couple of days.

Sergeant Trainer arrived late Sunday morning. "Hello, Mr. and Mrs. Marshall," he said.

"Did you find her?" blurted Rina.

"Not yet. But I thought you might like to know about the telephone tap yesterday."

"Oh, yes! Please come in, Sergeant." Rina still felt guilty about that call. Yesterday she had wanted to cry out, "Ginny, they're tracing the call!" But her yearning for her daughter's return had overcome her urge toward honesty. And now, she was eager to hear. "Please sit down."

"I can only stay a minute." He perched on the edge of the sofa. "I was hoping that you'd be able to tell us something about what we found out. We've traced it about as far as we can, but maybe it'll remind you of something."

"Let us try, Sergeant Trainer," said Clint, as eager as Rina.

"Okay. Well, the call came from a shopping mall near Trenton, New Jersey."

"New Jersey?" asked Rina, bewildered.

"Right across the river from Philadelphia. Just one big city around there."

"Yes. I remember now."

"It was a public phone booth, unfortunately. The police there checked around, found two people who had seen her."

"Really? They'd seen her?" Rina was dizzy with hope.

"Yes. She was with a woman, maybe one of those friends she mentioned. Both of them in jeans, Ginny in the poncho you described, the other woman in a trench coat. Two witnesses identified Ginny's photo and described the other woman. Caucasian, tall, maybe five nine, dark hair with a red scarf. That was it. Remind you of anyone?"

Rina shook her head. "I know two or three tall, dark-haired women, but I can't imagine what they'd have to do with Ginny." She gave him the names anyway.

"Okay. Well, the two of them had hamburgers out there at the mall, and on their way out to the parking lot they were seen by an employee of the soft-drink stand there. He saw them get into a car."

"Did he get the license number?" asked Clint.

"No. But he noticed it was a blue Toyota. When the New Jersey police took him out to look over the parking lot, he pointed out a car that he said looked very similar, parked in about the same place. But it didn't check out, so they must have been in another one nearby. Lots of blue Toyotas these days."

"Did they find out who owned the car?"

"The one parked there was owned by a guy named Jeff Smith. About fifty-five, five feet ten, blue eyes, glasses, thin. Recognize him?"

"No," said Rina sadly, and Clint shook his head.

"Well, we agree with New Jersey, he's probably not involved. He'd been shopping for flashlight batteries, he said, and the salesman at the hardware store backed him up. He didn't recognize your daughter's picture, or the description of the other woman. So the department there concluded that it must have been some other Toyota."

"I can't think of anyone I know with a blue Toyota," said Rina. "Can you, Clint?"

"Not offhand. But a lot of the high school kids have cars."

"Yes, sir, we'll be checking into that. Well, now." He stood up. "If you think of anything, let us know. The car is probably our best lead right now. The Philadelphia and Trenton police are looking hard."

"Good. Thank you, Sergeant," said Clint.

"And Mrs. Marshall, I probably should warn you, the press has been nosing around."

"The press?"

"Asking about the murder weapon."

Even Mamma didn't know yet about Ginny's scissors. Rina was horrified. "You didn't tell them! You told us not to tell!" Though she'd told Ginny, of course, so she'd know she had to come home.

"No, ma'am, we don't plan to give out that information to

the press soon. But we had to say something about where the victim spent his last hours."

"I see."

"And if your daughter doesn't turn up soon to straighten this out, we'll have to tell them about her. Sometimes publicity brings out new information about crimes. Helps us find people quicker."

"Yes, but not yet! We'll find her soon, and straighten this out!"

"Yes, ma'am, I hope so. Let us know when you hear from her."

"Yes, thank you, Sergeant Trainer."

"Yes, ma'am." He closed his notebook and went out.

A shopping mall in Trenton. Rina hurried to the den and pulled out the eastern U.S. map that Clint kept in his drawer. There it was, Trenton, north of Philadelphia where the river bent. She studied the map hopefully, as though the shapes and blotches of color, the lines and tiny printed names, could somehow bring Ginny closer. Clint followed her and looked over her shoulder.

Philadelphia. Trenton. Who could Ginny know there? Neither one of them could think of anyone.

"I'll call Paul Buchanan before I go to my deacon's meeting," Clint said. "He must know about this, although if she's across the river in Trenton, he won't have jurisdiction. But he'll have connections there."

"I'll get a sandwich ready," Rina said. She went into the kitchen and fixed them some tuna salad and a pot of coffee. Clint came in, but before he could speak the telephone rang. Rina answered.

"Hello?"

"Hello. May I speak to Mr. or Mrs. Marshall?"

"This is Mrs. Marshall."

"Joan Parson, *Washington Herald*. We understand that Mr.

John Spencer was visiting your home shortly before he died. Is that correct?"

Anger surged up in Rina, but she managed to say politely, "I'm sorry, Miss Parson, we have no comment."

"Can you tell us anything about Mr. Spencer? Friends, hobbies, and so forth?"

"We have no comment for the press. None at all." She hung up, her hand trembling. For the first time she was almost glad that Ginny was gone, missing all this.

Clint took a sandwich and glanced sourly at the phone. "Damn press. You did the right thing. No comment. We'll have plenty to straighten out with Ginny without having big exposés complicating her life."

"I know. We've got to protect her."

"Yeah. I spoke to Paul Buchanan. He'll call his Trenton contacts." He chewed on his sandwich. "She really said she wouldn't call back?"

"She said, not soon."

"Hell. Well, I have to go to this meeting anyway. They need my report. And it looks like there's nothing we can do here. But you know where to call me, Rina, if anything does come up."

"Yes, I know." He looked so haggard. It was gnawing at him too. "We should both keep busy," she said, and kissed him good-bye.

A few minutes after he left, the doorbell rang.

"Hello. I'm Michael Slayton, WCBA, Washington. You're Mrs. Marshall?"

"We have no comment," she said, and closed the door on the man and his film crew. She turned around to see her mother coming up the stairs.

"Who is it?"

"Newspapers, TV. They want to know about Mr. Spencer being here. Just tell them no comment if they catch you."

"Ghouls," said Mamma. She peered out the tall window

next to the door, through the sheer curtain. "What are they doing? Are they filming that young man out there?"

"Yes, it's Michael Slayton."

"Oh, yes, that one! I've seen him!" Mamma looked at Michael Slayton's back with fascination as he spoke into his microphone, their house the background to whatever he was saying. She glanced back, met Rina's disgusted glare, and said soothingly, "Don't get upset, *cara*. They'll go away soon."

They did. Rina used the next half hour to check again in the bathroom, the kitchen, Ginny's bedroom, even the downstairs laundry, to see if Ginny had left behind any signs that might point to Trenton, to Philadelphia, to blue Toyotas, or to women in trench coats. There was nothing.

Why had she gone? Rina's faith that her daughter had no guilty knowledge about the murder had been confirmed. Ginny's obvious surprise at the news of John Spencer's death proved that.

Well, surely she would be back soon to explain everything. She'd said she wanted to come home. She'd be back by now if it weren't for Mr. Spencer's death, if it weren't for those so-called friends in Philadelphia who wouldn't help her, that tall, red-scarfed woman with jeans and a trench coat and a blue Toyota.

"What are you looking for?" her mother asked suddenly from behind her as Rina looked through Ginny's clothes in the laundry basket.

"I don't know. That friend in Philadelphia—I just don't understand. Mamma, listen, would you be willing to ask Mrs. Deaver and Mrs. Gallagher over? Just to talk over what happened Thursday, and see if we can figure out what Ginny might have been thinking."

Her mother patted her on the back. "I've got a better idea. I came to tell you that Delores Gallagher already called to ask me over. She was going to get Marie too, to talk over a memorial for John Spencer. He went to Delores's church, you know. Why don't you come along too?"

"Yes, that would be perfect! Maybe the four of us can piece things together."

"She wants us there in about twenty minutes."

"I'll just run up to brush my hair."

"We'll take my car," Mamma decided. "I'll meet you in the garage in a couple of minutes."

"Fine." Rina ran upstairs. She took a minute at her mirror, because she hadn't fixed her hair or made up very carefully that morning. Her face, tired and worried, needed some freshening up. Mamma and her friends would discuss her state at great length if she didn't look normal. And she wanted so much to talk about Ginny. She managed to brighten herself a bit, then grabbed her coat and hurried toward the door to the garage.

The doorbell rang.

Rina hesitated. What if it was Trainer with more news? About the Toyota, maybe?

She opened the door a few inches.

"Mrs. Marshall?"

"Yes?"

It wasn't Trainer, it was the press. A tall young woman, stylish in a white rabbit coat, knee pants, dark glasses, a jaunty air. She said, "I'm Aggie Lyons, *New York Week.*"

"No, no comment. We have no comment for the press." Rina started to close the door, but the white furry corner of Aggie Lyons's coat had somehow blown into the opening.

Aggie said, "No comment about Ginny Marshall and her scissors?"

Rina froze. She knew they were Ginny's! She stared helplessly at the other woman, trying to fathom her intentions. The set of her mouth seemed friendly, sympathetic, but the reflective lenses hid her eyes, so it was hard to tell. Rina asked, "Did the police tell you that?"

"No." The clear voice was soothing. "I put two and two together. But Ginny has run away, hasn't she?"

"Did they tell you that?"

"They admitted they were hunting for her. I just wanted to ask you how things really were."

Rina debated. She didn't want to tell her anything, of course, but she needed to learn how she had found out.

"Rina?" came Mamma's voice from the garage door. "Delores will be waiting."

"I'm sorry," Rina said firmly to the reporter. "I have to go. We have no comment."

"Okay. I'll talk to you later, then. Thanks, Mrs. Marshall." The young woman smiled a friendly smile and turned cheerfully to go down the walk to her black sports car. The white coat, unfastened in front, fanned out behind her, as soft and elegant as egret's wings. Troubled, Rina closed the door slowly, relocked it, and went to join her mother.

"What's wrong, Caterina?"

"Oh, just another reporter. That young woman knew about Mr. Spencer and Ginny both." And the scissors! How had she learned about the scissors?

"I thought the police promised not to link them!"

"That's what I don't understand. I don't think they did. She said she put two and two together."

Mamma frowned. "That's too bad. Nosy people."

"Yes. I hope she doesn't write about it."

"Well," said Mamma, "I found out when your dad died, the press will print anything. But it blows over soon, cara."

"I hope so." Rina settled herself into the passenger seat. Dad's death hadn't been murder, hadn't been sensational. The errors in the obituary that rankled so in Mamma's heart had been careless errors. Not errors that could blacken a teenager's future. Had she been wrong to turn that reporter away? To make no attempt to correct the mistakes?

Her mother opened the automatic garage door, eased out,

and paused to make sure that it closed again. Then she drove, sedately and surely, through the suburban streets to Delores Gallagher's.

The Gallagher apartment was in one of those eight-story brick-and-glass buildings from the sixties, angled among similar buildings in similar landscaped parking lots, among a ring of similar developments that now surrounded Washington. Mamma found a spot under a young tree and positioned the car carefully. She was a very cautious driver. She had never been reckless, but a near accident with a young motorcyclist last year had made her realize that her reflexes were slowing a little. She overcompensated now. "What would I do if they took away my license?" she had asked Rina.

"Oh, Mamma, I'll take you anywhere you want. You know that."

"Yes, *cara*, I know. But you don't have to rush me into second childhood, just the same."

They went into the tiled lobby and up to the sixth floor. Delores had sold her house shortly after her husband's death and invested her money in a bank fund. She had kept up for a while, but inflation was so high these days that she had to cut down on everything, she said. Except rent, which was uncuttable. She worried a lot.

But today her friendly round face, fringed with artificially brown hair, was excited as she opened the door for them. "Oh, Rina, how lovely of you to come too! Leonora, how are you? Marie is here already."

"Hello, Delores," said Mamma, removing her coat. The little entry hall was painted a vivid turquoise, checkered with Delores's bright embroidered canvas squares in white frames.

Mrs. Gallagher took their coats and continued enthusiastically, "We have such an interesting visitor! The nicest young woman, interested in our problems." Delores opened the closet door, and Rina caught a glimpse of white fur inside. Her heart sank even before she stepped around the short wall that partitioned off the tiny entry from the apple-green living room.

Marie Deaver was sitting on the flowered sofa, her intelligent eyes amused. And sitting next to her was the stylish young woman in tweed knickers and sunglasses. A bright smile lit her face as she waved cheerfully at Rina.

"Hello again, Mrs. Marshall," caroled Aggie Lyons.

XIII

"Oh, Mrs. Gallagher!" exclaimed Rina in dismay. "She's a reporter!"

"Yes, I know." Puzzled at Rina's distress, Delores Gallagher smoothed down her skirt, a lime-green check that almost matched the walls.

"Well, it's just that we've been sending them away!"

"Yes, but I thought with all the trash they'd be publishing anyway, it would be good to have someone who could treat it more thoughtfully."

Rina's fury burst its seams. "What's so thoughtful about pushing her way in like this?"

"She didn't!" protested Mrs. Gallagher indignantly, and Mamma seized Rina's elbow to restrain her. Only Aggie Lyons was nodding sympathetically.

"Mrs. Marshall is right," the reporter said regretfully. Her clear voice was Middle Western, not New York. "I apologize for my profession. We're forced to be unmannerly just to get our job done. But Mrs. Gallagher is right too. I try to be fair, to get the whole picture instead of just a small, misleading part of a story."

"There! See?" Delores Gallagher beamed with satisfaction. "Now do come in and make yourself comfortable, Rina. I'll just go see if the coffee's ready."

Trapped. She mustn't insult her mother's friends. She couldn't even leave, because she'd come in Mamma's car.

Rina sat stiff as starch in a small straight chair across from the sofa, where she could watch Aggie Lyons. The reporter was relaxed but very proper, her knicker-clad legs modestly together, her stylish sunglasses unable to hide her sweetly sympathetic expression. No wonder Delores had been taken in by Aggie, who seemed to combine style and compassion, excitement and comforting safety. Rina realized she'd have to be very alert to head off any indiscretions these women might let slip into this reporter's supposedly sympathetic ear. Her desire to learn something about Ginny's departure was shattered, turned inside out; now she desperately hoped Ginny would not even be mentioned.

Mrs. Deaver, with an understanding glance at Rina, said, "Aggie, dear, there seems to be a difference of opinion here. Perhaps you could explain a little more about your work."

"Yes, of course." The young woman grinned, that bright engaging smile again. Rina had to steel herself against its haunting appeal. "Our magazine is still a small one, although the circulation is growing. We try to stress quality, you see, not sensationalism. The real stories behind the headlines. Real people. Have any of you seen it? *New York Week?*" She looked hopefully around the group, but they all shook their heads. "Well, I'd better tell our circulation manager to get more copies to Washington. Anyway, if you find a copy, you'll see that we try to give a rounded picture. The surface facts of a story seldom tell about the real problems people have, the real context. Reporting can be very unfair without the background."

A good line, thought Rina, not believing her. An explanation that would get a reporter into Delores Gallagher's good graces, without restricting the reporter in any way.

"Why aren't you covering a New York story for your New York magazine?" asked Mrs. Deaver. Rina was pleased. A sharp mind behind the mild tones.

"In a way, I am," replied Aggie Lyons. "We're doing a

series on problems older people face. Crime is one of them, of course. But we wanted something outside of New York City, so that our readers wouldn't think that was the only place people have problems. John Spencer's death bothered us. You'll have to admit that here in these nice suburbs you wouldn't expect it."

"Oh, no, crime is a worry here too," protested Mrs. Gallagher as she brought in a tray with the coffee. "We worry about muggers a lot!"

"But why didn't the muggers pick someone richer?" asked Mamma. Did she believe that reporter's story? Rina looked at her in dismay.

"Nobody's richer these days!" exclaimed Delores Gallagher. "At least, nobody our age. Of course we keep up appearances if we can. John dressed nicely. And look at us. I'm keeping this little apartment, but I have to cut down on food. And Marie has all the expenses of her son even though she's doing pretty well. And—"

"Most people eat too much, Delores," said Mamma uneasily, belatedly realizing what the presence of a reporter might mean.

"Oh, maybe. But I hate having no choice! My little grandson Donnie—well, his other grandmother gave him this wonderful automatic swing set for his birthday, and I—well, I don't want to spoil him, but there's no choice! And isn't it the same with you, Leonora? You might want to live with Rina anyway, but don't you hate being forced to do it?"

Mamma drew herself up stiffly. "Caterina is wonderful. She and her family are lovely."

"Oh, I know, dear," Delores said hastily, with an apologetic glance at Rina. "I don't mean that at all. I mean not having any choice."

"I think we all hate that," said Aggie Lyons thoughtfully. "Even when the results are good, even when we might have chosen it anyway, we still resent not having control."

"Just what would *you* know about not having control?" Rina asked, and wondered at her own sharpness.

"Well—" The reporter seemed to debate a moment, then shrugged. "For example, I know about ulcerated cornea." She gestured at her sunglasses. "If I could control things, I certainly wouldn't choose that. I wouldn't have to keep light out of my eyes. I wouldn't have to worry about maybe going blind."

"Oh, I'm sorry!" Rina felt stupid and callous.

"No, don't be. I'm glad you asked. You understand now, you didn't before you asked. Probably you thought I was a shallow-minded young twerp who wore sunglasses indoors because she thought it was fashionable, or because she was full of drugs." She smiled that heart-tugging, faintly familiar smile. "Anyway, I just wanted to explain to Mrs. Gallagher and Mrs. Rossi that I can understand some of the frustration of having no choice, even if I haven't yet had their particular problems."

Mrs. Gallagher beamed, pleased with her unexpected guest. "Is that what you mean by getting the real stories behind the headlines?"

"That's part of it, yes. Making sure I understand a little about the situation in its totality. Now, back to Mr. Spencer. He wasn't singled out for attack because he was rich, because you say he wasn't rich. You think it was just random, then? He happened to be in the wrong place at the wrong time?"

Rina tensed. Aggie Lyons didn't believe it was random! She knew about Ginny's scissors! But the glasses hid the subtleties of her expression, and Rina could not tell why she had asked.

"Well, doesn't it make sense?" said Delores Gallagher. "The police said there was no cash left in his wallet."

"Did he have friends or family who might inherit something?" Aggie asked.

"Do you mean they might have—oh, my goodness, what a terrible thought!" exclaimed Delores. "But he didn't have much of an estate. His wife had a lot of medical expenses before she died a few years ago. He had to sell the house. And after her, there was just his cousin in Florida."

"So Mr. Spencer had more than money problems," mused Aggie Lyons. "Family and friends dying. More and more alone. Some of my New York interviews said that was worse than money problems."

"Yes, being rich doesn't protect you against that," said Delores. "Or being poor either. You always think of poor people having lots of family, but it isn't always true. Marie even had to take care of the funeral for her maid a few years ago."

"Back when I could afford a maid," said Marie Deaver ruefully. "But you know, it's possible to make new friends. Look at Leonora, she's only been here a few years."

"And John did pretty well too," agreed Mrs. Gallagher. "He dated Lucille Barrow for almost a year. But he said she wasn't serious enough for him."

"Serious?" asked Rina.

"You young people may laugh," said Marie Deaver tolerantly, "but romantic feelings don't retire magically at age sixty-five, you know."

"Oh, Marie, don't exaggerate!" Delores Gallagher adjusted her emerald sweater self-consciously. "John did say that if the right person turned up he might be interested in marriage again. But he didn't expect it. Who would at our age? He was friendly, that's all. He used to have a sailboat, before his wife became ill. He said he'd rent one someday and take me out." She gave a little sob and then looked astonished at herself.

"He must have been pretty well-off once," said Aggie Lyons. "Was John Spencer a businessman?"

"An accountant. He said he was pretty well set for retirement before his wife became ill."

"Just like my Mike," said Mamma softly.

Delores nodded sadly. "John told me once that her death

took him completely by surprise, even though she'd been ill so long. He was always sure he'd die first."

"Where was he living?" asked Aggie.

"His house was in Arlington, but he had to sell that. He was rooming with one of our church families here. The Jenkinses. Just a little inexpensive room with kitchenette. They brought him along to the church suppers. He said he loved the home cooking. Always had a compliment for every dish."

"He did love good food," said Mamma with approval. "Asked so many questions about where I got my Italian cheeses and sausages."

"And he even remembered meeting Marie in the grocery," said Delores.

"Oh, yes, I met him in the Eastland grocery checkout line once. So it was amusing to meet again at the bridge party."

Aggie said, "Mrs. Gallagher, you drove him home the night he was killed. Did he give any hint of what he might be doing later?"

"Oh, I've thought and thought," said Mrs. Gallagher. "I guess I was the last one to see him that the police know about. But he hardly said anything about himself. We just talked about things in general."

"You talked about us, I imagine," said Mrs. Deaver, amused. Mrs. Gallagher reddened a little.

"Well, he was naturally interested. We'd just been with you. It wasn't gossip, really, he just wanted to know where you lived, where I lived. And he said how impressed he was with both you and Leonora, what nice friends I had."

Rina didn't dare ask if he'd mentioned Ginny.

"Did he say anything about going to the library?" asked the reporter.

"No, nothing."

"I've been thinking about the library," said Mamma. "Wondering why they found him there."

"Yes, I've been wondering that too," said Aggie Lyons.

"Well, you know they found him in those bushes by the turn in the drive, just before you get to the book drop. The street is lit, and the book drop is lit, but that turn is very dark. Dark before seven these days."

"That's true," said Mrs. Gallagher.

"Well, it could have happened right there," said Mamma. "But even if it didn't, it would be a good place to get rid of something. If your car was going slowly, everyone would just think you were dropping off your books. And he was found on the passenger side of the driveway. The book drop is on the driver's side."

"I see," said the reporter. "Just open the passenger door, kick the body out into the bushes, close the door, and drive on past the book drop. Then on to establish an alibi, only a few seconds late."

Marie Deaver shuddered. Delores Gallagher exclaimed, "What a horrible thought!"

"It's a horrible thought, no matter where it was done," said Mamma. "But Miss Lyons is right, no one could see you there, unless they were right behind you. And it's hardly ever that busy."

"So you think he was killed somewhere else, and just brought there by car," Aggie Lyons said.

"Well, there's no reason he'd be walking there."

"I'm sorry, I don't follow. Couldn't he walk to the library that way?"

"No," said Rina eagerly. Mamma was onto something. "I mean, he could, but the sidewalk is on the driver's side. Why would he be walking where there's no sidewalk? So it must be someone with a car!" Surely the police would see the logic. Ginny didn't drive yet, had no car!

"Well," said Aggie, "perhaps someone forced him to walk there. Or used a friend's car. A couple of young thugs wouldn't have any trouble, dead or alive, car or no car."

Rina felt deflated. Just when Mamma had produced a bit of reasoning that pointed away from Ginny, that Aggie Lyons thought of a way she could have done it after all, or could have helped Buck do it.

Aggie Lyons *knew* that Ginny's scissors had been used. That's why she thought Ginny had been involved. Rina had figured out what must have happened, though of course she couldn't say so here because she mustn't let anyone else know about the scissors. Ginny must have taken the scissors with her to the library for some reason. She'd probably put her backpack down, and the murderer had passed by and stolen them. Rina shuddered.

But this reporter didn't know Ginny, didn't know that the scissors must have been stolen from her. She thought Ginny could have done it. Or could have helped Buck do it. Buck, who had gone to the library to find her.

He hadn't found her.

Well, he *said* he hadn't found her.

"Young thugs," Aggie Lyons had said. Rina's fist clenched. It was clear that the reporter thought she knew who the young thugs were. In a minute she'd probably be telling them all that Ginny had done it.

But to Rina's relief she veered off in another direction. "What about this Lucille Barrow? Could she have been jealous?"

"Lucille?" Mrs. Gallagher stared at the reporter, astounded. "No, of course not! You know Lucille, Marie. Isn't the idea ridiculous?"

"I would say so. It's hard to see Lucille doing such a thing. Of course people surprise you sometimes."

"Mrs. Gallagher, may I use your bathroom?" Aggie Lyons asked.

"Oh, of course! It's at the end of the hall." Mrs. Gallagher pointed. "There's more coffee, everyone. Who wants some? And I'll bring in the cookies."

Rina took advantage of the reporter's absence to ask, "Did anyone hear Ginny say anything about going away? Visiting anyone?"

"We hardly saw her," said Marie Deaver sympathetically. Delores Gallagher, pouring coffee, frowned. "She wasn't very talkative. She came in for the cat, and ran after it, and that was all. Except for—well, you know."

"I just hoped she might have hinted something," Rina said.

"You talked to her longer than any of us," Delores said.

"But I thought maybe, if we compared notes, one of us might remember something."

"Good idea," said Aggie behind Rina, back already. She was carrying a big book as she sat down again on the sofa. "If we go over exactly what happened at that bridge game, someone might also remember a comment from Mr. Spencer that might throw light on what he planned later."

Oh, hell. Rina's worst fears were coming true. She sat rigidly on guard, but soon found herself listening avidly while the reporter led them through a careful account of the bridge game, the comments to each other, everything Mr. Spencer had said and done. They soon came to the argument between Mamma and Ginny over Kakiy. Rina's hands clenched in her lap. She was sharply aware of Aggie Lyons across from her. Mamma's story was quite fair; she admitted to losing her temper at the cat and regretting it instantly, and loyally refused to say anything against Ginny. It was Delores Gallagher who blundered and began to tell of Ginny's shouted insults to her grandmother and Mr. Spencer.

Rina broke in hastily. "Mrs. Gallagher, you know she thinks the world of that cat."

Mrs. Gallagher suddenly took the point and looked anxiously at Aggie Lyons. "Yes. That's right."

Marie Deaver's knobby hand gestured for caution. "Rina, you're trying to defend your daughter, I know. But it might be better at this point to let Delores tell us exactly what Ginny said, rather than leave it to Miss Lyons's imagination."

"I don't write from my imagination," Aggie protested gently.

But Rina understood what Mrs. Deaver meant. "She's right, Mrs. Gallagher. Please tell us," she said wearily.

Mrs. Gallagher, still upset, mumbled, "Well, you know how young people are. She just said Leonora was, um, an old, um—"

"Bitch," supplied Mrs. Deaver helpfully.

"Yes. And then when Mr. Spencer said she shouldn't speak to her grandmother that way, she said he was an old, um, fart."

"Well, that's rude, all right," said the reporter, with an apologetic smile at Rina. "But not completely surprising if the cat was hurt."

"I didn't mean to hurt the creature," Mamma said remorsefully. "Just scare it away. I was just so annoyed, I aimed too close."

"I know. And Ginny gets committed to people, or pets, and she's very loyal," Rina explained earnestly.

Aggie nodded and turned back to the others. "What did Mr. Spencer say then?"

They went through the rest of the bridge game and everything Mr. Spencer had said and done. But Rina heard nothing new. This had all been a waste. She had hoped for more, a comment or a hint of some type about where Ginny was thinking of going.

"Mrs. Marshall?"

"What?" She looked up, startled. Apparently the reporter had asked her a question. "I'm sorry. What was that again?"

"We were just talking about Buck Landon, and how he pushed his way in and went to your daughter's room. Your mother said you went back to the room and met him coming out."

"Yes. He's an impetuous boy. He was looking for her."

"Is he always that pushy?"

"He wasn't pushy, exactly. Just eager to find Ginny."

"Well, he certainly insulted Mr. Spencer," said Delores Gallagher indignantly.

"Did Mr. Spencer say anything about Buck as you drove him home?" Aggie asked.

"Yes, well, you see, he said he thought Rina was nice, and Leonora was nice, and he said teenagers these days were so hard to predict, even when they came from the best families."

Rina froze her face into friendly lines. She couldn't let this babble give away the secret Ginny so desperately wanted to keep! She said, "What did he say about Buck?"

Delores Gallagher looked away. "Well, John knew what a good doctor Dr. Landon is, and then his son acting like that—" Delores looked at Rina with a little frown. "I do have to agree, Rina. Why do you allow Ginny to date him?"

"Didn't you ever have any problems with Berta?" asked Rina tightly. "Mamma said she had to go away one summer."

"Well, that wasn't the same thing at all!" Delores flushed. "She had trouble with her science course, that's all, and we sent her to math camp, to nip it in the bud. And she did get into the University of Maryland!"

"Did you and Mr. Spencer talk about your children?" asked Aggie Lyons.

"Well, he always asks about them. I told him they were doing well. Tom is assistant manager now. And Berta's husband is principal of his school. And of course little Donnie is just precious. I'm sure *he* won't be a rude teenager!"

"Now, Delores, they were both upset," said Marie Deaver in a soothing tone.

"It's strange," said Aggie thoughtfully. "We always tell youngsters to be polite, but we often aren't very polite to them. When I was a teenager I used to give back all kinds of impudence."

Mamma was nodding. "Yes, you know, I was thinking about that. It's so hard to realize that they are nearly adults. And they do act like children sometimes, but then we all do, sometimes."

"Yes. We were as giggly as teenagers ourselves during that bridge game," said Mrs. Deaver, smiling. "We were all flirting with John, and he with us."

"Oh, Marie!" Delores Gallagher had turned rosy-red. "We were just having fun!"

"We were flirting," maintained Mrs. Deaver firmly. "Of course it was fun. Making him feel attractive and special. And why not? Aren't you glad you helped make his last hours happy ones?"

"But don't exaggerate, Marie! We were just making harmless little jokes. He was just friendly. Why, Donald Jenkins was saying only yesterday that he was an ideal roomer, always with a friendly word. We weren't flirting, Marie." She cast a worried glance at Aggie Lyons, whose thoughtful gaze was on her.

Marie Deaver, amused, said, "Have it your way, Delores."

"Well, what is Aggie going to think of us?"

The reporter grinned. "I'm going to think that you're like most of the people I know. You like to get together with your friends and kid around a little." Mrs. Gallagher looked relieved until Aggie added, "Would you marry again if the right person came along?"

"Why, what do you mean?" exclaimed Mrs. Gallagher, flustered.

Mamma joined in firmly. "Don't be silly, Delores. Of course we would. If it was the right man, as Aggie said."

Rina stared at her mother in amazement.

"Well, I hadn't thought about it," insisted Mrs. Gallagher.

"Oh, I think you have," said Marie Deaver. "I've thought about it, Delores, and I've decided I value my independence too much. But it still is a very appealing idea. Having a man to take you to a movie or a concert, or to call the plumber, or just to bring you a cup of tea when you have a cold."

"That's right," said Mamma. "Be honest, Delores. It's your children you're worried about, isn't it? Berta and Tom would be shocked, you think."

"Well, they would! And the school board! So I don't think about it."

"Well, I do!" declared Mamma. "It's all right for Marie, Frank left her pretty well set. Independent, as she says."

"There are still expenses," said Marie.

"Of course," admitted Mamma. "But leave Marie aside. You and I, Delores, we're having a little trouble with our independence, aren't we? It's hard to have independence on our little incomes. A husband who could add his own little income would help in a lot of ways."

Rina, who had been listening in fascination, suddenly recalled that a reporter had been listening too. It was time to call this off.

"Mamma—"

"Oh, well, let's talk about something else," said Delores at the same moment. She had remembered too.

"But—" said Mamma.

Rina stood up decisively. "Mamma, really, we'd better be going."

"Oh, no!" Delores Gallagher was horrified. "I haven't even brought out the cookies yet!"

"I'm sorry," said Rina firmly. "We do have to go back. Come on, Mamma." She was annoyed at herself for having left home for so long. Ginny had said she wouldn't call again for a while. But what if she'd changed her mind? This whole afternoon had been a wild-goose chase, and Rina had learned nothing of value, and that reporter had learned too much.

Aggie Lyons was standing now also. "I'd better zip off too," she said. "I'd like to thank everyone for letting me talk to you."

"Oh, of course." Delores was beaming. "But I've been so busy talking, I forgot to bring out the cookies. I want you to stay for some."

"Oh, thank you, no." The reporter pulled something from her bag and moved, quick as a bird, to the side of the room. "Just one more favor. Say cheese." And the four of them were caught in the flash as they looked at her, startled. She dropped the camera back into the big bag, explaining rapidly as protest sprang into their faces, "I need a snapshot to jog my memory of who you all are, because I talk to so many people each day. If the magazine needs photos, our photographer will get in touch and we'll have a regular photo session. We probably won't need any more, actually, but it would help to have one of Mr. Spencer. Do you have a photo of him in your album, Mrs. Gallagher?" She indicated the book she had brought from the back hall and left on the sofa.

"Oh, yes, here." Delores fumbled through the pages. How could she still be so cooperative, Rina thought? The gall of this reporter! But Delores was pointing things out eagerly. "It's right in here somewhere. There's my Tom. There's Leonora at Easter. Oh, there's Berta with little Donnie, my grandson."

"He's a darling." Aggie Lyons beamed at the photo. "Is that stiff fellow Berta's husband?"

"Yes. He's nice, really, he just has to wear a suit all the time. Berta says they all have to watch themselves. Can't even go to the grocery in curlers for fear she'll meet a school board member."

Aggie grinned. "Nothing scarier than a school board member."

"Let's see, John Spencer—" Delores Gallagher flipped hastily through the pages. "Oh, here it is! Just these two snapshots."

"Wonderful! Let me borrow this one, all right?"

"Well . . ."

"I'll get it back to you within two days. Thank you!" Aggie dropped the photo into her bag.

Rina had had enough. She strode to the front closet. Suddenly Aggie Lyons was next to her in the entry hall.

Mrs. Gallagher urged, "Rina, Aggie, do stay! I didn't serve the cookies yet!"

"Thank you, no. Come on, Mamma," said Rina in a tight voice.

"We should stay, *cara,*" said Mamma, who hadn't budged from her chair. "We haven't discussed the memorial yet."

"Oh, Mamma, really, we must go!"

"Nonsense," said Aggie Lyons briskly. "You want to leave, so I'll drop you off, Mrs. Marshall. Let your mother stay."

"Oh, no!" said Rina, appalled. It was the last thing she wanted. But the logic of the solution appealed to the others.

"Are you sure it's no trouble?" Mamma asked the reporter.

"None at all."

"Well, I wish you would both stay," said Mrs. Gallagher, who nevertheless bustled to the coat closet and handed out the furry white coat. Aggie Lyons shrugged it on.

"Rina, dear?" Mrs. Gallagher, assuming everyone had agreed, held out her trench coat.

Rina bowed to reality. "Thank you, Mrs. Gallagher." What a fiasco!

"Don't worry now, dear, we'll send Leonora home in good time."

"Thank you."

"Thanks, Mrs. Gallagher. I'll be back in touch soon!" The bright Lyons smile flashed at Mrs. Gallagher, and then the young woman followed Rina into the hall. They walked in silence together to the elevator. Seething, Rina jabbed the button.

The reporter said mildly, "Please excuse me for kidnapping you, but we really should talk a little."

"Miss Lyons, I'm sorry I can't help you. But really, I have

no comment." Then her control snapped and she flared, "I'd think you had plenty to write about already from what they said in there!"

"Oh, I do." The elevator came, and Aggie Lyons held the door open for Rina. "But Mrs. Marshall, I don't think I have the whole story yet."

"Well, you'll just have to make do with what you have, I'm afraid."

"Sure, if you insist." They emerged from the elevator and out the lobby doors. Aggie Lyons unlocked the passenger door of a black Camaro with muddy New York plates. Still angry at the trick that had left her at this woman's mercies, Rina could see no alternative now; she got in and slammed the door. The reporter put the key in the ignition but did not turn it for a moment, just sat with her bony hands resting on the wheel, a slight frown half hidden by the sunglasses. She said, "Maybe it would help if I summarize what I have right now. Hero: a friendly old man, behaving very properly but with a nice sense of humor, bringing a pleasant bit of spice into the lives of three warm and friendly widows his own age. Okay so far?"

"Yes," said Rina, her voice tight.

"Good. Villains: a rude teenage boy and his girlfriend, who are angry with the heroic old man because he scolded them for talking back to her grandmother. Question: Do they get their revenge by killing the old man with her scissors?"

"No!" cried Rina. "No, no, no! It's not like that at all!"

Aggie Lyons gave her a broad smile and turned the ignition. "Well," she said as she steered skillfully out into the traffic, "I really don't think it's like that either, you know."

"Well, then, why did you say so?"

"Because you tell me I must make do with what I have. That's what I have, Mrs. Marshall. You haven't told me anything about the girl or the boy, you see. What I have is that they both yelled at Mr. Spencer, and that her scissors were used to kill him, and that she ran away at just that time. Doesn't that look odd?"

"Yes," said Rina, glowering at the other woman for telling the truth. "But it's ridiculous. You don't know Ginny."

"That's why I was hoping you'd tell me what she's like."

"She's wonderful! She's bright, straight A's. And loving, and beautiful, and talented. Everything you'd want a daughter to be."

The reporter negotiated a turn onto the highway in silence, then said, "Talented, you say. At what?"

"Soft sculpture. Wonderful little creations from scraps of cloth. She's won prizes in adult competitions."

"Really?"

"Yes. She's very good. And also, she dances very well. Ballet."

"I see. She certainly sounds perfect."

Rina realized she was overdoing it. She said, "Well, she's got a temper sometimes, but no worse than any of us. I mean, we don't bottle things up in our family. And she had good reason to be angry Thursday. You heard about it. Even Mamma admits that. Ginny's very attached to her cat."

"But not attached to her grandmother?"

Trapped. Rina fought back. "Of course she is! But sometimes they have little disagreements. It's perfectly normal, just what you'd find in any family."

"True. So why did she run away?"

Anger and unease were playing tag in Rina. She said, "Look. You asked me what she was like, and I told you! She's not a villain for your story. She shouldn't be dragged into this kind of affair at all!"

"I'm sure you're right, Mrs. Marshall."

"Of course I am. I know her. She's a wonderful daughter."

"And she'll come home, and you'll all live happily ever after."

"Yes! Yes, why not?"

Aggie Lyons shrugged and drove in silence for a block or two. Then she said, "Would it be imposing on you too much to ask if I could see your house?"

Rina wanted to scream, *Yes, idiot, it would be imposing! Damn you, damn your misconceptions!* But she managed to say levelly, "I'm really very busy. I appreciate the ride home, but I have a lot to do."

"Just a quick look?"

"No. I'm sorry. I just can't manage it."

The reporter shrugged again. The black car bore them up Ridgewood. She pulled into the driveway.

"Well, thanks for the ride," said Rina, relieved enough to be civil. "Good luck with the story. I'm sure you'll be fair." She leaned forward to open the door.

"I try to be," said Aggie Lyons. "I'll do my best, I promise. By the way, my sources on Long Island say that Ginny is adopted."

Rina froze, her fingers on the handle of the door she was opening, her eyes closing in reflex against the blow. Headlines danced in her mind. Adopted girl reverts to type! Innocent family friend slain by changeling! Bad blood infects suburbs! Ginny would never forgive her, never come home, if she let the adoption get into the news. She had to stop this woman, had to explain somehow. Mrs. Farnham's round face drifted into her mind, as vividly judgmental as it had been all those years ago. Bruised, Rina forced her eyes open to look at the woman who had just slashed open the fabric of her life.

"Okay," said Rina, defeated. "I guess you'd better come in."

XIV

The reporter was silent as Rina unlocked the front door, the pleasant enigmatic face in the sunglasses shifting to survey the shingled walls, the begonias still bright in the reflected sunlight, the little flagged front terrace. Rina turned the knob and motioned her in with forced courtesy, and in response a little mocking smile twitched at Aggie Lyons's mouth. But as Rina followed her in, the younger woman stopped abruptly.

"My God," she said, "that is beautiful!"

She was looking at Rina's quilted hanging, glowing on the wall across from the stairs, where the light from the tall sheer-curtained windows beside the door brought out the warm fairy-tale colors of the calicos that made up the happy country scene. Rina's pleasure in the compliment was soured with suspicion, with a sense of violation. She didn't answer for a moment, just walked stiffly past the reporter and up the half-flight toward the living room. At the top she paused and looked back down. "Thank you," she said politely.

Aggie Lyons laughed and bounded up the steps past her, the white fur fluttering. "I meant it," she said. "But I wouldn't want a compliment from me either, if I were you. A pushy reporter, half blind, who blackmails her way into your home, and could publish all your darkest secrets to the world if she isn't stopped. Evil personified, that's me." She slapped her chest extravagantly. She was striding around the living room, inspecting the piano, the furniture, the fireplace, the plants, the window that looked out on the late flowers in Mamma's garden.

"What do other people do with you?" asked Rina in despair.

"Oh, they differ. Some love the attention, like Mrs. Gallagher. Some clam up completely. I always worry about those, because it's hard to be fair when you don't have their side of it. A few have even written me thank-you notes. But I don't expect you to believe that, yet." She was circling the living room again, like a hawk looking for prey, Rina thought. She stopped at last in front of Rina. "Is your husband home? You should tell him I'm here and ask his legal advice."

So she knew Clint was a lawyer. Rina was not surprised. "Why do you even bother to talk to me? You know everything about us already."

"Of course I don't, that's why I'm here. But it saves time if I do my homework before I bother people."

"I see. I think I will call Clint." Rina went to the kitchen phone. As she dialed the church number, she found herself gripping the receiver as though for support.

"Hello? This is Rina Marshall. May I speak to Clint, please? He's at the deacons' meeting."

In a moment Clint's warm, concerned voice came on. "Hi, honey. Are you okay?"

"Yes." She glanced at Aggie Lyons, who was watching from the kitchen door. "But there's a new complication. A reporter."

"You don't have to tell them anything."

"I know. Most of them I've turned away. But this one knows so much already. It's a question of getting it all in context."

"What do you mean, knows so much?"

"About Ginny running away. About her scissors. About her being adopted."

"Damn. And she's threatening to print this? Nothing proven, and she'd ruin a kid's life?"

"Well, she says she wants to be fair."

"Yeah, they all say that, don't they? What the hell else does she want to know?"

"I don't know. She says background. And—well, she didn't say anything about the scissors and the adoption to Mamma's friends just now. She could have, but she didn't. So she's been discreet so far."

"Mmm. I see. May I talk to her?"

"Just a minute." Rina handed the receiver to the reporter, who was lounging against the kitchen door frame, her knicker-clad legs crossed.

"Hello, Mr. Marshall? This is Aggie Lyons." Her free hand played with the clasp of her shoulder bag as she listened.

"Yes, Mr. Marshall, I realize that she's young, and that publicity could be very damaging. My problem is that the surface facts already seem rather damaging to your daughter. I'd like to get a more rounded picture of the situation. Obviously there's a problem, or she wouldn't have run away. But the only problem that's clear so far is the murder. And the murder was committed with her scissors. You see my difficulty."

Clint said something, and she nodded earnestly at the phone. "Right. I know a story like this could damage her unfairly if she's innocent. So I don't want to jump to conclusions. I'm a fanatic for fairness. Had a bad experience myself once." She shook her head. "No, the police didn't tell me. They're searching for your daughter, of course, they aren't keeping that secret. But the other information was from private sources, which I can't reveal." There was a pause. "Libel law? Sure, I know a bit about it, and one of my friends works with Morgenstern and Wilcox in New York. Besides, as I say, my interest is in a fair account of factual material. I'm sure this situation is more complex than it seems on the surface, and I don't want to jump to conclusions."

Clint made a long comment.

"Yes, Mr. Marshall," the reporter agreed. "I'm very concerned about the effect on your daughter too. I have a daughter myself. And I promise that nothing will be used if it's not necessary to the story of Mr. Spencer's death." She smiled. "Okay, here she is." She handed the receiver back to Rina.

"Hello again."

"Well, Rina," said Clint, "she appears to understand the problem well enough. There's no way to stop her from publishing facts, or using the public records. So possibly a fuller account would be better. Fairer. And you say she was discreet in front of your mother's friends. I just hope—well, that's irrelevant. Just try to keep the emphasis on Spencer so she won't get sidetracked into making Ginny the center of the story."

"I see. Okay."

"I've got to give my report. But I'll be back as soon as I can, maybe an hour or two."

"Bye, honey."

Rina hung up and looked wearily at Aggie Lyons, who was leaning against the door frame again. "I'm to minimize the damage if I can," she said.

"I'm a bully," admitted the younger woman cheerfully. "But it's a sincere attempt to avoid doing damage. To anyone besides the murderer, I mean. Now, where was the card table set up?"

Keep the emphasis on Mr. Spencer, he had said. Good. "In here," Rina told her, leading the way to the spot near the sofa.

"They used a folding table and chairs?"

"Yes. We keep them in the closet there. Do you want to see them?"

"No. I can imagine them, I think. The cat comes from the hall down there, and hides behind the plant here." She was talking to herself, moving around the room again, as though photographing the scene. "And your mother blows up, kicks him. The cat splits for the hall, Ginny after him yelling insults over her shoulder, the older people clucking up here. Okay, I've got that." She smiled at Rina again. "You're very patient, Mrs. Marshall."

"There's not much choice, is there?"

"I'll try to be quick. Fast forward, now, to the point where you arrive home. Front door? Garage door?"

"Garage door, into the hall of the lower level."

"So you came up these stairs?"

"Yes."

"And then?"

"I said hello to my mother and her friends, and she introduced me to Mr. Spencer. Then I asked if Ginny was home, and she told me she was in the den, and that the cat had gotten out."

"I see. Where had you been?"

"Damn it, I can't watch them every minute!" Rina burst out.

"My God, why should you watch them every minute?" Aggie Lyons seemed astounded.

"Well, yes. That's what I mean." Rina felt uncomfortable. She had to keep control. She knew that the eyes behind those glasses were studying her.

"Were you somewhere you're ashamed of, Mrs. Marshall?"

"No, of course not! I have a part-time job at a college crafts center. This term, twice a week, I have a quilting and soft sculpture class."

"That beautiful thing in the entry hall is yours?"

"Yes."

"My God, Mrs. Marshall. I'm impressed."

"Yes, thanks, but that doesn't have much to do with Mr. Spencer," said Rina coolly.

"You're right. Okay. Next, you go into the den and talk to

Ginny." She moved so swiftly, Rina didn't catch up until they were in the bedroom hall looking into the den. "Then Ginny decided to go to the library, right?"

"Yes. She went to her room for the backpack."

"This is her room? No, this is the bathroom."

"Next door."

"Okay." The reporter walked in as though invited, and straight across to the worktable under the window. "The scissors were here?"

"That's where they usually were. So I suppose they were."

"May I touch the doll?"

"Yes, it's nearly finished."

The younger woman picked it up almost reverently, and studied the unhappy little face. She said after a moment, "She's really good, isn't she? I wouldn't have expected this much talent. Most teenagers do pretty sappy stuff."

"Last year she won a prize at the State Crafts Fair," said Rina. "The youngest person who's ever won in this section."

"Really?"

"There it is." Rina gestured back at the wall over Ginny's headboard, next to the door. The reporter turned around and froze for a moment, as though stunned.

The doll figure Ginny had made was not large, perhaps ten inches tall, unromantically ugly but full of character. It was all of cloth, very old-fashioned in general effect, despite the fact that the muslin body was dressed in denim. Anguished embroidered blue eyes stared hopelessly; the mouth, a slash of dark thread, appeared to be moaning. The unbleached muslin head and hands were carefully primitive in form. The whole was twisted, suspended in a large stuffed fabric frame about two feet square, complete with quilted curlicues. Slender white filaments of thread from the frame held the doll's body in midair, stretched in agony. The long black hair was stretched too, so that it appeared to be buffeted by a stormy wind. From the waist, where the figure's navel might have been, a single pale filament of support thread dangled unattached, the only loose end in the construction.

Old-fashioned sampler-style letters stitched to the stuffed frame spelled out the title: "Self-portrait 1978." Next to them, a little red ribbon announced that the work had won a prize.

Aggie's fingers had clenched around the post of the footboard. "Damn, damn, damn," she said huskily.

"It makes me cry," admitted Rina.

"Me too," said Aggie, and Rina saw that it was true. She felt a flicker of hope that perhaps this odd young woman would understand after all.

"You see what I mean," she said hopefully.

"Yes. It's eloquent. Damn." The ambiguous sunglasses turned to Rina, and Aggie took a deep breath. "Mrs. Marshall, you're right. You have a remarkable daughter. But why the hell do you—" She clipped off her sentence unfinished and became restless again, moving around the room. "Cat toys. Novels." Her fingers paused on Haley's *Roots*. "Does she read all this stuff?"

"Yes. Sometimes to the detriment of her schoolwork."

For a moment Rina thought that her blunder had not been noticed, because Aggie seemed to be absorbed in riffling through the notebooks on Ginny's desk. But she pulled out a paper and handed it to Rina as she answered.

"Yes. The detriment of her schoolwork. Tell me about her grades again, Mrs. Marshall."

The paper was marked "D."

Rina said miserably, "She'll make A's again. It's the school's fault. She's bored. Too bright for them."

"Yes. Maybe. But maybe you should think it through a little more, Mrs. Marshall. Look at all the evidence." There was a hard edge in her voice now.

"What do you mean?"

"Tell me. Who killed John Spencer?"

"How should I know?"

"You were here in this house. So was Spencer. So were the scissors. Implication: So was the murderer. Who was it? Who took those scissors? Who wanted to kill him?"

"I don't know!"

"You say it wasn't Ginny. Why not?"

"I *know* Ginny didn't do it!"

"Well, who did?"

"I don't know! I've been so worried about her, I haven't thought!"

The reporter sighed. "Well, start thinking." She turned abruptly to the dresser. "Is this the young man in her life?"

"Yes. That's Buck."

"Nice-looking fellow."

"Yes," Rina said guardedly.

"If she marries him, will she live happily ever after?"

"No. I mean, I don't think she'll marry him."

"Why not?"

"He's not good enough for her. Not smart enough. She won't throw herself away."

"Doesn't that mean she's throwing herself away now?"

"Well, everyone makes mistakes when they're young."

Aggie Lyons sat down on the side of the bed and looked up at Rina. "Let's count up mistakes," she said. "One, the boy-friend isn't good enough for her. Two, her grades are lousy even though she's bright. Three, she yells at her grandmother and at the guests. With good cause, maybe, but running away —that's four—is an overreaction. Now, none of that means she murdered John Spencer. But it means she's got a problem, Mrs. Marshall. Something is eating her. Right?"

Rina said nothing. Finally she shrugged.

The reporter asked, "Does she do drugs?"

"No!" Rina flared. But the relentless unreadable lenses went on regarding her steadily, and she realized this woman would implacably track down Jan, Buck, Linda. She shrugged again. "Sometimes."

"Heroin?"

"No, of course not! Pot, ludes. Not often."

"Okay. Another symptom. Pot's not very unusual, maybe, these days. Ludes I'd worry about."

Rage was bubbling up in Rina again. "You want me to throw her out of the house for an experiment? Is that what Dr. Spock recommends?"

"No, no. All I'm saying is, put all those symptoms together and they say something is wrong, don't they?"

"Look, who are you to tell me there's something wrong? You don't know anything about it! You don't have a teenager, you don't know what it's like!"

"True."

"You haven't said one single thing that isn't true of a lot of teenagers. She's just a normal kid. It's hard to grow up these days. But bad grades or even a few ludes don't make her a criminal!"

"Of course not. But you telling me she makes straight A's and is just a normal kid doesn't clear her either. She needs more concrete help than that. Besides, she's not just a normal kid."

"What do you mean?" Angry tears blurred Rina's eyes. She wanted to rip at that white coat, that enigmatic face, to give back some of the pain this invader was causing.

"I mean she's very bright. Look at what she's reading. And she's enormously talented." The reporter gestured at the sculptured doll. "And she's enormously unhappy. How can you say she's just a normal kid?"

The truth of every word rang in Rina's heart. She sat down, suddenly exhausted, on the bed next to the younger woman, and faced facts. She picked up the soft little bear Ginny had made at age ten and ran her fingers over its round little ears.

"It was the genealogy chart," she said at last, in a low voice.

"What?"

"A school assignment a couple of years ago. She wrote down Clint and me on the chart and didn't comment. But she knew it was a lie. I should have said something."

Aggie seemed off balance. "What could you have said?"

"I don't mean I could have told her anything concrete. I've told her everything I know, but it's almost nothing. Her mother was very young and couldn't keep her. That's all I know. No names, nothing. But at least I could have told her I knew it was rough for her."

"What did you do?"

"Nothing. I mean, I just answered her questions about my parents and Clint. It's hard for me to talk about the—the adoption. I thought maybe she wouldn't think about it much if I didn't make a big thing of it."

"When was all this?"

"A couple of years ago. And she avoided the subject too. Once or twice I brought it up, and she said, 'Skip it, Mom.' Maybe she sensed that I, well, didn't like to talk about it. But that's when she started ignoring her schoolwork. She quit ballet, took up with Buck, and so forth."

"Meaning drugs?"

"Not often. Look, I've read all the stuff about how to tell if your child is using drugs. And yes, she's tried ludes. But only a couple of times! I bet you can't find more than half a dozen kids in this county who haven't tried them!"

"Yeah, that's true in New York too."

"No, what really bothered me was the self-portrait."

"And you didn't say anything even then?"

"I didn't know what to say! They didn't tell me what to say! They said everything would be normal, like a real family."

"Like a real family." The other woman's voice was very tight.

"You know. A birth family."

Aggie bounced up, strode away to the window, then turned

back, the light behind her now. "Tell me what a real family is like."

"What do you mean? Everyone knows."

"For starts, a mommy and a daddy who are married, right?"

"Yes, of course!" Rina was puzzled. Why did this reporter care?

"For the first, last, and only time." Aggie Lyons's face was shadowed, unreadable against the misty brightness of the window behind her.

"Well, yes, ideally."

"And there is a child."

"Or children."

"And the daddy earns the money, and the mommy doesn't work."

"Not when the kids are little. Maybe part-time."

"You've eliminated my family twice already," said Aggie.

"I don't understand."

"My husband was married once before. And I work, full-time. And we have kids."

"You told Clint you had a daughter."

"A six-year-old. And a three-year-old son. A relative is taking care of them at the moment."

Rina said stiffly, "I'm sorry. I was talking about a sort of abstract ideal. I didn't mean to insult your family." She had been wrong, this woman did not understand. She got up from the bed and started out the door.

The reporter followed. "No, I refuse to take it as an insult. Because I don't care whether my family is ideal or not, as long as I can have the one I have. The husband I have, the kids I have. We muddle along pretty well together, whether we're ideal or not."

Rina was silent, bitter. For a moment, as they had looked at Ginny's sculpture, she had thought they were communicating, but the chasm was too great. This woman had children, had given birth. Rina had entrusted Ginny's secrets to someone as blind as all the rest. Except that this one could publish them for all the world to see. What a stupid, stupid fool she'd been.

Aggie Lyons said uncertainly, "Did I say something wrong? I'm sorry. I just think that your family is a lot closer to that abstract ideal than a lot of others, including mine."

"No doubt," said Rina acidly, stalking down the hall. "I've heard that before. How ideal things are, how lucky I am. Next you'll probably say you think I'm lucky because I didn't have to go through all the annoyance of pregnancy and childbirth, right? And then you'll say Ginny is luckier than most kids because she was chosen, right?" The younger woman raised her hand in dismay, but Rina charged ahead. "And you'll say that Clint and I are just unbelievable saints because we can love someone else's child, right? And then you'll say that after all, you don't even know how your own will turn out, right? And, let's see, you probably will think that Ginny looks more like me than most daughters look like their mothers, right? Look!" She dodged into the den and pulled a photo album from the bookshelf.

"Mrs. Marshall, I'm sorry!" Aggie Lyons sounded shaken.

"Look!" Rina insisted. She flipped the album open. Ginny, age three, beamed up at them from the page, the wide smile, the big blue eyes. "You'll say she looks like me, right? All but the eyes, you'll say. Look!" She flipped the pages again. Ginny, a serious ten, in a ballet pose, the black hair pulled back into a ponytail. "See what a saint I am to love her?"

"Stop it!" Aggie cried.

Shocked at the anguish in the voice, Rina glanced at her for the first time. Aggie was not looking; she had bowed her head, and was shielding her already hidden eyes with one angular hand. With a mixture of regret and bitter triumph, Rina closed the album.

The younger woman lowered her hand. "Spare me your kiddy stories," she said in a ragged voice.

"My God!" The last threads of Rina's control snapped; she slammed the album down on the table. "I didn't invite you in! I've tried to explain, tried to be polite to you, tried to answer your questions. What the hell are you trying to do to us?"

"I'm trying to tell you that you've got a wonderful daughter! And it doesn't matter what's ideal or not ideal, she's lived with you! That's a wonderful truth! What difference does it make what the rest of us think? Why are you making yourselves miserable with this fairy-tale 'real family' thing? Don't you realize how lucky you are just to live with her?"

"Of course!" Furious, Rina glared back at her, astonished at Aggie's intensity. "Is that all you want, for me to tell you I feel lucky? My God, you'll never, never know how lucky I feel!"

Aggie too was struggling to bring herself under control. The long capable hands flapped once, uncharacteristically helpless. "Well, okay, I guess I knew that, really. Look, forget it, I'm sorry. Most unprofessional of me."

Rina's anger was waning. She could almost touch the younger woman's unhappiness. She said uncertainly, "You said you had kids. You aren't infertile."

"Infertile?" The dark head cocked toward her, puzzled.

"It's just that when I found out that I couldn't have children, I was so jealous, so sad. Almost as though the babies I'd never have were dead. Every child I saw made me want to cry because it wasn't mine. You just—it's silly, but you just seem to be feeling the same way, somehow."

Aggie was silent a moment. Finally she said, "I can't really talk about it. But I've been so rude, I owe you an explanation. You see, I lost a baby girl once."

"Oh, Aggie!" A rush of tenderness filled Rina, and she reached toward Aggie. "I know how terrible that must have been!"

"Yes, okay." She jammed her hands into the pockets of her knee pants, withdrawing, cooler now. "But it's like a lot of other things, you can't understand it, really understand it, unless it happened to you. So—"

But Rina was not to be put off that easily. She shook her head, sympathetic but determined. "I think I can, Aggie. Maybe it's not exactly the same, but I really can understand. You mourn for one of your children. But you see, I mourn for all of mine."

"All of yours." Aggie was very still a moment, studying her, then suddenly reached out and took both of Rina's hands. "What a smug, insufferable boor I've been! Of course you do. You do understand, and I'm the one who's been dense. God! God, Rina, I didn't think."

"Well, how could you know?"

"God." She shook her head, intent on Rina, reevaluating her. "Look, I need a lesson, okay? A minute ago I said something pompous about not caring if my family was an ideal family or not. Tell me why you care."

"It's not that I care. I adore my family, just the way it is. Like you. But it is different from that ideal. I mean, we went to such lengths to try to have children, and gradually accepted that we couldn't, and we grieved. We still do, in a way. You look back at the unbroken chain of your ancestors and realize that the thread is cut forever. It hurts. And it hurts to know that for some reason you can't do this thing that most loving couples can do, have a child together in your love. And—well, this is kind of frivolous, but I had looked forward to being pregnant, to giving birth, almost as though it was proof of my womanhood." Aggie was shaking her head, and Rina said, "Oh, I know, with my mind I know it's not true, but it's hard to shake the expectations you grow up with. Even so, we came to terms with it, Clint and I. We cried together, and grieved, and finally decided that even though our biological children would never be, we still wanted to be parents together. We could love and care for a child, and that was what we really wanted most. So we applied to adopt a child."

"I see."

"Not to replace the children that would never be. We knew that it would be different, but wonderful. And we were right. But there are problems. You see, to adopt a child you have to pass tests."

"Tests?"

"Interviews. Home studies. Someone checking to see if you're good enough to have a baby. Most people just go ahead and have one. They don't have to convince someone they're great housekeepers, great nurses, great personalities, great cooks, great wives. They don't have to prove that their only problem is bum tubes. Prove they aren't psycho for wanting a child." Rina smoothed back her hair. "My God, Aggie, all your life you're told you'll have a family someday. You just assume it. And then when you don't have a baby, it really hurts. And everyone thinks it's a tragedy. And you go to doctors and have operations, and when it turns out that you're in the ninety percent that the operation doesn't help, it's a tragedy all over again. And after all that, the agency wants you to prove that you really want a child!"

Aggie's hand touched hers again. "Rina, I didn't know. I never thought what it must be like."

"Nobody does."

"So ever since Ginny came you've been trying to be a real family. What the agency calls a real family."

"How can you argue with them? You've already spent years praying to God. The agency is above God." Rina looked at the other woman, whose sympathy was written in the tilt of head and shoulders, in the softness of the wide mouth, in the earnestness of the voice. She realized she was being indiscreet. She also realized she didn't care. She smiled a little. "Those quilts you admire so much. That's the agency's fault too."

"How do you mean?"

"I was working on a little pillow when we had our first

home visit, there on Long Island. First one I'd ever made. I was trained as a commercial artist, you know."

"No, I didn't."

"Yes. And I wasn't especially excited about that pillow, we just happened to need one. I was working then, freelance, catalog illustrations. Mrs. Farnham from the agency wasn't impressed. But she liked my dumb pillow. Said at least I was able to turn my talents to homemaking too."

"She said that? God, Rina!"

"Well, then, I was stuck. I started making the baby a quilt for the next visit. And maybe you know, there's a long period before the adoption is final, when they can still take the baby away if they decide . . ."

The doorbell chimed.

"Your husband?" Aggie asked hopefully.

"He'd use his key. Probably some reporter."

"Yeah. Damn press." Aggie stayed in the background while Rina hurried to the door and peeked through the curtained sidelight.

It was not the press. It was Rosamond Landon. Rina unlocked and opened the door. "Rosamond! Come in!"

Rosamond stepped in, her cashmeres charcoal-colored today. A diamond pin glittered on her collar. She patted absently at a stray strand of blond hair, her eyes fixed accusingly on Rina. "Rina Marshall, just what have you told the police?"

"The police? About what?"

"Oh, don't play dumb! They have my poor boy down there still! Three hours they've been there! Where's your daughter?"

"She's—not back yet."

"I'll bet she's not back yet! You've sent her into hiding somewhere, haven't you? You're trying to make Buck take the blame!"

Aggie was drifting toward them from Ginny's room. Rina said, "Of course not! I just told the truth! Rosamond, let's not make things more difficult than they are. I'm sure the police have good reason to—"

"They have the reasons you fed them! Really, Rina, to take advantage of a young boy's romantic feelings—well, you're just going to have to go down there and tell them it's not the truth!"

"What's not the truth?"

"Buck wasn't here Thursday! He never saw that dreadful old man!"

"But he was here! And high as a kite on Quaaludes!"

"What?" For an instant something fractured deep in Rosamond's eyes, then glazed over again. "So that's what you've been telling them! No wonder! Well, Rina Marshall, I warn you, you're going to be—who's this?" She focussed suddenly on Aggie, who was standing near them now, closing the catch on her shoulder bag.

"Aggie Lyons. *New York Week.*" Aggie stepped forward, hand extended, and shook Rosamond's hand vigorously. "I'm so glad to meet you, Mrs. Landon! I've been wanting to ask you some questions!"

XV

"A reporter?" Rosamond stepped back in shock.

"I'm trying to find out the whole truth about Mr. Spencer's death," Aggie said. "Not just the sensational headlines."

"A reporter! Rina, we'll sue you! How could you bring in a reporter—spring her on me like this—" Rosamond was backing toward the door.

"I would have been ringing your bell pretty soon anyway," Aggie said in a soothing tone of voice. She edged around Rina to stand next to the door, so that Rosamond's advance toward it brought her closer to Aggie too.

Rosamond stopped and said, "You wouldn't get in! I've told Maria, no reporters!"

"Look, all I want is to find out the truth. You say Buck wasn't here Thursday. Mrs. Marshall says he was."

"She's just trying to dump the blame on Buck!"

"Where was he, then?"

"With Chip. His friend. A congressman's son."

"Ah. A congressman's son." Aggie wrote it down. "You saw them together, Mrs. Landon?"

"Together?"

"Chip and Buck."

"Yes! Well, later I saw them."

"Buck was here, about five o'clock," said Rina mulishly.

Aggie waved her down. "Okay, we'll worry about that later.

I wonder if Mrs. Landon can tell me now why Mr. Spencer was dreadful?"

Rosamond, her mouth open to argue with Rina, was startled by the change of subject. "Dreadful?"

"You said he was a dreadful old man. You knew him?"

"No! Of course not! I never saw him in my life!"

"You spoke to him, though."

"No! Who told you that, the Playmate of the Month?"

"She implied it," said Aggie smoothly. Rina, bewildered, wondered who they were talking about.

"Well, *she* may have spoken to him. None of us did." Rosamond smoothed her hair. "You can't believe anything she says about us. That one has other fish to fry."

"Okay, I'll keep that in mind," said Aggie cooperatively. "Now, Mrs. Landon, the police are talking to your son, but you say he's not involved. So why are they talking to him?"

Rosamond pointed her chin at Rina. "Because *her* daughter's trying to put the blame on him! Her daughter got into this terrible mess, and she'll stop at nothing to shift the blame! Let me tell you, you're right to be interviewing Mrs. Marshall. She's the one who knows the truth. But she'll probably give you nothing but lies!" Rosamond shoved past Aggie and out the door.

Rina said despairingly, "It's not true. He was here. She's just upset, trying to defend her son."

"Yeah, I can understand that," Aggie said. "But she might think a little more clearly if she weren't reeking of alcohol. Who do you suppose the Playmate of the Month is?"

"You mean you didn't know? I have no idea."

"How about this Maria she mentioned? Is she a maid?"

"Yes. Nice Mexican woman."

"Young?"

"No, maybe forty."

"Not the Playmate of the Month, then. Well, we'll figure it out. I have to go make a few phone calls now. But maybe tomorrow we could team up and talk to some people. You know the area and the people. It would be a big help."

"Rosamond Landon would slam the door in my face," said Rina ruefully.

"So we'll save her till last." Aggie smiled encouragingly. "Tomorrow, then, okay?"

Well, why not? "Okay," said Rina.

She waved good-bye to Aggie with much more optimism than she had any right to feel.

The problem was that Will was just not sick enough to stay quietly in bed.

Ginny, already exhausted by late afternoon, was putting dishes in the dishwasher when she heard a blood-curdling scream from the front hall. Hands still streaming water, she sprinted to the front of the house, and discovered Will shrieking in purely psychological agony while Sarah hugged a very uncomfortable Kakiy to her chest.

Will was beyond coherence, but Sarah realized that some sort of justification was called for. "It's my turn to hold Kakiy," she explained, a hint of guilt in her brown eyes.

Ginny said, "Sarah, Kakiy looks squeezed. He doesn't like to be held quite so tight."

Sarah loosened her grip a little, and as Ginny had expected, Kakiy exercised his basic feline constitutional rights to life and liberty by writhing out of her arms and leaping away to the side of the room.

"Kakiy!" squealed Sarah, and dove unsuccessfully after him. Will continued to bawl. Ginny swooped up one child under each arm and marched out to the kitchen with them. They were both startled into momentary silence.

"All right, you two," she said in her best Cagney imitation, settling them onto a pair of chairs. "You sit right there and don't move! And have your milk and graham crackers. Because if you don't, I'm going to throw you out the window so high that you'll bump into the clouds."

Will's brown eyes widened in shocked apprehension, but Sarah gave a delighted giggle, and then he laughed too.

"No, no!" said Sarah. "You can't throw us that high!"

"Well, then, I'll throw you so high, you hit the moon!" Swiftly, Ginny was pouring two glasses of milk and getting out the remains of the graham crackers.

"No! You can't!"

"Oh, dear. Let's see. So high you hit a bird?"

"No!" They were eating gleefully now. Maggie's red book had been right. If they get really awful, feed them, she had written. It was certainly working with Sarah. Will was a sour-face today, but he had real problems. At three and a half it's hard to pinpoint the source of your unhappiness.

At sixteen too.

Maybe, thought Ginny, I ought to eat something myself. She made three peanut butter sandwiches and sat down with the children at the table. "How high then?" she asked, handing around the sandwiches.

"So high we hit an airplane!" suggested Sarah. They really were cute, the lively brown eyes fixed on her expectantly. Even Will looked momentarily adorable, his happy expression overriding the flushed and pimpled skin.

They continued this not overly intellectual conversation until the snack was finished. Then Sarah seemed to want some privacy and went into her own room, where she looked at books, happy and solitary, for an hour. Will was not so helpful. After a while he began to whimper, "Want Mommy!" Eventually Ginny managed to coax him back into bed.

The phone rang at about seven o'clock. Ginny answered in the upstairs study.

"O'Connors'," she said, praying that it wasn't the police.

"Hi, it's Maggie. How're you doing?"

"Okay. What's happening there?"

"I met your family. No, no one recognized me. Your mom's a terrific person, Ginny. One hundred percent on your side."

"Yeah. She's okay," admitted Ginny. She stood in the study door, where she could see the children's rooms.

"Your dad seemed very sensible. I only talked to him on the phone. He seemed worried about what this publicity might do to your future."

"Yeah, he's a little hung up on my future."

"Typical of those of us who have already lived through a bit of our own futures."

"Yeah."

"I talked to your grandmother briefly."

"What did you think?"

"A very frustrated woman. Loves you all, but feels degraded having to live on your parents' charity."

"Charity!"

"It seems that way to her."

Ginny decided to think about that later. "What about Mr. Spencer?"

"I'm still fishing for facts. Talked to your grandmother's friends, checked out the bridge party. I had an interesting talk with Buck's mother. But if she knows anything about Mr. Spencer, she's not telling."

Ginny's stomach was tight again. "God, Maggie, be careful! Don't tell them I'm adopted!"

"I'll be very careful. Mrs. Landon mentioned someone she called the Playmate of the Month. Who would that be?"

"Playmate of the—oh, yeah, Buck said his parents had a fight about her. You mean the assistant at Dr. Landon's office."

"I bet that *is* who I mean!" said Maggie happily. "Thanks. Listen, how're the kids?"

"Fine. Will is asleep already."

"Has he been beastly today?"

"Well, he's sick."

"He has been beastly then. Sorry."

"We'll manage. Do you want to talk to Sarah?"

"Please."

Ginny called Sarah from her room and handed over the receiver, and Sarah, sparkling, discussed her day with animation before handing the phone back to Ginny.

"Hello again, Ginny. I'm at the Adams Motel, 301-555-2343. Got that?"

"Yes, thanks. Listen, Nick called. Just to say hello."

"He's next on my list. Anything else?"

"I guess not."

"Well, try not to let Will get you down. He's really a pretty reasonable little fellow most of the time."

"I know. I've seen him on better days. None of us do very well when we're itchy and headachy."

"Right. See you soon, I hope."

"Me too. Bye."

Ginny hung up, feeling suddenly desolate. She checked Will, who was still in an exhausted sleep, and then went into Sarah's room.

"It's time for gymnastics," announced Sarah.

"Oh, Sarah, I don't know how!"

But Sarah insisted, and they trooped up to the big top-floor room. Ginny soon found herself matching her little sister cartwheel for cartwheel and enjoying it. Her genes were the genes of gymnasts. After the workout she helped Sarah with her bath, and finally settled her down for a bedtime story.

"How about *Alice in Wonderland?*" Ginny asked casually.

"Okay."

Ginny read three chapters before Sarah let her stop, and she wondered at the way the half-familiar words chimed softly in her memory. Mom and Dad had read it to her when she was small, she remembered now, and she had been fascinated because the girl's name was Alice, like her own middle name.

But the book had been put aside along with most of her other youthful books as she grew older.

With Sarah finally settled, Ginny went up to the exercise room to bring her sheets down to the sofa in the little study, so that she would be closer to Will in case he needed her at night. It wasn't until she pulled off the quilt that she saw the cardboard box under the window, about a foot square and almost as deep, labeled "For Ginny."

Inside was a pair of bookends and a photo album, and a note. "I've been keeping this scrapbook for you, in case you were interested. The bookends were a gift from your father. They're for you, if you want them."

She looked at them, little copies of Notre Dame Cathedral. From her young father to her young mother, in those happy months long ago. Those happy months that had given Ginny her existence, and her anguish.

Obscurely disturbed by them, she closed the box and took it down to the study along with the sheets. She made up a bed on the sofa there. Sarah was still reading to herself, and Will, hot and scabby, was still drowned in sleep. Ginny kissed her little brother's roughened forehead, and left the doors ajar so she could hear him if he woke during the night. She got into one of Maggie's nightshirts, looked hard at the box, and lay down. She wasn't quite courageous enough to look at the scrapbook tonight.

She dreamed again of people who flew away from her.

Monday, September 17, 1979

XVI

Monday started early and didn't let up.

At about six Will woke her, shaking her shoulder, demanding to go to the bathroom. He was smelly, whiny, and thoroughly disgusting. Ginny closed her eyes a moment, remembered the friendly little boy she had met Friday, remembered that he was her brother, and got herself up to help him. Luckily she had followed the advice in the red book to diaper him at night when he was sick; he was soaked, the caustic smell of staling urine like a pungent cloud around him. She decided to start him off with a bath. But while she was tending to the soaked diaper he jumped down from the toilet and ran downstairs, naked except for his pajama shirt with its unspeakable damp hem, and whined for breakfast until she gave in.

And so it went. She finished with his breakfast, got cleaner clothes on him, and realized Sarah needed breakfast too. She got Sarah off to school against the background of Will's complaints, and finally got him into the bath. Halfway through the bath Zelle, in an anxious frenzy of barking and scrabbling, reminded her that she too needed a run. Those jobs completed, she figured out how the washing machine worked and had just started a load of Will's foul-smelling sheets and diapers when the telephone rang.

"O'Connors'." Will was whining behind her.

"Hi. It's Maggie. Just wanted to tell you, I'm sending an express package. They promised to get it there this afternoon.

It's to Alice Ryan. I apologize, but I thought you'd better not sign your real name."

"Oh. Okay. What is it?"

"Schoolbooks. I borrowed them from your mother. I saw Linda and Jan last night and got some homework assignments."

"So you do want me to make better grades!" Ginny felt triumphant at exposing Maggie in a lie at last.

"I thought you deserved a choice," came the mild reply. "I saw a few of your papers. You seem to have your precise level of underachievement down to a science. I didn't want these few days to throw you off too much. Is that my son yowling in the background?"

"Yes. I'm not beating him, honest."

"I know. He sounds just the way Sarah did two weeks ago. Ask him if he wants to talk to me."

Will and Maggie had a serious conversation about how far away she was, and how many chicken pox pimples he had, and whether Zelle and Kakiy might catch it next. Then he gave the receiver back to Ginny.

"Tell me about Buck," Maggie said.

"I've told you already. Did you see him?"

"I talked to him last night on the phone. He seems puzzled by the whole situation. Misses you. But I couldn't get a lot of sense out of him. He was pretty high."

"Yeah. He is, more and more these days. It's a bore. Well, what can I say about him? You talked to him."

"Would he take your scissors?"

"No. I mean, he might borrow them if he had a reason, but he wouldn't have a reason."

"Mr. Spencer and your grandmother were scolding him, you see. He was also stoned when he came looking for you, and he bumped into Spencer. Sassed them when they complained."

"So that makes him a murderer? Come on!"

"Or your accomplice. You sassed them too."

"Jesus!"

"I'm just mentioning some of the possibilities the police are probably considering. Buck went straight from your house to the library. Where the body was found."

"God, Maggie."

"You think he'd never pull a pair of scissors on someone?"

"Never."

"Even when stoned?"

"Oh, hell, Maggie," said Ginny in despair. "What am I supposed to say? I don't know exactly what happens in his head. He gets happy, not mad, when he's stoned. I don't think he'd do it. Listen, I've been thinking, what if Mr. Spencer took the scissors himself? He could have. Then a mugger got them away from him! Doesn't that make sense?"

"And then the mugger put them in Buck's car?"

"Oh, hell."

"Where does Buck get his drugs, Ginny?"

"I don't know."

"But you have an idea." Ginny was silent, and Maggie added, "Look, this is murder we're talking about. Maybe the drugs aren't relevant, but maybe they are. It's up to you, but we're not talking about a rap on the knuckles for possession. You and Buck are in deep shit, kid."

"Yeah."

"His dad is a doctor."

"No. The accounting system is too complicated. Coded."

"You think he gets it from a regular connection, then?"

"Maggie, I never asked. I didn't really want to know. But he does get an awful lot somewhere. I don't think he was lying about his dad's accounting system. But Buck gets enough to supply the football team sometimes."

"Wow. Has he ever been in trouble with the cops?"

"No. Not officially, anyway. Some of the guys on the team are from pretty important families. Political appointments, senators, judges. The football booster club is like Who's Who. So the school doesn't hassle them much. I don't know if the police would hassle them either, even if they knew."

"I see. Buck's father isn't political, though, is he?"

"Physician to the stars, you know. And Chip Wilson is Buck's best friend. A congressman's son."

"Chip's the one who says he was driving home with Buck at the time Mr. Spencer was being stabbed."

"Well, he probably was!"

"Yeah. Okay, thanks. I'll call you again later."

Ginny felt a moment of panic because Will was suspiciously quiet, but when she checked, he was all right. He was twitching his frog-shaped beanbag back and forth while Kakiy batted at it with his paws. Ginny started the dishwasher and, during the brief respite that Will's game with Kakiy offered her, made a plan. Graham crackers would stay in the kitchen today. Baths would be at logical Ginny-determined times. She'd get things picked up and vacuumed and keep them that way. Will would take a nap, like it or not, and she'd get something done.

It was a good plan, except that while she was putting the diapers into the dryer Will helped himself to a peanut butter sandwich and dribbled globs of peanut butter and jelly all the way up the stairs, and while she was opening the door for the delivery man and signing "Alice Ryan" with a queasy feeling in the pit of her stomach, Will decided to take a bath on his own. She searched frantically for him all over the house before finding him standing next to a half-full tub of water.

"Will, for heaven's sake, you'll drown yourself!" Exasperated, she pulled the plug. Will's little crusted face wrinkled, and he began to breathe in gasps that were clearly headed for all-out bawling. Demolished by this Excalibur of the small and weak against the powerful and logical, Ginny gave up her grand plan and sat down with him to read some more *Alice in Wonderland*.

Kakiy observed them from Will's sunny windowsill, serene and unruffled.

Mrs. Deaver's house was brick with a white porch on one of the older streets of the suburb. The neighborhood had good-sized yards and mature trees. Once it had been inhabited by middle-class civil servants like the Deavers, but values had risen sharply. "We couldn't afford it today," Marie Deaver explained in response to Aggie's question. "And the sad thing is, the rise in price doesn't help me at all. I can't borrow on it, because I couldn't afford the monthly payments. And if I sold it, I'd end up like Delores, rent going up every year. No, the best thing for me to do is to hang onto it for Bobby. The estate can sell it for him, and invest the money so he can stay out at Shadyland."

"It's a lovely house," Aggie said. Rina agreed. It was not as large as her own home, but the brick fireplace and colonial-style furniture, set off by Marie Deaver's collection of antique blue-and-white plates, gave a friendly charm to the house. Aggie walked to the big window at the rear of the living room and looked out. "Pretty garden too."

"Thank you." Marie Deaver closed the closet door where she'd hung their coats. "Those are the mums your mother just gave me, Rina."

"Oh, yes, I remember." Rina joined the others at the window. Several young bushes of showy golden chrysanthemums blazed against the black soil in the neatly hoed and weeded flowerbeds, just as they did in Mama's garden at home. "They're doing well."

"Thank you. But no one's thumb is as green as your mother's."

"Certainly not mine!" Rina agreed.

"Excuse me. May I use your bathroom?" Aggie asked.

"Certainly, dear. Here, let me show you." Marie led the way halfway up the stairs, then paused. "There you are, on the right side." She watched as Aggie trotted up past her, then she turned back to Rina. "How about some coffee or tea?"

"Oh, don't go to any trouble."

"No trouble. I usually fix some tea for myself this time of the afternoon." They went into the kitchen, and Rina helped arrange the lovely old cups and saucers on a tray while Marie put on the kettle and measured tea into a fat blue-and-white pot. She took a few butter cookies from a tin and set them on a plate. "I always feel like apologizing for my cooking when I'm with you Rossis," she said, smiling.

"No need. But it is one of Mamma's passions," Rina admitted.

Aggie appeared in the kitchen doorway. "Oh, a proper tea!" she said enthusiastically. "What a good idea!"

Rina picked up the tray. "Where do you want it?"

"Let's take it in the living room."

"Mrs. Deaver, I couldn't help noticing the room across from the bathroom," Aggie said as they followed Rina to the coffee table. "The one with all the clocks."

"Bobby's projects," said Marie. "He's very good with mechanical things. He built some of the clocks, but of course he can't keep many at the home. So I put them in his room here. He can have them when he's ready to come home. Do you want lemon, Rina?"

"Thank you." Taking the cup from Marie, Rina thought of Bobby's room upstairs, kept ready for him just in case. Ginny's room was ready for her too. But Ginny would come back, really, she reminded herself fiercely. She would!

Aggie and Marie Deaver were talking about the rest of the family. "Frank worked at the Federal Trade Commission," Marie explained. "I took care of Bobby for a few years, but when we saw he'd do better in a special school I went to work too."

"For the government?"

"Yes. Various departments. Under Johnson—the War on

Poverty, remember?—I worked on implementing some of the welfare legislation. Getting it into the computers and so forth. It seemed like they had a new law every two days. A crazy time. I helped make sure we didn't cut out eligible people by mistake. It was a madhouse some months. But we did pretty well on average."

"That was important work. Do you miss it, now that you've retired?"

"I miss my friends. I still visit the old office occasionally to say hello. And I miss the excitement. But a lot of it was drudgery too."

"Most jobs have a lot of drudgery. Mine—I love talking to people, but writing it down is a chore sometimes. Quilting must be the same, Rina. The excitement and fun of design, and then all those little stitches, thousands of them."

Rina nodded. "That's true. But there's a satisfaction in completing a project well, too. In trying to live up to the vision. Tell me, Marie, does Bobby like his quilt?"

Marie placed her cup carefully on the tray and smiled. "Oh, yes. He was very engrossed in it. Stroked it."

"I'm glad he likes it. It has nice bright colors."

"Yes. Now, tell me why you're here," said Marie. "You said you had some questions."

"Yes," said Aggie. "Who do you think killed Mr. Spencer?"

Marie picked up her cup again. "I'm not a detective, Aggie," she said mildly. "Or a reporter. And I certainly don't want to point a finger at an innocent person, perhaps lose a friend."

"Well, let me put it more delicately. Suppose you were a detective—what would you be looking for? Just supposing."

Marie Deaver smiled. "Yes, that question is better. But I can't think what I'd do that the police aren't doing already. I'd try to find out something about John, in case it was a friend or acquaintance who did it, and I'd also try to work backward from where he was found, because it may have nothing to do with him, it might have been pure chance."

Aggie took a butter cookie. "Do you think they're right to ask so many questions of his friends?"

"It does get tedious," Marie admitted. "And I can't imagine any of us doing it, can you? So it does seem that they're paying too much attention to us. But maybe they hope we'll remember something about him, because it is possible that it was an acquaintance. These days, with such a drug problem, it's difficult to trust anyone."

"Was Mr. Spencer too trusting, you think?"

Marie shook her head sadly. "Of course I knew him only slightly, but my impression was that John was sensible. No more gullible than the rest of us. Still—the facts don't bear that out, do they?"

"You mentioned drugs," said Aggie. "You think they may have been involved, then?"

"I don't know. I just said there were a lot of them involved in crimes these days, and young people—" She glanced uneasily at Rina. "I just meant that was one possibility."

"You needn't be polite on my account," said Rina wearily. "I know Buck Landon has problems. And Ginny's interest in him is a problem. I just don't understand what she sees in him."

"It's hard to understand youngsters," Marie said sympathetically. "I have trouble understanding what Bobby needs sometimes, and he's my own blood!"

"Yes." Her own blood. Rina felt that Marie had struck her, sideswiped her careful props from under her.

"But as for young Buck Landon, we can hope he gets straightened out before long," Marie continued. "He really was acting very strange. We had to tell the police, you know that, Rina."

Rina murmured, "Yes, of course you had to tell them."

Aggie glanced at Rina with a hint of worry around her

mouth, but her words didn't help much. "Ginny ran away just then, too," she said. "That called the attention of the police to her."

"Yes," Marie Deaver agreed. "Forgive me, Rina, but she was a bit difficult that afternoon. So was Buck."

Quit pouting, Rina scolded herself. *Use this opportunity.* "I know she was, Marie," she said. "Do you remember anything she said? Anything that would account for her being so upset?"

"Why, the cat, of course. I was upset—well, goodness, your mother was upset too, the minute she realized what she'd done. But Ginny does feel motherly toward the cat. She over-reacted, but we were all upset."

"Yes, but I mean, did she say anything that might be related to wanting to leave?"

Marie frowned. "Leave? No, I don't remember anything like that. In fact, when she first came after the cat, she apologized that he'd escaped. Very mannerly, I thought. But then when the cat was hurt, she got upset and ran off to the den. That was the last I saw of her. No, any thought about leaving must have come afterward."

Meaning after the murder? Rina put down her empty cup. "Well, if you do think of anything else, please let me know. I just can't imagine where she's gone."

"Oh, she'll be in touch soon, I imagine." Marie smiled reassuringly at Rina.

"One last question," said Aggie. "You're familiar with the area near the library book drop, where Mr. Spencer's body was found."

"Yes. And Delores and Leonora and I went to have a look at it afterward."

"Did you notice anything out of the ordinary? I mean, besides the police tape and so forth."

"Oh, dear. I hardly looked at it before all this happened, you know. It did seem to me that the area looked very trampled down when I went with the others. But we thought that was probably the police walking around."

"The police I know are very careful about that," Aggie said. "Trampled down, you say. Could you see footprints?"

"No, that's not what I meant. Goodness, I'm not an expert! It just seemed that a lot of twigs and branches were broken. More than I'd expect."

"Interesting," said Aggie. "So the killer might have taken a few minutes out of the car, you think? To arrange the body there?"

"It occurred to me."

"I wonder what needed arranging?" Aggie looked at her watch. "Oh, dear, the high school will be getting out soon. I wanted to try to catch some of Buck's friends before I spoke to him. Thank you, Mrs. Deaver. You've been a good sport." She stood, and Rina and Marie Deaver followed suit.

"Well, I'm afraid I haven't been much help, it's so confusing," Marie said.

"Oh, we're all confused." Aggie opened the closet and took out her white fur and Rina's trench coat, then straightened the remaining hangers so Marie's winter coats weren't crammed into the corner. "But if we get enough facts, some sense may emerge. Thanks for the talk and the tea, Mrs. Deaver."

"Thanks for the company. I'll see you soon, Rina."

She stood smiling at the door as they left, a small white-haired woman in a big empty house.

Nick snuggled the receiver to his chin. "What am *I* doing? Well—I'm in the hotel room." The phone had rung a couple of minutes after he'd come in. He was sitting on the bed and could see himself in the wide mirror across the room: unkempt and still sweaty from rehearsal. Undershirt and old gray sweatpants, decidedly undecorative. He lowered his voice to a more romantic pitch. "I'm in my tux, of course. Bow tie slightly loosened. Room service brought me a glass of champagne and a bud vase with a single lovely marguerite." He could hear Maggie's giggle. "Glass in hand, I gaze longingly across the Mississippi to the east, and all alone beweep my outcast state."

"Lovely!" There was relish in Maggie's voice. "Tears on your satin lapel, and sighs."

"Yep. Sighing like a furnace, with a woeful ballad to your eyebrow and all that."

"Lovely. I get the picture. You've been working like a dog and probably haven't showered yet."

"Got it in one."

"Rehearsals went well?"

"Yes. They forgot to tell us about a support column right in the middle of the stage area, but we worked it into the action. Breakfast and lunch shows tomorrow, we'll be fine. Now, what have you been doing?"

"Talked to Buck Landon on the phone last night. Kid's got a major drug problem. Ginny says he supplies the football team."

"Uh-oh."

"Yeah. I want to do some research before I talk to him face-to-face. And today I talked to Mrs. Deaver, one of the bridge party. Smart woman. I managed a quickie tour of her house while I supposedly went to the bathroom. Files are neat, stuff on her husband, her autistic son's institution, even her cleaning ladies. Insurance, financial stuff in order. She used to work for the government, everything in triplicate, I guess."

"Wish we had someone like that around the house."

"Me too. But it was sad, Nick. She has this big house—her own bedroom, a den, even a little servant's room. And she's still got a bedroom for her son, even though everything in his file seems to say he'll never recover."

"It's hard to give up on a kid," Nick said.

"Yeah. I still admire her. You called Ginny?"

"Twice. No problems, she's doing fine," he admitted. "No more frantic than I'd be in her place."

"That's my feeling too. I'll check tonight and tomorrow morning, you do the afternoon again, okay?"

"Fine. I can work that around the second show."

"What else. I talked to a few high schoolers here, but of course no one said, 'Hey, wanna know where I get my drugs?' "

"Youth is so secretive."

"Right. And, uh, I did go to the bus station. Found the guy who drove to New York at five-thirty Thursday. Ginny was definitely on the bus. He recognized her photo, even volunteered that she was wearing a fedora."

"Thanks, Maggie," said Nick after a second. "I didn't want to ask, but—"

"I know."

"Will asking the driver about her give away her trip?"

"Possibly. I don't think so. The same bus stops in Philadelphia, so she could have gotten off there."

"Good. What else?"

"Well, after that I tried to call you and failed, and then I went for a run, and then I came back and called you again and here you are."

"So you need a shower too."

"Yep. We're two of the most bedraggled on the continent just now."

Nick smiled, visualizing her. "Bedraggled becomes you, love. Gives you a delicious glow."

"Mmm. Thank God for your kinky taste."

The conversation degenerated to murmured unprintables, but when he'd finally hung up and was heading for the shower at last, Nick was cheered. Maggie was learning a lot, though there was much more to learn. And Ginny was doing fine.

Still, he'd be glad to get this damn show over and get back to his kids.

• • • •

By Monday night, when she finally got them both to bed, Ginny was exhausted. She flopped down on the chair in Will's room for just a minute, and woke up at two A.M., cold and stiff. Rubbing her neck, she limped into the little study and looked around. There were her schoolbooks, untouched. There was the box, too, with the bookends and the slender scrapbook. She sat down on the couch and, hesitantly, opened the scrapbook.

There wasn't much, a few newspaper clippings and dated photographs. 1960: a young Maggie doing gymnastics. 1964: graduating from high school. 1967: lounging with jaunty grin against a Hargate Theatre lighting instrument. 1968: standing in front of a square brick house with three other young women. 1969: snowy day, Maggie laughing, dressed in white, next to Nick in a horse-drawn sleigh. "Our wedding," that one was labeled.

There were pictures of other people too. A smiling professor with spectacles and curly gray hair, Maggie's father. A professor. A lean, robust white-haired woman, Maggie's mother. Her own—God, it couldn't be! Her own grandmother! Grandma, it appeared, was mayor of a town in Ohio. And as advertised, there was Aunt Olivia, the reporter, sitting next to a handsome man with curly black hair and the same dark-blue eyes that Ginny and Maggie shared. Maggie's brother, Jerry. My uncle, thought Ginny. My Uncle Jerry. Uncle Jerry was a doctor, said the note.

Bad blood.

She could not quite believe in them, these attractive half-familiar faces. Fairy-tale faces.

There were two black-and-white photos in the back of the album. Ginny looked at them for a long time. In one, a teen-aged Maggie was dressed in a dark skirt and jacket, knee socks, prim white blouse, but the demure outfit was belied by the radiant smile shining on the young man next to her. A handsome man, straight black hair cut in the oddly short early sixties style, returning Maggie's smile with a look of warm affection.

The other photo of the same pair was fuzzier, full-length, against a row of shops: charcuterie, boulangerie, said the signs. Again, the two were laughing, holding hands; but the detail that mesmerized Ginny was Maggie's coat. A white furry coat. The same coat she had worn to Maryland yesterday.

Ginny had a sense of doors crashing closed. A sense of loss. She frowned at the photos, trying to understand. It was all just as Maggie had said—the school uniform, the handsome young Frenchman with straight black hair, the affection. And the coat that Ginny herself had touched. It was real.

Real.

The coat was real. The bookends. The homemade sausage.

Until this moment she had not quite believed in it. In Maggie, yes; she had known from that first instant in the dining room that this was her mother. There was no doubt of that. She had known in her deepest self that they were family. *Il sangue chiama,* Gram said. For days Ginny had been riding the flood of confused feeling that this new connectedness engendered, striving to cope with these fierce new loves and hates.

But she had not had to believe in the story Maggie had told, although it had found a place among her own fantasies. The schoolgirl in Paris had been no different from the prostitutes and princesses who had lived in Ginny's imagination for so long. Maggie might have been any of them, might have played any part, just as she was now playing a journalist. The schoolgirl was just one more possible character in one more possible story.

Except that this story was real. The coat, the bookends, the sausage, the photos all showed that. And Ginny was dismayed as this new account shouldered its way brutally through all the others and established itself confidently as the only truth. She was so used to the other stories, so used to explaining herself to herself by one or another of the familiar shifting host of fantasies. How could she learn to live with just the one? Not knowing had been agony; her amputated past had left her adrift. But knowing, she saw, would be painful too. It threatened her. Walled her in. Forced her to be real too. Rooted in facts, not in shifting fairy tales.

Frightened, she threw the album back into the box. The schoolbooks were still lying in the package that the express company had brought. To Alice Ryan. Damn. She scratched out the name, then pulled out the books and took them to the desk. Concentrating fiercely, she worked all of the English assignments through next week, and started on the social studies.

A little after four A.M., sitting on the sofa with the text open on her lap, she finally fell into an exhausted sleep.

At six, Will's whine awakened her again.

Tuesday, September 18, 1979

XVII

"I'd like to see Dr. Landon's office. This is the place, right?" Rina nodded, and Aggie turned the Camaro into the parking lot of an office complex, landscaped with fruit trees and dark-leaved azalea bushes, glossy in the morning sun.

"Are you sure I won't be in your way?" Rina asked as they got out.

"You know more about this area. You may make a connection I can't." Aggie led the way to the entry, and the dark glasses turned toward the directory. "Here it is, second door."

Dr. Landon's waiting room was done in Early American, beige, blue, and cream. Rina's eyes were drawn immediately to an authentic crib quilt hanging on the wall, its faded calicos and tiny hand-stitched squares tugging at her heart. She looked away to find Aggie smiling at her. "The furniture's real too," she murmured.

"Their own furniture is very modern," Rina remembered. "But expensive too."

"Different decorators. Do you recognize the receptionist?"

"No."

A couple of people were seated on the padded deacon's bench, reading magazines. Aggie went past them to the receptionist, a brunette in her twenties who looked like a cosmetic ad. She looked Aggie over carefully, as though price-tagging each garment, and said coolly, "May I help you?"

"I'm Aggie Lyons. *New York Week,*" said Aggie. "I'm doing a story on the murder of John Spencer."

The people in the waiting room had looked up from their magazines with interest. The receptionist said, "That has nothing to do with this office."

"Yes, but you see—oh." Aggie intercepted the nervous glance toward the waiting patients and leaned forward, her voice too low for even Rina to hear.

The receptionist stood up quickly. "Follow me."

"Come on, Rina!" said Aggie breezily, explaining to the receptionist, "She's our capital-area stringer."

They went through a door into a short hall. The receptionist led the way into an office on the right and murmured something to the young woman seated behind the desk. Angela Warner, said her nameplate. Even in businesslike nurse's whites, Angela Warner was stunning. Translucent skin, dimples, a halo of strawberry-blond hair. Aggie whispered "Bingo" to Rina. Rina felt a jolt of sympathy for Rosamond Landon. Playmate of the Month, she'd said. Clint, like most men, met plenty of attractive women in his job, and Rina trusted him as she supposed most wives trusted their husbands. But if Clint had actually gone out of his way to hire someone who looked like this, if he'd chosen to work alongside her for hours every day—

"Ms. Warner will help you," the receptionist said briefly, and scurried back to her post.

"Ms. Warner, I'm Aggie Lyons, *New York Week.* Rina Marshall, my area specialist."

"Yes?" Ms. Warner had warm brown eyes, cautious and intelligent. She stood up to close the door to the hall.

"I understand that Dr. Landon's son is being questioned about the death of John Spencer. The boy quarreled with Mr. Spencer the day he was killed. I wanted to get the doctor's reactions to this situation."

Ms. Warner was already shaking her head. "Dr. Landon has

cooperated fully with the police. They can tell you whatever is necessary."

"Okay," said Aggie cheerfully, flopping down into the only other chair in the office. "I know he's a busy man. I can wait."

"No, the doctor can't see you. I mean it." Ms. Warner was firm.

"I mean it too. Unless—well, maybe you could answer a couple of questions. Is Dr. Landon close to his son?"

"He's a good father, if that's what you mean, but—"

"You have a chance to observe them together, Ms. Warner?"

"Not often." Ms. Warner seemed a little off balance. She arranged herself behind the desk again before continuing. "This is a busy office, of course. But Dr. Landon talks about the boy from time to time."

"Here at the office?"

"Of course!"

"Oh, I'm sorry, Ms. Warner," Aggie gushed. "You see, Mrs. Landon said you were on extremely close terms with Dr. Landon, so I just assumed—"

There was a flash of anger in the beautiful eyes. "Oh, you assumed, did you? Well, you'd better stop assuming! Mrs. Landon has a vivid imagination. Lurking around—"

"Well, sometimes women worry as they get older," Aggie said soothingly. "Even if there's nothing happening."

"Of course there isn't!"

Aggie pulled out her notebook. "So I can say, 'Dr. Landon's assistant denies accusations that she and the doctor are having an affair?' "

"Hey, wait, that's not fair! You shouldn't mention it at all! Look—Dr. Landon is a good doctor, okay? I like working in this office. But romance—no way! He's fifty, for God's sake! My boyfriend is a surgeon, and he'll be making twice as much as Landon in a few years. Plus he's twice as cute!"

Aggie looked puzzled. "Well, then, I don't understand

about Mrs. Landon. She knows you've got another boyfriend, and she still lurks? You said lurk?"

"I see her, almost every week! Dr. Landon generally leaves for hospital rounds about four-thirty, and Debbie and I straighten up and leave a little later. Mrs. Landon is parked under those crabapple trees in the west corner of the lot. And I think a couple of times she's followed me. I keep seeing a beige car back in the traffic."

"You're sure it's her?"

"She's parked in the shade, but there's no missing her hairdo."

"Does she ever come into the office?"

"She makes excuses sometimes and drops in. Dr. Landon does try to discourage it. Debbie thinks she wants my job."

"She used to work for him, didn't she?" Rina said.

"That's right, that's how they met. She had my job. Quit when the kids arrived. And of course she's ages out of date by now. In medicine, you can't just pick up twenty years later, you really need to go back to school. But she—anyway, Debbie and I think she's jealous on a lot of fronts."

Aggie nodded. "Yes. It must be annoying. Still, you have to be kind. Well, obviously you're right, I'd better not mention any of this in the story, if it's just Mrs. Landon's imagination. I will have to check it, of course."

"Go ahead." Ms. Warner didn't seem worried. "You won't find anyone saying that except her."

"Can you tell me what you do here?"

"Medical assistant and chief bottle washer." Ms. Warner smiled, the dimples lighting her face. "Debbie keeps track of the people, I keep track of supplies. And I give standard immunizations, explain treatments, assist while Dr. Landon examines female patients. The usual."

"Okay. Now, does Dr. Landon's son ever come by?"

There was a brief hesitation before Ms. Warner said, "Not really."

Aggie cocked her head. "Never?"

"Well, just to say hi to his dad, maybe. Look, I've got nothing against Landon's family, unless they're making some kind of accusation against me."

Aggie said, "Buck Landon is a heavy drug user, Ms. Warner."

"Buck is? The football kid? Well, I know that's no guarantee these days." Ms. Warner frowned.

"Could he get it from his father's supplies?"

"No. Impossible. I keep the records, I know." She gestured at the file cabinets behind her.

"There's really no way?"

"Dr. Landon has a special code. I sign for all the deliveries, double-check everything. I know how important it is."

Aggie glanced at the small window. "Has anyone ever broken in here?"

"Never. In fact, there have been a couple of attempts. But one reason we're in this building is the top security. All the doctors are aware of possible problems. Wherever the kid's getting it, it's not here."

Aggie shrugged. "Well, fine, Ms. Warner. Now, Mr. Spencer."

"Who?"

"John Spencer. The old man who was killed. Was he a patient of Dr. Landon's?"

She hesitated. "You should really talk to the police. They've been over all this."

"Okay. But you could give a yes or no, surely."

"No, he was not a patient."

"Not a patient. But he did contact you. Recently?"

"I can't say any more."

"Is Dr. Landon free now?"

"No. And he won't be." The firmness was back in her voice.

Aggie shrugged and closed her notebook. "Okay. Thanks, Ms. Warner."

Back in the car, Rina said glumly, "That didn't help much, did it? Every question we ask seems a dead end. Or makes it even worse for Ginny."

"Do you think Ginny was involved?" Aggie turned the ignition.

"No!"

"Then the truth can't hurt her."

"But maybe parts of it can! It frightens me, Aggie."

"Yes." But after a moment Aggie added gently, "Still, we have to have faith that knowing is better than not knowing. So let's keep digging."

"Did John Spencer know that Ginny is adopted?" Aggie asked them that night.

Clint shrugged and looked at the others—Mamma erect in her rocking chair, Rina next to him on the sofa, Aggie on the rug in front of the waning fire.

"I don't think so," Mamma said. "He didn't mention it, and I didn't tell him."

Rina, on the verge of answering, hesitated and said instead, "Why do you ask?"

"Well," said Aggie, and Rina had the impression that she too was holding back, "the people I spoke to this afternoon all commented on his curiosity. His landlords, Mr. and Mrs. Jenkins, said they were very fond of him, but they had to admit that sometimes he was a little too helpful. He would bring in their mail for them, for example, and they'd seen him inspect the envelopes. A friendly gesture, maybe, but a little more personal than they'd expect. And he was always asking questions."

"Well, that's natural, in a friendly person," said Mamma.

"Of course it is. God, that's how I got into this journalism business, loving to ask questions! But you see, the point is,

Ginny wants you to keep the adoption secret, and so you've told very few people here. And it just seemed to me that a person like Mr. Spencer might be interested in such a secret. Like me. Naturally nosy."

Again Rina hesitated. It was getting late. Aggie had given them a leisurely description of Mr. Spencer's rented room—the neatly made studio bed, the table with a few books, the easy chair before the color television, the photo album with pictures of his wife and his sailboat, the cans of beef stew and soup, tired fruit and vegetables, a souring half-gallon of milk. "Mrs. Jenkins was very apologetic. She said the police had sealed the room, and she hadn't had time to clean it up. It was really very good of her to let me in."

"You can be quite persuasive," observed Clint. "Tell me, did the Jenkinses have any idea where he was going Thursday?"

"They said they didn't. Mrs. Jenkins heard him come in about five-twenty. That's about right, according to Mrs. Gallagher. Mrs. Jenkins thought she heard him leave again about thirty minutes later, but she wasn't sure because she was very busy fixing dinner. They were expecting friends."

"Was he alone when he left?" asked Clint.

"She didn't hear any voices. But of course that doesn't rule it out, especially since she was busy. She said he might have been catching the bus to the mall. He often went there. And the bus driver said—"

"You talked to the bus driver?" asked Clint unbelievingly.

She grinned up at him, the dying firelight glowing on her cheek. "Oh, I'm thorough," she said. "Woodward and Bernstein and Barbara Walters all rolled into one, that's me. No stone unturned. Unfortunately, what the bus driver said didn't help. It was a busy evening and he couldn't remember. I showed him Spencer's picture, and he said the man was a frequent rider but he didn't know about that particular night. Said he told the cops the same thing."

"No help then." Clint, dissatisfied, leaned back in the sofa, looking at her appraisingly. He still did not share Rina's trust in the reporter, but he was coming to believe in the sincerity of Aggie's claim to want to know the truth about the murder. He continued, "You're working on the theory that all his curiosity might have turned up a guilty secret. Something that somebody didn't want spread around. Hence the murder."

That was why she shouldn't tell about the call, Rina realized. Then she saw that Aggie was studying her, and she struggled to compose herself. After a second Aggie answered Clint.

"That's right. I'm a nosy type too, and I've been threatened by people when I've learned something they didn't want known. John Spencer might have run into the same kind of trouble."

"Do you like that sort of life?" blurted Rina. She desperately wanted to shift the direction of the conversation.

"Yes," said Aggie. The reflective lenses turned to her gravely, and somehow Aggie spoke directly to Rina's conflict. "The truth is worth some risks. Physical risks, or emotional risks."

"But safety is important too. What about your children?"

"Of course I want them to be safe. But I also want them to value truth. And a lot of other corny things—justice, love, mercy. I have to set an example. It's part of the obligation we take on as parents."

"You said love. Keeping your family safe is part of the obligation too. Part of love."

"Yes. Of course you're right. But sometimes love demands very painful and risky things too."

But did it ask you to accuse your daughter of having a motive for murder, when you knew she didn't do it? Rina said evasively, "Well, maybe you're right."

Aggie headed off her escape. "For example, when you adopted Ginny you took a risk, didn't you? Don't they keep the child's background secret? That must have taken courage."

"They told us some things," Rina assured her. "Her first mother was just a girl. Middle teens, they said. But it's true, I've always wondered what her situation was. I wanted a child so desperately for so long, and I just can't imagine giving one up. But of course if it was best for the baby, if I couldn't—I don't know. It's so hard for me to imagine. I think that young mother must have loved her. But she did sign the papers right in the hospital. So I don't know."

The lenses turned toward Clint. "Clint, what do you think?"

"I'm bewildered too. Grateful to her, because she gave birth to Ginny and let us have her. Bewildered because I don't know the circumstances. And the other father, I wonder about him sometimes. How he felt."

"Yes, I wonder too," said Aggie.

"I mean, it's easy to forgive a young unmarried girl, who just wasn't able to take on that responsibility. In the early sixties she would have been thrown out of school, ostracized. She couldn't have made any kind of life for herself or for the baby. So I feel angry at the man who put her in that situation. You think of rape, of funny uncles—you know. But then I think, maybe he was young too, just as helpless as the girl. Maybe he would have married her if they'd let him."

"There's just no way to know," said Rina. "But I feel very protective toward that girl. I hope she's doing well."

"Do you think Ginny would be interested in meeting her?"

"Oh, she wouldn't want to see Ginny! It would remind her of a very sad time in her life. She's put it all behind her, I hope. Gone on."

Clint said, "But Aggie was asking about Ginny's feelings. Not the mother's. Yes, I think Ginny would like to meet her."

It was a blow to her heart. Rina shook her head wordlessly,

and Mamma said sharply, "Rina's been the best possible mother to Ginny!"

"Of course she has," Clint said. "But I think Ginny would like to know more."

Rina appealed to Clint. "I keep hoping she'll stop worrying about it."

"Maybe, honey. But if we wonder, she must wonder too. Anyway, it doesn't really make any difference what she wants. The records are sealed." He patted her arm. "And the important thing is that you'll always be her mother, and I'll be her dad."

"Yes, but . . ." Rina's hands twisted together. "It's just frightening to think about."

"Why frightening?" asked Aggie.

"She doesn't need another mother," said Mamma firmly. "And certainly not that one."

Rina said, "That's right, Aggie. If she looked for that girl, who knows what she might find? The circumstances might be horrible."

Aggie said, "Yes. But *these* circumstances are great. With this good family to fall back on, don't you think she'd be strong enough to cope?"

"Yes, but—but wouldn't it mean she didn't need us anymore?"

Aggie pushed her fingers through her curls. "Maybe it would just mean she wanted to know."

"I don't know. It just frightens me." The tears in her eyes turned the embers into smears of light. "I couldn't bear to lose her. I just couldn't."

Clint scowled at Aggie. "Why are you so interested in this question?"

Aggie leaned back on straight arms, pointing her toes at the fire. "It's just that there are so many emotions connected with this case," she said in a dissatisfied tone. "Some connected with the murder. Some connected with kids on drugs. Some with growing old and poor. Some with this adopted girl who's run away. It's a tangle of nice people with strong feelings."

"People do have strong feelings," said Rina.

"Of course. But—well, take this adoption, for instance. You have a very nice normal family that everyone approves of. Even the agency. You have normal problems too, of course— adolescence, different generations trying to live together. Tough problems, but normal ones. Yet lurking behind this nice normal family, there are ghosts. The pretty picture is full of society's favorite villains, people nobody approves of. A bastard. A slut who abandons her child. A wicked stepmother."

No one said anything for a moment. Even Mamma was silent. Then Clint cleared his throat and said, "That's society's problem, isn't it? Not ours. We love each other."

"Yes," said Rina honestly, "but it's ours too when we're afraid of it. Those ghosts are really there. And I'm afraid sometimes, Clint."

"We all are, sometimes," said Aggie. "Who really has the perfect, seamless life that Mrs. Farnham dreams of? But there is one consolation."

"What's that?" asked Rina.

"You showed me, Rina. In your hanging there in the hall. With your skill and your love, you've stitched little rags and scraps together into something beautiful. Much more beautiful than any seamless piece could be."

Rina couldn't look at her. So few people understood her work. Her soul. She said huskily, "Thank you, Aggie."

After a moment Mamma said with forced jollity, "Now don't go giving her a swelled head!"

"Okay." Aggie smiled, sat up straighter, and turned to her. "Back to business. Mrs. Rossi, tell me. How could Mr. Spencer find out Ginny was adopted if none of you here told him?"

Rina, caught unawares, scrambled to get her defenses up again. "Do you know he found out?"

"We're playing just suppose. If he did know, Mrs. Rossi, who could have told him?"

Mamma considered. "Marie and Delores knew. But I made them promise not to tell anyone else."

"Mm. Who else knows?" asked Aggie.

Clint said, "The McCormicks, our good friends. And a lot of people on Long Island, including whoever told you."

"And Dr. Panolous," added Rina. "He asked about family diseases for her medical records, so we had to tell him we didn't know."

"God, it permeates everything you do, doesn't it?" said Aggie glumly.

"It's part of our life. We have to deal with it," said Rina. "Stitch it in."

"Yes." Aggie smiled at her, then became businesslike again. "That's not many people, though. Unless, as Clint says, we count Long Island. But that's probably not necessary."

"Is there anything else you need from me?" asked Mamma. It was very late for her, Rina realized. "All of this worry is giving me a headache."

"Oh, I'm sorry, Mrs. Rossi. Don't let me keep you, please." Aggie seemed apologetic, but made no move to go.

"I'll just be downstairs if you need me. Good night, Aggie. Good night, *cara.*" She kissed Rina and Clint, and went off slowly down the steps. Aggie stared absorbed at the fire until they heard the door close downstairs. Then she swiveled abruptly on the rug to face Rina directly.

"Okay, now," she said quietly. "I must ask you to be discreet about what I'm going to tell you. I didn't feel free to speak in front of your mother because they're her friends. But Clint was right when he said I was hunting for motives. And I've found a couple of things. The police may find out soon too."

Rina was alarmed. Clint, frowning, said, "What do you mean?"

"Number one, the landlords. Mr. and Mrs. Jenkins. I asked them how Mr. Spencer came to rent their room, and they showed me the little ad in the paper. And they showed me his room, as I told you. And there were rent receipts in his desk. But they were for about half the advertised price. So I asked Mr. Jenkins why they were giving the room to him so cheap. Mrs. Jenkins started crying, and Mr. Jenkins hushed her and said that Spencer preferred to pay every two weeks instead of every month. Okay, a reasonable story, except that she wouldn't cry about that. So I looked at the chits again. Very orderly, you could tell he'd been an accountant. The receipts were all dated the first of the month. I pointed that out to Mr. Jenkins."

"I see," said Clint.

"And Mrs. Jenkins was still blubbering, and she said, 'Let's tell her, honey, or she'll think it's worse.' "

"A familiar line to you, no doubt," observed Clint acidly. "You carry a big stick."

"And I don't always speak softly, do I? Anyway, it turns out that their son did something or other shameful. I didn't ask what. But they said Spencer had found out about whatever it was, and had come in, with his usual sympathetic air, and said how sad it must be for them to have such a secret in their family. And then he added that it would be a great boon for him that month if he could pay the rent in two installments."

"And the second installment never came," predicted Clint.

"Exactly. He didn't say another word about it, and neither did they, but from then on he paid only half for his room."

"Well, then, *they* might have done it!" exclaimed Rina, and then was ashamed of her eagerness to shift the blame to the kindly Jenkinses.

"Possibly," said Aggie, displaying no such guilt. "We have only Mrs. Jenkins's word that Spencer went out again after Mrs. Gallagher brought him back. Some friends visited the Jenkinses a little later, arriving about six-thirty. Unless the friends are lying, Mr. and Mrs. Jenkins didn't do it between six-thirty and eight, when the body was found. And they didn't do it unless Spencer himself took Ginny's scissors. I don't know why he'd do that."

"Maybe a kleptomaniac?" suggested Clint.

"Possibly," said Aggie again. "Though no one I've spoken to has mentioned any leanings in that direction."

"You said the Jenkinses were number one," said Clint. "I take it there's a number two?"

"Number two is Delores Gallagher. I went back to see her because Sunday I noticed that there were quite a few photos of Mr. Spencer in her album. More than you'd expect of a casual friend. But she'd claimed there were only two. She admitted he was very nice to her, and she appreciated the companionship."

"Just what Mamma and Mrs. Deaver were saying," said Rina.

"He even proposed marriage to her," said Aggie.

"Really? I had no idea! They seemed—well, more distant than that."

"She said she was flabbergasted too. Wouldn't say yes, wouldn't say no. She was very worried about what her children would say. But then she sat down to take stock, and discovered that over a period of about eighteen months she had spent hundreds of dollars on restaurants, gifts, even the color television I saw in his apartment—all things she had charged and he had said he'd pay back. Finally she confronted him and asked him to start paying her back."

"And?"

"And he looked very sad, and said he had thought that their relationship was above such things. Then he added that they had given each other proofs of their love that no one else in the world should know about."

Clint snorted. "Proofs of their love!"

"Her euphemism," said Aggie apologetically.

"She told you all this?" ask Clint unbelievingly.

"In confidence, you see. I'm afraid I, ah, thought of a way to construe those photos that made her look absolutely felonious. She told me all this so I wouldn't publish something far worse."

"I don't understand," said Rina. "Do you mean Mr. Spencer told her that he'd tell?"

"Exactly. Blackmail's the word. He really knew her weak points too. He said he'd write to the school board that her daughter Berta is trying so hard to please."

"My God!" Rina was horrified. What was considered normal in Ginny's generation could still dismember a reputation in her mother's. And to threaten Berta's livelihood! Suddenly the playful flirting she had overheard at the bridge game seemed more ominous. "But—but Mrs. Gallagher brought him in as though he was her friend," she protested.

"They'd come to an understanding," Aggie explained. "Mrs. Gallagher actually stood up to him pretty well. She told him if he caused her any trouble she had the charge records to show what a freeloader he was. That was pretty shrewd, if my theory about him is right, because he could only play his confidence games if people thought he was a thoroughly aboveboard sort of person. So her weapon against him was pretty powerful too. It was a standoff. He immediately claimed he had no such thing in mind, her friendship was all that mattered to him. I think she still had hopes of getting her money back someday."

"God, poor woman," said Rina.

"You wouldn't talk about these things in front of my mother-in-law," said Clint thoughtfully. "That shows admirable discretion. But it would be even more admirable if you didn't break Mrs. Gallagher's confidence at all. Or the Jenkinses'. Why are you telling us other people's dark secrets?"

"Because Rina knows something about John Spencer, and

she's afraid to share it. I just wanted to show her that there's a pattern here. A lot of people could have a motive if he's a small-time blackmailer. And every fact we learn about Mr. Spencer could help solve this puzzle."

"Is that true, Rina? You know something?" asked Clint in surprise.

"Yes." She looked at him. "He called, Clint. Thursday, about six, before you arrived. Mamma was out buying dinner. He asked me if it was true that Ginny was adopted. I said yes, but that she preferred not to have people know, so I would appreciate it if he didn't tell people."

Clint whistled. "You said that!"

"Yes. I didn't realize." Rina too was appalled at the implications of his call, now that she'd heard Aggie's report.

"Did he say anything else?" Aggie asked.

"Well, at the time I thought he was reassuring me. He said that he understood perfectly that we wouldn't want people to know. And then he said he'd call back later, because he had to meet someone."

"Who? Where?" Aggie's tone was suddenly urgent.

"He didn't say. Just hung up quickly. But there was something, noise in the background—I don't know. It was familiar. I just had the feeling he wasn't at home. There was music— well, it could have been his TV."

"But your impression was he wasn't at home?"

"Yes."

"Mrs. Jenkins thought he might have gone to the mall."

"That's it, Aggie! Cash registers! People in the background, and Muzak, and cash registers. A phone booth in a mall."

"Good. Okay, now. He called, asked about the adoption, then hurriedly hung up."

"Yes. It was odd, because at first he seemed to be taking his time. Very courteous."

"Maybe the person he was meeting had arrived."

"God!"

"And so he hung up. But he was going to call back, probably to find out in dollars and cents how much his silence was worth to you."

"Oh, God!" Rina was shaken. "How could he threaten a young girl like Ginny?"

"You would have paid?" Aggie asked sympathetically.

Rina started to nod, but Clint burst out, "Hey, wait just a minute here! What does all this mean? Are you trying to blackmail us too?"

"No, of course not!" said Aggie.

"Because I find this whole setup fishy! Here you are, asking us to take your word that this old man, dead now, was a blackmailer. Asking about the value of his silence to us. Or are you really asking about the value of *your* silence?"

"No. You've got my silence already." She sounded very sad.

"Because if that's your game, you'd take our money and get away clean, wouldn't you? We couldn't even describe you to the police! You'd drive off, take off that curly wig and those sunglasses you wear even in the dark, and we'd never know you again!"

He reached forward suddenly, rising from the sofa, grabbing for her glasses. Rina expected Aggie to dodge back away from him. But instead her forearms snapped up to shield her lowered face, and she lunged straight into startled Clint, butting the top of her skull hard into his chest. His arms stretched uselessly past her. Then her strong bony fingers were digging deep into the hollow of his throat. Gagging, he clawed at her fingers, shoved himself away from her, and fell back, gasping, into the sofa.

Rina had not had time to move. "Clint!" she exclaimed, jumping up. "Are you all right?"

He nodded, hands still protectively at his throat.

"Sorry, Clint," Aggie said politely. "I'm afraid I've got the reactions of a street fighter. But look here." She knelt beside him, guiding his hand to her hair. "Pull some out if you want.

You'll find it's real. But please don't mess with my eyes. I want them to last every day that they can."

Clint dropped his hand to his lap and shook his head. "All right, all right," he wheezed.

Rina said uncertainly, "We're all upset."

"Yeah." Clint's voice was stronger now.

Aggie was sitting back on her heels, still watching them. "It's sensible to be suspicious," she said. "I know these glasses make me look like a walking disguise. But please believe me, Clint. I'm interested in finding the person who killed Mr. Spencer. No one else's motive will be published. And if we find that person, your daughter will be cleared."

"I know," said Clint. "Look, I'm sorry I doubted you."

"I'm glad you did. I'm glad you stick up for your daughter. But I guess we've done what we can for tonight. I'll run off and leave you in peace for a while. You've been good to put up with me, both of you."

They said their good-byes, and Rina closed and locked the door after her. Everything seemed hopeless. Why should Ginny ever come home, when things were so terrible? Clint came down the steps to her and held her.

"It'll be all right, Rina."

"Clint, do you really think Aggie would try blackmail? She seems so understanding!"

"I don't know, Rina. I'd like to believe her." He coughed.

"Mr. Spencer really did call me, Clint. That fits with what she said."

"Yes. And the hair was real too. And the street fighting. God."

"I think I believe her."

"Yeah. It'll be all right."

"I know. But Clint, I miss Ginny so much! I wonder what she's been doing."

• • • •

" 'I'm a Fawn!' it cried out in a voice of delight. 'And dear me, you're a human child!' A sudden look of alarm came into its beautiful brown eyes, and in another moment it had darted away at full speed. Alice stood looking after it, almost ready to cry with vexation at having lost her dear little fellow traveler so suddenly. 'However, I know my name now,' she said: 'that's *some* comfort. Alice—Alice—I won't forget it again.' "

Ginny's voice had grown thick. She stopped reading and tried to collect herself.

"Are you sad?" asked Sarah. Damn sharp little sister.

"A little."

"Because the fawn ran away?"

"Because for a long time I didn't know my name either. Like Alice in the wood. It's scary."

Sarah was puzzled. "Your name is Ginny."

"Yes. It's hard to explain. A long time ago I was Alice Ryan, and that's the name I lost. That's why it took me so long to find you."

Sarah was frowning, trying to understand. Ginny laughed and hugged her. "It's okay. I'll explain it when you're a little older. It's a happy ending, really, it's just hard to get used to. Like Alice: 'I know my name now, that's *some* comfort.' "

This metaphysical discussion made Will impatient. "Read Tweedledum and Tweedledee," he demanded.

"Okay," said Ginny, and went on with the story.

She and Sarah had become good friends, except for the times that Sarah was hungry and therefore irritable. The little girl was insatiably curious and quizzed Ginny on every subject that came up. She also loved the wild stories and extravagant mock threats that Ginny made up, and giggled at them in a most gratifying way. Being adopted was good for one thing, Ginny thought, it developed your imagination. Useful in dealing with children.

Though it didn't help much with Will. Incessantly out of sorts, the boy responded to her efforts only occasionally. During the day Ginny found herself missing Sarah's cheerfulness. She was becoming very tired of this caged and friendless existence. Ellen stopped by for Sarah each morning, sometimes with groceries and always avoiding any mention of the law. But Claudia brought Sarah back each afternoon without coming in, so except for Ellen and Nick and Maggie's frequent calls, Ginny was isolated, trapped by the sick little boy's obvious needs. By Tuesday night, after Maggie had called to report on her visits to Dr. Landon's office and to John Spencer's landlords, Ginny felt lost and depressed. She cleaned up dutifully after the children and even polished the bathroom, and she finished her social studies assignment and started her math. But all the activity did not distract her from the unpleasant truth. Mr. Spencer's murder, a threat and a puzzle, was always with her. And though she adored Sarah and Will, she dreaded the thought of even one more day spent at their beck and call. She needed time to think about herself—about who she really was, about what this new family meant to her, about her future. And how the hell could a person think while Will was whining for attention?

Mom had gone through all this for her when she was little. Ginny was overcome with homesickness. After she stopped snuffling she thought about doing a lude. Just one, just for a little time out from her problems. But Will was sick. She'd better not, he might need her.

She slept uneasily. In her dreams, the people no longer flew away. They turned and waited for her, expectantly. But she still didn't know how to reach them.

Wednesday, September 19, 1979

XVIII

Wednesday morning was overcast. The weather report had said there was a chance of rain, a break in the clear cold weather that Friday's storm had brought. Ginny went through her depressing morning routine of damp diapers, breakfast, getting Sarah out to school, bathing Will, and tending to the animals before she became aware of an astonishing truth.

Will was not whining.

"Hey, Will. How do you feel?" she asked him.

"Fine." He looked up at her with a sunny expression.

"Does your head hurt?"

"No."

"Let me look at you." She drew him nearer the kitchen window.

He didn't actually look any better, aesthetically. His face and body were still covered with the dried crusts of the pox blisters. But there were no fresh ones, no more of the little yellow bubbles that had been appearing in inexorable succession for the last four days, only to break and crust over.

"Hey, I think you're getting better!"

"Can we go to the park?"

"No, not yet." Ginny was alarmed. She hated being housebound, but she feared the police even more. Clearly, having Will well would present a whole new set of problems. "When your mom calls I'll ask her if we can do anything different.

But for now we'll just take it easy and finish getting well. See, the chicken pox haven't gone away yet."

Will looked somberly at his arm. "Mommy says I have several hundred chicken poxes."

"I wouldn't be surprised."

Then he smiled that enchanting small-boy smile that had been so rare the last few days, and changed the subject. "I'll build a house for Kakiy!"

"How?"

"From blocks!"

"That's a great idea!" She went up with him to his room and got him settled to his task, then went back to the study to work on her math assignment. It was hard to concentrate, though. Partly it was because Will kept interrupting, wanting to know if Kakiy needed a bathroom in his house (no, said Ginny, just a corner for his litter box), or if he needed a window (sure, he likes to sit on windowsills). But the biggest problem was her own dark thoughts. Fear of the police who were searching for her. Worry that Mom and Dad would figure out who Maggie was, and be heartbroken. Anger at Maggie, and love. Jealousy of this family, and yearning for her own. For Mom and Dad. And disappointment. For years she had hungered to know the truth about her background; and Maggie had given her truth, unstintingly. But Ginny's image of herself, nobly accepting her mother's misfortunes and forgiving her heinous sins, had not come to pass. Maggie—perversely, inexplicably—refused to be ashamed. Claimed to love Ginny even while she admitted she would do it again. That made her sins even more heinous, right? At any rate, Ginny could not forgive.

She wondered again if it was some fault in herself. She had dreamed of great sins or great misfortunes, of degeneracy or tragedy. Genetic wickedness that would account for her own defiant feelings, genetic misfortunes that would account for her inability to live up to Mom's dreams for her, or to her own dreams. Wickedness and misfortune she had lived with, in fancy. She had been ready to forgive.

But instead she had found talent and brains and compassion, a close good-humored family, song and laughter. Her genes were the genes of Ph.D.s, engineers, professors, mayors. Good-bye to bad blood. Good-bye to all those possible mothers: the prostitutes and murderers, the rape victims and drug addicts and fallen princesses, who had accompanied her through her follies and rebellions. They had been an ever-changing yet constant explanation and solace. She missed them. She was ready to cry with vexation at having lost her dear little fellow travelers so suddenly.

Poor Alice. Poor Ginny.

She had been staring at the same math problem for five minutes. In commemoration of her prostitutes she had pulled in a D on the first quiz. A D for the daughter of an engineer and a statistician.

"Oh, God, who am I?" she murmured. After all this pain, she still didn't know!

"You're Ginny Marshall," said Will's voice.

She turned in surprise and looked at him, a small and scabby and cheerful boy. A future statistician or doctor or mayor. Or actor, in his case. She pulled herself together. "Yes," she said, considering, "but I was asking God."

He giggled. "I'm just Will."

"So you are. Come on, little brother. Lunchtime." She stood up.

"But I need Kakiy so he can see his house."

"Oh, is it finished?"

"Come see!"

She admired Will's construction, then suggested having a sandwich.

"But I want Kakiy to see it!" he said.

"Okay, but I don't know where Kakiy is right now. How

about lunch first? Then nap. Then you can put Kakiy in his house."

Miraculously, he agreed, and chatted with her pleasantly over cheese sandwiches and apples. The surface of her life was certainly a lot nicer when Will was healthy. But underneath she was floundering more than ever. She had lost all her excuses, but had not found a direction.

And that was why, when Will stretched out contentedly on his bed for his nap, telling himself the story as he turned the pages of a Dr. Seuss book, Ginny gave up on the math and did a lude. Just for a break, she told herself, just a respite from these awful thoughts. Will is okay now. And it'll be worn off by the time he wakes up and Sarah comes home. She sat in the corner of the sofa in the study, fingers tingling, smiling dreamily at the rows of math books on the shelves. Pretty soon she couldn't see the titles very well anymore, and she floated peacefully above her confusions and worries, gliding toward a dreamless sleep.

Except that after a time there was a noise somewhere, something she should pay attention to. Annoyed, she held her hands to her ears, but when she dropped them the noise was still there. It was important. What? She tried to stop floating, to listen.

Her name. "Gin-nee!" A small voice. Well, she'd answer later.

Again. "Gin-nee!" It was important.

She had to stop the noise so she could float again.

She stood up, bumped into the door, straightened again, and looked out at the unsteady hall. One foot forward, then another. The next doorjamb lurched toward her.

"Gin-nee!" It was louder now.

She stumbled into the room and looked around. Her eyes weren't working very well. Nobody was there in that blurry room. It was very cold.

"Gin-nee!" There was a whimper this time, too.

She looked toward the sound. The window was open. Have to close it. Cold. She started toward it and fell on the bed, giggled, struggled up, reached the window, and stumbled again.

"Ginny, help me, okay?"

Her abused eyes managed to focus a little. Gloomy brightness outside. Tree, gold-edged leaves, like her tree upstairs. Branches. Will. Silly Willy.

She laughed. "Whasha doing, Will?" Her tongue wasn't working very well either.

"I wanted to get Kakiy."

"You look shilly!"

"Help me, Ginny."

She frowned. He looked frightened. Not silly.

"Come here, Will."

"I can't. Help me, okay?"

"Okay." Confidently, she started out the window toward the tree. Her muscles seemed to go their own way. She stumbled, flailed, caught the frame before she fell through. For an instant panic cut through the blurriness, and a bit of her mind suddenly grasped the situation.

Little Will was somehow stranded in the tree, frightened, clinging to a high broad branch, pleading for help.

And she, his caretaker and sister, was stumbling about in the window frame below. Stoned. Mindless. Zombied out.

"Buck Landon, right? I'm Aggie Lyons, from *New York Week.*"

Buck had emerged with a swarm of young football players from the high school gym. He'd slowed and dropped his book bag. Now he paused, hand on his back pocket, and looked at Aggie. From where Rina sat in the passenger seat of the Camaro, parked a few yards away, she could see that his hair was still damp from the after-practice shower.

"Yeah?" Buck said. Chip had paused with him, Rina saw,

but their teammates had moved noisily on to the cars left in the parking lot.

"We talked a minute on the phone. I'd like to ask you a few more questions," Aggie said.

"You're a reporter? See, I'm not supposed to talk to reporters."

"Just a few questions."

"He means like no comment," said Chip.

"No problem." Aggie smiled sweetly and gave Buck a friendly slap on the back. "I'll just tag along, write an eyewitness account."

"But he's not going to talk to you!"

"You're Congressman Wilson's son, right?" Aggie reached into her bag and pulled out her notebook.

"Hey, no comment from me either!" Chip stepped back with an apologetic glance at Buck. "Buck, I better fade. See you at the usual place later."

"Yeah." Deserted, Buck stared after Chip a moment, then back at Aggie. "Really, I can't talk to you."

"No problem. Mrs. Marshall and I will just tag along, as I said."

"Mrs. Marshall?" For the first time Buck noticed Rina in the Camaro. "Oh, hi, Mrs. Marshall."

"Hi, Buck."

"I didn't know that you—see, I'm not supposed to talk to reporters."

Aggie had been watching Buck's teammates. Most had piled into cars and were pulling out of the high school lot. "You're going somewhere now?" she asked.

"Yeah, I'm going—" He glanced at Rina again. "Well, you know. Home."

"Okay. See you later." Aggie got into the Camaro and turned the ignition.

"You usually don't give up so easily," Rina observed.

"Nobody's giving up," Aggie informed her. She had not

put the car into gear, but was sitting, watching Buck. The teenager had hurried across the lot to his car, fumbled in his back pockets a moment before finding his keys in his front pocket, and was now steering for the exit. It wasn't till he had slowed to pull out onto the highway that he seemed to realize the Camaro was right behind him.

He put on a burst of speed and changed lanes twice, but Aggie kept up easily. When they reached Monroe Boulevard, Buck turned left, as he should have, and drove sedately home.

Aggie didn't follow him into the looped drive, but went up the other arm, so that he couldn't continue around and out again. Their cars met nose to nose, and all three of them got out together.

"Mrs. Marshall, see, I'm not supposed to talk to reporters," Buck said in some desperation.

"I know, Buck. But Aggie thought you might know something that would help bring Ginny back."

"It's about Ginny?" Uneasy, he looked around at the trimmed hedges, the porch, the lawn, as though help lurked there. His hands seemed shaky. "Well—okay, come in. Maybe Mom's here."

But when he unlocked the door and they entered the spacious hall, the only person who answered his call was Maria. The maid nodded politely to Aggie and Rina, her broad brown face unsurprised, and hung their coats in the closet. Buck kept his jacket on. Aggie was already on her usual whirlwind tour of the living room, looking over the furniture, the draped windows, the Braque over the fireplace.

"Mom's not around?" Buck asked Maria.

"She said she'd be back before dinner."

"Okay." He followed Aggie into the living room and dumped his book bag on the leather sofa. "I guess it's okay to talk about Ginny."

Aggie turned from the painting. "It's Mr. Spencer you're not supposed to talk about, right?"

"Yeah."

"And the police questioning you about his death? You're not supposed to talk about that?"

"Who told you—" He looked accusingly at Rina. His hands were definitely shaky.

"Your mother told me, in fact," said Aggie easily. "She came in to tell Mrs. Marshall you were being questioned. I happened to be there too."

"Oh. I see." He licked his lips.

"Well, let me ask about Ginny then," said Aggie. "What do you know about why she disappeared?"

"Nothing! Honest! I told Mrs. Marshall, she didn't say a thing to me about going away!"

"How did her scissors get into your car?"

"God, I don't know! She must have dropped them—hey, wait!" Buck looked at Rina in frowning alarm. His hands were clenching and unclenching. "Her scissors—I mean that's something I'm not supposed to talk about."

"Oops. Sorry," said Aggie.

"Buck, listen," said Rina urgently. "It's part of why Ginny's staying away. If we can figure out how those scissors got into your car, we'll be halfway toward finding out who killed Mr. Spencer! And then she can come home!"

But Buck had stopped listening. His eyes were on Aggie, who had quietly pulled an envelope from her bag. She opened it and nodded.

"They're all here, Buck," said Aggie, dangling the envelope by its corner.

"How did you—" He stared at her, fists clenched.

"I picked your pocket back at the gym door. Where did you get them, Buck?"

His mouth worked a moment before he said, "From a guy."

"What's his name?"

"I don't know. He doesn't say."

"Is his name Dr. Landon?"

"No!" Buck looked around the room, panicked.

"What's his name, Buck?"

"It's not my dad! This guy—he doesn't tell his name. The guys call him Shorty."

"Shorty. Uh-huh." Aggie dropped the envelope on Buck's book bag next to her on the sofa. "Buck, it turns out to be hard to talk about Ginny without bringing in other things. She's under suspicion, because her scissors—"

"Listen, I'm under suspicion too, and I didn't do anything! It was my car! But I don't know how the damn scissors got there!" Buck kneaded his thighs with his fists. "And I'm not supposed to be talking to you!"

"Hey, don't get upset. You don't have to talk to me. We can wait till your mom gets back and talk to her." Aggie lounged back in the sofa, stretching her arms expansively along the back. "Or we can talk to your dad. Maybe they can help."

"No, look, you can't—don't bring them into this."

"Up to you, Buck."

Rina sat on the arm of the sofa and stared at the envelope Aggie had dropped on the book bag. "Buck, this Shorty. Is he from Philadelphia? Is Ginny there because of Shorty?"

"No, Mrs. Marshall, she's not much into—" He licked his lips again, as though his brain weren't working despite his obvious agitation. "Well, maybe—I mean, I don't know where she is."

"Did she talk to Shorty? Would he have done anything to her? Sent her anywhere?"

"No! I mean, I don't know."

"Rina—" Aggie cautioned.

But Rina felt that at last she had a real clue. She leaned forward eagerly. "This Shorty. Where can I find him?"

"Rina, for God's sake, back off! He's not going to tell us about his connection!" Aggie said.

"But it's just to find Ginny! He thinks a lot of Ginny, he

says!" Rina turned back to the boy. "Buck, tell me how to get in touch with Shorty. I just want to find Ginny! When you need him, how do you reach him?"

"He, uh—look, I have to go to the bathroom." Buck started for the hall.

Rina sprang from the sofa arm and grabbed his arm. "How do you reach him?"

"The, uh, the record store in Eastland mall." He shook her off and bolted up the carpeted stairs.

Aggie was standing beside her now. Rina turned, excited. "Aggie, let's go! This man Shorty might be able to say where she was Thursday!"

"Take it easy, Rina." Aggie was watching the stairs. "You know it won't be that simple. You don't just walk up and ask for a drug dealer, the way you ask for a shoe salesman. Not even at the mall."

"Oh. Yes." That was a problem. "And I'm just an average middle-aged woman, I don't look like one of his customers," Rina said, discouraged.

"Actually, you probably do." A grim smile flicked across Aggie's face. "But even if you find him, you won't get anyone like Shorty to tell the police anything." She started up the stairs.

What she said was true, Rina realized with sinking heart as she followed. Even if they overcame all the obstacles and found Shorty, he'd have no reason to cooperate, and plenty of reason to avoid the police. And it wouldn't help Ginny much either to tell them that she might have been with a drug dealer. Still, this was the only new direction they'd found, they had to follow it.

At the top of the stairs the hall branched right to the rooms over the dining room and kitchen, and straight ahead along the wing of the house that led away from the street. Aggie went straight, glancing in the open bathroom door and continuing to the last room. The door was barely ajar. Aggie pushed it open and paused.

There was a quick gasp from within.

Rina peered around Aggie. It was clearly the master bedroom. Champagne-beige carpeting, expensively textured pale walls, four big beds—no, only two, one of the walls was mirrored and reflected the two beds. It reflected a wide teakwood double bureau too, and it reflected Buck, bending over the bureau but face toward Aggie with a stricken look. The middle drawer was half open. Rina could see piles of satin and lace in it. In his hand Buck clutched a bunch of champagne-colored, large-cup bras.

Aggie swept across the room, grabbed the drawer he was trying to push closed, and peered in. "My oh my, what a lot of pretty pills! It's a regular cornucopia in there," she said, and was back at the door before Rina had quite seen that the boy's fists were tightening and his teeth clenching. Aggie said, "It'll only make things worse if you hit us, Buck. They're already asking if you're violent, right? If you do anything else—"

The boy stopped, arms falling, the bras dangling from his fist like a wilted bouquet.

"Fine," said Aggie. "Okay, we're leaving now."

She closed the door and propelled Rina briskly back down the stairs. By the time they reached the hall, Maria had reappeared to help them quietly with their coats. Her broad-boned face showed no emotion except patience.

"Thanks, Buck! See you later!" Aggie waved at the stairs.

Rina looked up. Buck stood on the landing, relaxed now, but a frown on his face. She raised her hand halfheartedly, then followed Aggie to the car.

As they backed out to the street, she said, "Aggie, Rosamond must know, don't you think? Wouldn't she notice that he was hiding things in her own drawer?"

"That he was hiding things?" Aggie looked at her in surprise. "Rina, for God's sake! When are you going to learn that not all mothers are as good as you?"

It was an hour till showtime. Nick picked up his room phone and dialed Brooklyn.

The phone rang. And rang.

Odd, he thought, Ginny usually answered soon. She didn't go out, after all. Although she might be in the little backyard, if Will was feeling better. Or of course she might be rocking him to sleep, or bathing him. Some things couldn't be easily interrupted.

He'd try again from downstairs after he got into makeup.

"Rina, have you been cleaning my room?" asked Mamma anxiously.

"No, I haven't been in there."

"Well, someone has." Mamma was clenching and unclenching her hands.

"What do you mean?"

"Someone has been through my handbag. And gone through my papers."

"Are you sure?"

"Yes. Were the police here again?"

"No. And they wouldn't search your room without telling you."

The two women stared at each other, uneasily.

"When did it happen?" asked Rina.

"I'm not sure. I had it with me when I went shopping at ten."

"Yes, I remember. I was working on my quilt." And becoming more desperate by the minute. Aggie's suggestion that they go together to see Buck after school had seemed a godsend, although what she had learned depressed her even more.

"And this afternoon I was out in the garden," said

Mamma. "When Aggie brought you back I was still there. She came out to say hello before she left."

"Yes."

"Do you suppose someone got in while I was in the garden? I did leave the door open."

"Wouldn't you have seen them?" Rina felt jumpy, cranky.

"Yes, but—well, weeding by the evergreens there, I might not have noticed. Should we call the police?"

"It's not much. But with everything else, maybe so."

Sergeant Trainer, when they reached him, noted it down with his usual neutral questions. Then he said to Rina, "You haven't heard anything from your daughter, Mrs. Marshall?"

"No. Nothing. But she said she wouldn't call again for a while," said Rina defensively.

"It really is important for us to get in touch with her."

"I know, Sergeant Trainer. But she hasn't called."

"Yes, I know, and I wonder why not."

Rina was indignant at his persistence. "You can't blame her, can you, if she doesn't want to face questioning? For murder? At her age?"

"No, no, but—"

"Why don't you find out who did it? Then she'd be back like a flash!"

"Now, Mrs. Marshall—"

"Just find him! It's your job!"

"We're doing our job, Mrs. Marshall." Sergeant Trainer was not made of stone after all; Rina could hear splinters of anger in his cool voice. But she was too upset herself to stop.

"Well, what do you have to show for it, besides a trumped-up charge against an innocent teenaged girl?" she demanded.

"Mrs. Marshall, the lab report came in today, and there's no doubt at all. The only fingerprints on the scissors that killed Mr. Spencer belong to that innocent teenaged girl."

Fear washed the anger from her. "To Ginny?"

"I'm sorry, Mrs. Marshall. I shouldn't have told you that.

But we're being as reasonable as we can. Really. Try to see it from our point of view."

"Yes. Yes, I see that. Thank you, Sergeant Trainer. I'm sorry."

"Yes, Mrs. Marshall. I'm sorry too."

Rina replaced the receiver slowly and leaned back against the kitchen counter for a moment, thinking.

There was one way out, she realized suddenly. One way that might save Ginny, might bring her back.

Aggie had said it. Sometimes love demands very painful and risky things.

Tomorrow, thought Rina. If they don't find the murderer today, I'll do it tomorrow.

XIX

Everything was fine, of course. But how had Will gotten into the tree? Ginny tried to think, but her mind seemed wrapped in cotton. The roof below the window slid down at an alarmingly steep pitch. The lower branches were high above it. The branches blurred again. She should be laughing, but she was worried. Maybe another lude would help. She could worry later.

But Will was her brother. Her own blood. *Famiglia.*

"Will. Howjoo get—up there?"

"Ladder."

Ladder. She frowned, looking around. Finally she was sure. "There's no ladder!" She giggled. "You're kidding!"

"It fell down."

"The ladder?"

"Yes." Will whimpered. He wasn't giggling.

"Wherezit?"

"It fell down."

The world was misting over again. She said, "Jusha minute," and lurched out of his room again. Everything was fine. Except her legs weren't working very well. Maybe she should wake herself up more. Cold water. She took aim at the bathroom door and managed to reach it. There was a problem getting into the shower, because the side of the tub was in the way. But she succeeded at last and turned the faucet.

It worked. She turned it off again, gasping, and thought almost lucidly for a moment.

Will had to be rescued. He was small, and sick, and could not hold on to that branch forever.

Police? No. Impossible. She forgot why, but it was impossible.

She'd have to do it herself. She couldn't get to the branches from the roof of the porch. But upstairs, from the exercise room window, the branches were very close. If her muscles would do what she told them to. It would be safer with a rope. But there was no rope.

No rope, no hope. She giggled at the silly rhyme.

Better take a nap, think later.

Some hidden vein of determination pulled her back into coherence. Rope. Something tight. Tighten your belt.

Still dripping, she stepped carefully across the hall, and after some difficulty found the knob to Nick and Maggie's closet. For a minute everything swam before her again, but then the determination prevailed and she saw Nick's belts, four of them on a hanger. Tighten your belt. She put one on but then couldn't buckle it. Her fingers didn't work, and things kept blurring. Then she carefully looped his belt over her own, so that it dangled down before her, held in its middle by her belt. She was so pleased at this success that she looped three more belts through, beaming, before she noticed the noise again.

"Gin-nee!"

"Coming!" she called. Where was he? Oh, yes. Tree. Her window upstairs. She struggled up the steps and found it was easier on all fours. Like Kakiy. Whee. At the top she hauled herself upright with the banister, started confidently toward the window, and stumbled only once before she got there.

She heaved up the sash triumphantly. Hey, everything was fine! There was the branch she knew so well.

A long way down to the roof, warned some part of her

mind that was still awake. And further still to the hard cement of the walk between the porch and the side fence. Not
soft like the mat under her. Well, then, throw the mat out
there! She seized the corner, pushed and squeezed it through
the window. Then she shoved it exuberantly and it popped
through. Whee! It hit the roof, skidded down rapidly and over
the edge. She heard it smack against the cement below.

Will was crying. Poor little kid.

"Will! Hey, Will! I'm coming!"

"Ginny?" snuffled Will.

"I'm up. Here."

Cautiously, he looked up. "Help me, Ginny."

"Okay. Jusha minute."

"Silly Kakiy went in the tree."

"Yesh."

"You come here and get me, okay?"

"Okay." Get him. Get Will. Silly Willy. She reached out of
the window, grabbed the branch happily. It was rough in her
hands. She pushed herself cheerfully out the window. Whee!
She laughed.

But her hands hurt where she was dangling from them. A
gust of wind slapped her, icy on her wet clothes, and another
moment of clarity came. Far below, the steep roof of the
porch sloped down. A little nearer, Will clung to his branch,
waiting for her. And Ginny, chuckling like a fool, was hanging
by her hands from a higher branch, eight or ten feet up from
his. No way to reach him from here. Her hands hurt.

She should get her leg up on the branch, lie on it like Will.

"Jusha minute, Will," she said cheerfully.

The panic inside her was not quite submerged in the flood
of well-being. The panic made her concentrate. Throw a leg
up over the branch. Whoops, missed, try again. Throw a leg
up and pull at the same time. There, done! She wrenched
herself up, teetered on the top. And slid off the other side. A

stump of a twig ripped into the inside of her thigh as she slid over, breaking into her sense of peace.

Hang on.

Have to do it again. Throw a leg over, pull hard, stop. This time she balanced, though the world swirled. Hold on.

Will was still holding on.

"How you, Will?" she asked.

"I want to get down."

"Wait. Ish hard for me too."

He whimpered. Poor little guy.

"I'll get you, Will. I promish."

"Okay." The snuffling stopped.

She had to slide backward along the branch to the trunk. Things would be fine then. She could get to the next branch down, then to Will's. She couldn't quite trust her muscles, but she was sure everything would be fine. Obeying the stubborn panic that would not be quieted, that was spoiling her high, she clamped her arms and legs around the branch, slid back just a little, moved her arms and legs back, clamped again and slid again. It was hard to avoid the twigs.

She clamped, slid, clamped, slid, bumped into the trunk and almost fell.

She might feel cold if everything didn't seem so fine.

"Ginny, hurry up."

"Okay. Everything's fine."

How could she get down to that next branch? She tried sitting up, still straddling her branch. Her back was to the trunk. One of the belts looped through hers slithered out and fell, startling her. She swayed but hung on.

She had to get Will. She had promised.

There was another branch a couple of feet above her head. She slowly lifted one hand, concentrating, still holding tight with the other. Hard not to lose her balance. Like ballet. Up went her hand. Up over her head, whee! It bumped into the branch and she clutched it. That was what she wanted. Everything was fine. Why had she wanted it? Oh, yes, to stand up. She grabbed the branch with her other hand too and stood up happily, and her feet slipped, and once again she was dangling from her sore hands, and the pain was prodding her awake again.

It was a long way down. She remembered the mat skidding down. Better not to skid like that.

Behind her was the branch she had slipped from. She groped with her foot, found it, slowly stood again, still holding to the upper branch. A few feet further out that upper branch, she noticed, was Kakiy. Serene. Unworried. Cheshire cat. She giggled.

"Gin-nee!"

Get Will.

She clamped one hand, let go with the other. Then she turned carefully to face the trunk. She could see a branch below her. Hold tight, said the panic, even though everything was fine. She put her free arm around the trunk, made sure her feet wouldn't slip, and threw her second arm around. With enormous care she chose the correct foot, the right one, and hugged the trunk, and stepped out toward the lower branch. After a long time her foot reached it, and, still clasping the trunk, she shifted her weight to the lower branch.

The bark was rough, sliding against her wet sweater. Her leg hurt. But she had to reach Will. She'd promised.

"How ya doing, Will?"

"I'm tired."

"Me too. I'll be there shoon."

Better not fall. It would scare Will.

But another blurry time came, and the panic made her hold still, embracing the trunk. When she was little she had been good on monkey bars. Trees too. Why was this one so difficult?

"Ginny?"

"I'm coming." She had promised. She began again. Hug

the tree, left foot down slowly, touch, shift weight. She had to think through and double-check each part of the automatic actions. Finally she found herself standing on Will's branch.

"Ginny, I'm cold."

"So am I. Jusha minute, Will. I'm thinking."

Together maybe they would be warmer. Warm. Sleep.

Not now, snapped the panic, think! Be careful! Tighten your belt!

Why had she brought the belt?

Tighten your belt. Your seat belts.

Carefully, with her right hand, she withdrew one of Nick's belts. Carefully, she reached as far around the trunk with it as she could. On the third try she caught it with her other hand. She pulled it back, lost it, found it again, and managed to pass the end around her waist. Now she had to buckle it. Then everything would be fine. She leaned against the trunk, fumbling with her stubborn hands. Finally the pin slid into the hole and she had buckled herself to the trunk. She giggled in delight.

God, this was a beautiful tree. A fine tree.

But she was supposed to be helping Will. She'd better turn toward him. She grabbed the tree with one arm, eased herself around inside the circle of Nick's belt, then slowly lowered herself to a squat. The belt caught a couple of times as it slid down the trunk, but finally she was sitting, one arm still around the trunk, the belt circling her body and the trunk.

Will, his rump to her, tried to look back at her. "Come get me, Ginny."

"I better not. You hold on tight. And back up, very shlowly. Slowly."

He moved a little, trustingly. Now that she was so near he was confident again. The tough little body that swung on the parallel bars upstairs contracted, stretched, contracted, and then he was there, his little feet against her thighs, his corduroy-clad bottom only inches away.

"Good, Will!" What a wonderful, wonderful brother. "Do you want to sit up?"

"I want to go down."

"I know. I do too. But we'd better wait a little. I can't do it yet."

"But I'm tired of the tree."

"Lesh rest a little while, okay? I bet you want to sit up."

"Yes. My hands hurt."

"Okay." She gripped the trunk tighter, put out her arm. "Okay, Will, I'll put my hand out. You hold it and lean against me."

She bent her efforts toward holding steady, and Will, coordinated and no longer fearful, nestled back against her. Ginny was flooded with love for her little brother. Little trusting brother.

He shouldn't trust you, said the panic. Tighten your belt.

"Now let's put on our seat belt," she said.

"Seat belt?"

"Here." She pulled out a second of Nick's belts. "Around our legs and under the branch. To Grandmother's house we go." She giggled.

Interested, he helped pull the belt around. "I can buckle it," he announced proudly, and did so.

"Good! Now one more." She pulled out the last belt, carefully passed it between her waist and the trunk, and then gave the two ends to Will to buckle around his own little belly. And finally the panic in Ginny subsided a little.

"Your clothes are wet," observed Will.

"I'm all wet," she giggled. "But ish okay. We'll be warmer together."

They snuggled, and she began to drift away. But Will was restless enough to keep bringing her back. He made her sing songs. They giggled, and told stories. Every now and then he asked wistfully if it was time to go down, but the high was beginning to wear off and the panic was swelling within her.

Her legs and back were very cold, and her thigh throbbed where the twig had torn it, and her butt was sore from the constant hard pressure of the supporting branch. But she knew better than to move.

After a while Kakiy came down a little from his high branch, eyed them disdainfully, and then ran lightly along the branch into the exercise room. Will was quite interested, and prattled along for a while with conjectures about what Kakiy was doing inside, maybe going into his new house. Ginny made appropriate noises, but she wasn't really listening. There was something about the way she felt right now, as the drug's haze receded. Something to do with Mr. Spencer. Something she had seen as she left home.

But then a more important question pushed through the waning mists of the drug. What the hell was she doing in a tree?

Objectivity was returning, and terror, and with it came shame.

She was a total idiot.

She should have done something sensible. Maybe not the police; she still flinched from that. But she could have called Ellen. Or better yet, she could have prevented the whole problem, if she'd been paying attention to what Will was doing. She could have stopped him in time. Or at least she could have found a way to help him down, a rope or a ladder of some kind. There were a million sensible things to do other than that drunken lurch through the tree to hold him and sing to him. What a total idiot she was! And there was no way out now, she realized. They were stranded. There was no one to call for help.

Why had she taken that damn lude?

Well, she thought defensively, what could you expect? She did pretty well really, considering that her biological mother was probably a half-witted junkie and . . .

Her mother was a bright athletic Ph.D.

Damn.

A bright athletic Ph.D. would not get herself stranded in a tree. Would not abandon her responsibilities to a sick little boy and get wrecked on ludes just because she was tired of being stuck in the house and was feeling sorry for herself.

Not even if she was accused of murder? And homesick? And had just learned the brutal news that her genes gave her no excuses?

Especially not then.

So what the hell was Ginny doing in this tree?

She loved Will. Her little brother. Okay, she had done dumb things for love before. For love of Kakiy, she had yelled at Gram and Mr. Spencer, and gotten herself accused of murder as a result. For love of Mom, she had let Maggie go snooping to Maryland instead of telling the police where she really was, and had gotten herself stuck with this interminable baby-sitting as a result. For love of Buck, she had risked getting pregnant, and as a result—well, she had lucked out on that one.

What if she hadn't? God, Will was three and a half, and still needed so much attention. Look at what her hour's lapse had done. If she'd actually had a baby—God, twenty-four hours a day, for years, all alone. Well, Mom might try to help, but that wouldn't be fair. Ginny couldn't bear to think of disgracing her like that. And Buck—she couldn't imagine Buck with a baby. In her romantic visions she had occasionally pictured him playing with a child, but she knew that in reality he'd get bored fast. Go off with his buddies. Get stoned. Luded out.

And Ginny? After only three days of it, she'd luded out.

She had betrayed her own brother.

She had betrayed herself.

Well, yes, but remember, she had problems. Real problems! Being accused of murder was a real problem. So was being trapped in a house, the only protector of a sick three-and-a-half-year-old boy. She was only sixteen, for God's sake! How could Maggie expect her to do it? There was no way out, and no one to help, and no end in sight. It was unfair. It was tragically unfair to little Will. It was—

Jesus.

Jesus, that was the point, wasn't it? That was the goddamn point.

XX

She still wasn't answering the phone.

Nick replaced the receiver slowly and straightened his handlebar mustache. It had to be the backyard. She'd said nothing about Will getting worse, and he'd sounded okay this morning. Ginny had sounded fine too—just the right degree of frazzle, coping well but not trying to pretend there were no problems. They must be out back.

The stage manager was calling places for the beginning of the show.

But it was still his watch. Maggie wouldn't be calling them till late afternoon. Hastily, Nick dialed again and left a message with the secretary of Ellen Winfield-Greer, Esq., to please check on the O'Connor kids.

He went on with his mustache slightly askew.

"Hey, Ginny!"

"Yeah?"

"I gotta pee."

"Oh, dear." Ginny turned her attention to this new problem. "Well, we'll just have to manage it here. First the belt." She unbuckled the one that held their legs. Her fingers were working better now, though still awkward with post-lude sluggishness. She stowed the belt carefully around her own neck, and then removed the one that circled their two waists, holding Will tightly with one arm.

"Okay, Will. Now I'll unfasten your snaps. You stand up very carefully and pee on the roof down there."

He looked around at her, brown eyes wide. "On the *roof?*"

"Yes. It's okay because this is an emergency."

"Mergency." He was impressed by the solemnity of the word.

Ginny braced herself and, holding him tight, helped him face sideways on the broad branch. He did pretty well, only dribbling a little on her knee at the very end. They got his clothes up again and he sat down.

"Good job, Will," she said, slipping the belt around their two middles. "Here, you buckle this one."

"I want to go down."

"Yes, I do too. But we have to wait for help."

"Can't you help?"

"I can help keep you warm. But we need a ladder to get down."

He buckled the belt while he considered. Then he said, "The ladder fell down."

"Yes. That's the problem." Well, one of the problems. She pulled the third belt around their legs again. God, but her butt was getting sore. The branch was wide, but not wide enough. And it was very hard.

"I want a snack," announced Will.

Oh, God. If he started whining again it would be hell. But no matter, she was responsible for him, and would keep him safe. Whether he liked it or not. Whether she liked it or not.

"We have to wait," she said. "Why don't I tell you the story of Kakiy?"

"Is there a story?" He was immediately distracted from his woes.

"Of course!" she said. She began a story of a little kitten whose mother belonged to a beautiful ballet dancer. Will listened, intrigued, as the fictional Kakiy visited Moscow and Paris and Oz and Wonderland and finally Washington, D.C., where he went to live with Ginny. Will was so delighted when Ginny came into the story that she had to embroider the narrative with lots of details about Kakiy's life in her room. But he became troubled that an old woman who lived in the house didn't like Kakiy.

"Was she a wicked stepmother?" he asked.

"No, no! The stepmother wasn't wicked. She was wonderful. This was another old woman. She wasn't really wicked either, I guess. But some people don't like cats because sometimes they walk on the table, or their hair gets onto the furniture. Or they make people sneeze. Or they climb trees when they shouldn't."

"I like Kakiy anyway," decided Will.

"Yes, so do I." She went on with the story. Eventually the feline hero went to New York and rode on the subway.

"He was coming here!" crowed Will.

"You have to wait. That part comes a little later," admonished Ginny. "In this part of the story, Kakiy isn't very happy. The subway was louder than anything he had ever heard before." She continued, drawing it out; but eventually, when Kakiy went out into a tree and his friend Will tried to get him, there was no more to tell.

"Is that the end?" he asked.

"Oh, no, of course not. But that's all we know so far. We'll find out the rest later."

"Let's go in and have a snack."

Ginny eyed the branch she had used to get into the tree, and was amazed that she had managed. Right now, less sluggish but more sensible, she wouldn't dare. "We still have to wait a little more, Will."

He whimpered, and this time wouldn't stop. For twenty minutes, despite her best efforts, he refused to be consoled. Ginny finally began to sing some of the Italian lullabies Mom used to sing to her, not because they soothed Will—they didn't—but because she herself felt calmer. God, she missed Mom.

"What are you doing?" A little voice interrupted them.

"Sarah!" Ginny, delighted, looked down at Will's window. Sarah, still in her outdoor jacket, was holding Kakiy and observing them in some puzzlement.

Will started to complain because Sarah had Kakiy, but Ginny hushed him firmly. "We're trying to figure out how to get down," she said.

"Where's the ladder?"

"It fell down," volunteered Will.

"Shall I go get it?"

"Can you?" asked Ginny, amazed.

"Oh, sure!" Before Ginny could inquire further, the little girl disappeared from the window. After a time there was scuffling under them, on the back porch. "Hey, there's a mat here!" said Sarah's voice. "But no ladder."

"I bet it's under the mat," called Ginny. Sarah was very small. Could she manage the mat?

After a while her voice came up again. Ginny said, "Will, shh. Sarah is trying to tell us something. What, Sarah?"

"I found it. I'm pulling it out."

"Terrific!" Ginny tried to imagine the little girl with a ladder, struggling to get it from under the mat. It made her lose heart again. Sarah was too small. It would have been better to tell her to phone Ellen. Ellen, no doubt, would call the police. So much for all their elaborate plans. But Ginny would face that when it came. This mess was all her fault, she'd take the consequences. She'd run away again, or something. Somehow she'd keep Mom from finding out.

"Sarah? Maybe you should call Ellen," she called.

There was no answer. Will continued to whimper and squirm. He had been very good for a long time, and she couldn't blame him now. Hell, she'd be squirming herself, if she could.

"Sarah?"

No answer. Maybe Sarah had locked herself out, or had forgotten them and gone off to play with a friend, or had fallen and hurt herself. Ginny felt desolate.

"Here it is," said Sarah, appearing at Will's window.

"Where?" Was the little girl teasing them? Then Ginny saw it. "Oh!"

The ladder was a sturdy pair of chains with aluminum rungs strung between, and big hooks at one end. There was no way that small Sarah could throw it to her.

"Sarah, do you know where there's some heavy string?"

"Yes. In the kitchen drawer."

"Can you tie a tight knot?"

"Sure. Except sometimes I get mixed up with the bow."

"That's okay, we won't need a bow. Just a knot. Bring the string to the window and bring Will's frog. The beanbag frog."

"How come?" asked Sarah, the ever-curious.

"It's a secret plot," said Ginny portentously.

That was answer enough. The little girl skipped away and then reappeared with a thick ball of string. "Here it is!"

"Hey, terrific! Now the first thing you do for this secret plot is unwind lots and lots of string."

Sarah did so, with gusto. "Is that enough?"

"Yes." Ginny hoped she hadn't tangled it too much in her enthusiasm. "Now cut it off."

"The scissors are put away. So I'll chew it," decided Sarah.

She was right. Protective Maggie kept scissors, knives, and poisons locked up in a high cabinet. Nothing was in reach. Except for Ginny's ludes. Ginny shivered suddenly, wondering what would have happened if Will had found her stash.

Sarah was still chewing. Finally, she accomplished the task.

"Good girl! Now tie one end around the frog. Very tight. And the other end around the ladder, very tight."

Sarah busied herself at her task. Will was grumbling, "Not the frog!"

"Okay, all done!" said Sarah.

"Good. Now, throw me the frog."

"Not the frog!" whined Will. Fortunately, Sarah ignored him and threw the little green beanbag at Ginny. Ginny missed. Because of the belts, and Will, and general sluggishness, she couldn't reach out very far.

"Sorry, Sarah. Pull him back and try again, okay?" she said encouragingly.

On the fifth try, Ginny caught the frog. She tied the string around the branch, carefully working around the wriggling Will.

"It's all right, Will," she explained. "This is the next part of the story of Kakiy. The frog comes to help his friend Will. And now you can help. You pull on the string. Sarah, you help the ladder along slowly, so it won't get stuck in the window, okay?"

Together, they hauled the ladder close. Ginny inspected it and saw how the hooks could be placed safely around the branch.

"Where does it go, Will?"

"There." He pointed to a spot a little further along the branch. Parallel scuff marks on the bark showed the location. "But I wanted it there so I could get Kakiy." He indicated the branch above.

"So you moved it?"

"And it fell."

"I see. Well, Kakiy usually gets back in without any help. So don't try to help him again, okay?" She was tying the string onto the first rung of the ladder and up to the branch to be sure they could get it back if they dropped it again. Then she undid the belts and, very carefully, they slid forward along the branch to the correct spot. Together, they put it in place.

"I guess it's okay now, Will," said Ginny, testing it. "Be

careful!" But he was eager, and far better coordinated than she. He swarmed down the ladder to the roof and then quickly up the shingles to the window. Ginny followed more slowly, her numbed legs still hard to control, and went up the roof slope on all fours, carefully. She clambered in, closed the sash, and collapsed onto Will's bed.

"No!" shrieked Will from downstairs. "My turn!"

Ginny roused herself again and hurried to rescue Kakiy from death by hugging, to dole out food, to make peace, and to praise them both for their excellent help in the emergency.

"I had to pee on the roof," boasted Will.

"On the *roof?*" Sarah was fascinated. Clearly that was going to be the highlight of the episode for the children.

There were three calls. Ellen said, "Hi. I just got out of a meeting and found a message to check on you guys. Everything okay?"

"Oh, yes, thanks." How had she known? Well, the important thing now was to keep her from calling the cops. Ginny said, "Since you called, we could use some more milk and peanut butter."

"The staples. Listen, I'll bring you some take-out lasagne too. You must be pretty tired of sandwiches."

"Oh, sandwiches are okay. Easy to fix."

"All you have to do with this is warm it up. Oh, you were raised Italian, weren't you? Is that the problem? Well, listen, I'm not talking about frozen stuff. You're in Brooklyn now, and I'm going to bring you the real article baked today by real Italians."

"Sounds wonderful," Ginny admitted, suddenly ravenous.

"Okay. See you soon."

The next was from Nick. "Hey, where were you the last couple of hours? Outside?"

"Uh—yeah. Outside."

"Is Will feeling better then?"

"Yes. He's a lot better. Still looks scabby, but he's acting normal again."

"Probably running you in circles. I can hear him in the background now telling Sarah something about a roof."

"Yes, uh, Kakiy went out the window for a little while. I was just getting ready to fix them all a snack."

"Okay. I'll talk to you later then. Want to get my spirit gum off." He sounded very relieved.

The important call came a few minutes later. Ginny asked first, "Are they coming to arrest me yet?"

"No, but things aren't looking very good for Buck. Or his mother," said Maggie.

"His mother? Rummy Rosamond?"

"It ain't just rum, kiddo."

"Yeah. I suspected that."

"I think she's his connection, Ginny."

"His mother? His own *mother?*"

"Yeah. Buck found her stash and raids it. Of course she can't complain to anyone. I think she gets it after hours from Dr. Landon's office. She used to be his assistant, so she knows the code. Hangs around pretending to be jealous, then lets herself in, helps herself, and doctors the books."

"God. I'm not really surprised. But listen, I've got an important question." She handed bananas to the children. Bananas would keep them busy quite a while.

"Fire away," said Maggie.

"Before I was born. Did you think about keeping me?"

There was a pause. Then Maggie said, "Ginny, can we talk about that later? I don't know how to answer so that you'll understand. I've been thinking about Mr. Spencer. See, if he noticed that Buck was—"

Ginny refused to be deflected. "Yeah, but listen. Did your parents say you couldn't keep me? They'd disown you or something?"

"No, no. They said it was up to me. They'd back me up

whatever I decided to do. But you see, I knew it was my responsibility. Not theirs. They both had lives to lead, important work to do. I wasn't about to mess up any more lives than I already had. It was my problem and my kid, so it was up to me to decide."

"So you did consider keeping me."

Silence.

"Why did you change your mind?" Ginny persisted. The children were engrossed in unzipping their bananas.

"Who says I changed it?"

"Maggie, I know you better now. Why did you change your mind?"

"My mother found me a—look, we'll talk later, okay?"

"Tell me, damn it!"

Silence.

"Maggie, you said your mother found you a summer job. Please, you promised the truth."

"It was full-time for six weeks," Maggie said reluctantly. "For a couple who were going away to Europe. Housekeeping and stuff while they were gone."

"They had a kid, I bet."

Another pause. Then Maggie said in a weary voice, "Two toddlers."

Bull's-eye. Ginny's heart was singing. "So your mother the mayor prescribed a summer of toddlers! But before that, you were going to keep me!"

"All right, damn it, yes! I was absolutely determined to keep you! You were going to be my own little baby and friend, and no one else was going to have you! I refused to think about any other way. I made great plans. Noble Maggie and noble baby in rose-covered cottage. You were going to college with me, in a backpack. Never mind that they wouldn't even have let me back into high school. And then I was going to find a glamorous high-paying job with a sympathetic boss, and you'd never cry, you'd sleep peacefully by my desk while I made pots of money."

"And when I learned how to crawl? And walk? And climb trees?"

"Oh, they were great plans." Maggie sounded very sad.

Ginny wanted to dance and cheer. But first she had things to explain. She said, "That summer, Maggie, did the kids do anything really scary?"

"Occasionally. Kids do." Then, suspiciously, "Such as what?"

"Such as climbing into a tree after a cat and then dropping the ladder by mistake. Stranding themselves."

A noise came over the line.

"What?" asked Ginny.

"French. Not for beginners. It was Will, right? Is he okay?"

"He's fine. We're all fine."

"Damn, I meant to take that ladder down before I left! What did you do?"

"I, uh, climbed out to him. We sort of kept each other's spirits up until Sarah came home and got the ladder to us."

"Sarah? Why didn't you take the ladder with you when you climbed out?"

Ginny hedged. "Okay, Maggie, listen. Right now I'm about five years older than I was this morning, okay? I swear that they'll be one hundred percent safe as long as I'm here. This very minute I can see them both eating bananas. They're singing a mushy-mouthed version of 'Five Fools in a Barrow.' Everything is fine. So don't—"

"*Ginny!*" squawked Maggie. "What dumb thing did you do?"

Ginny still couldn't quite say it. Couldn't quite admit that she was as rotten as Rummy Rosamond. "Well, I was so tired of everything, the cleaning up and whining and not knowing who I am, and he was settling down for his nap very nicely, and—"

"What did you *do?*"

"I, uh, took a lude. And then he went out the window. And I couldn't think very well, so I went after him."

"*Stoned?*"

"Well, uh, yes."

Another French noise.

"Maggie, are you okay?"

"Fine. Sure. Perfect. I mean, for a woman who's just learned that two of her kids almost killed themselves today!"

"Well, I wouldn't have worried you, but I knew they'd tell you. Maybe scare you more."

"You got into that tree stoned!"

"Blown away. I, uh, took along a bunch of Nick's belts. Seemed smart at the time. When I got to Will we buckled ourselves to the tree. Later Sarah came home and threw us the ladder."

"Jesus. You goddamn idiot!"

Ginny propped the receiver between her ear and shoulder so her hands were free to pour the children some milk. She said humbly, "You're right."

"I could shake your teeth out! But I probably won't. And hell, it's my fault too, I forgot to take down the ladder."

"I didn't know he could get to it. Even so—Maggie, how come you trusted me?"

"Ginny, if there's one thing you've made clear the past few days, it's that you'd never hurt or abandon a little child. Never. And you didn't. Also, you've been really responsible about your parents. Besides, you've been through hell with me already without trying to drown your sorrows. I figured—well, let's just say I'm the kind of person who sometimes takes risks."

Her voice sounded breezy. She still didn't quite understand. Ginny returned the milk carton to the refrigerator and took the receiver in her hand again. She said carefully, "Well, I know why you took this risk. And it paid off, damn you. I learned a lot in that tree."

"You learned a lot?"

"About you and me. About love. Your mother the damn mayor is pretty sharp, you know. Her prescription really does cure illusions."

Silence. A long silence. Finally there was something like a snuffle.

"Is that more French?" asked Ginny gently, feeling a little snuffly herself.

"Yeah. Must be."

"Okay. Um, speaking of that tree?"

"Yeah?"

Ginny grabbed the cookie tin one-handed from the top of the refrigerator and handed it to the children, who were now caroling "Pop Goes the Weasel." She said, "I want to tell you something else I found out in that tree."

"Good God, you mean there's more?"

"It was the lude. That hazy feeling, you know? I remembered feeling the same way when I was leaving home. Happy but not really, you know? Well, at home when I was getting Kakiy, feeling hazy like that, I looked over at my worktable. And Maggie, the scissors were gone."

"Gone? You're sure?"

"Absolutely. But I was too foggy just then to worry."

"That means—oh, hell, and I thought—well, it's back to square one. Unless—listen, Ginny, does the name Caroline White mean anything to you?"

"No, not really."

"How about Maybelle Darcy? Or Belinda Johnson?"

"Belinda and Caroline seem faintly familiar."

"Kids in school?"

"No, something else. I'm sorry, I can't place them. Except —you said Darcy?"

"Yes."

"You know, when Mr. Spencer first arrived I think he said something about Mrs. Darcy."

"He did? Darcy? You're sure?"

"No. But—"

"Hey, good-bye. I have to go to the grocery, love." And the line was suddenly dead.

The grocery? What could be so important about the grocery? Ginny shook her head at the receiver in fond exasperation. Not motherly, that one. Not at all. But that was okay, Ginny had a top-notch mother already. Mom was as good as they came.

But Maggie, admirable and flawed and loving, was going to be a damn good friend.

Thursday, September 20, 1979

XXI

By Thursday morning they had not arrested anyone. Rina saw Clint off to work, sorrowing for the new furrows she saw in his forehead, and then pulled out pen and paper. She wanted to phrase everything exactly right, and had already torn up two versions when the doorbell rang.

It was Delores Gallagher in her bright magenta raincoat. "Hello, Rina. How are you? You look a little worn. Children are such a worry, aren't they? And all this about John—" She shook her head sadly.

Mamma came up the stairs in time to hang up Delores's coat. "Hello, Delores. Let's go down to my room to work. Oh, wait, here comes Marie now."

"What are you doing this morning?" asked Rina.

"We have to write an insert for the church bulletin, about donations to John Spencer's memorial fund," Mamma explained.

"Well, good. I hope it goes well," said Rina lamely. This was not a helpful development. But they'd be downstairs. "You have coffee made downstairs, Mamma?" she asked anxiously.

"Of course. And *biscotti.*"

"Leonora, you spell doom to any diet," said Marie Deaver, coming in. "But if we're quick, maybe Delores and I will escape only a few pounds heavier."

The three trooped downstairs. Rina returned to the kitchen

table, where she'd been working, and finished the page. Quickly, before she lost her nerve, she phoned Sergeant Trainer.

"I have something important to tell you," she said.

"You've heard from your daughter?" he asked with unprofessional eagerness.

"No. But it's probably more important than that. It would be easier to tell you face-to-face."

"Okay. We'll be there, let's see, in thirty minutes or so."

She spent the time in an oddly detached calm, straightening the house. She put a log on the charred remnants of last night's fire and lit it. She put all her scraps of fabric and thread and scissors into her sewing box and vacuumed the room, looking regretfully at the half-finished quilt. She tidied her bureau drawers and put her toiletries into a kit, and combed her hair carefully. She didn't want to look disheveled and silly.

When Sergeant Trainer and his officer arrived, she asked them in and sat at one end of the sofa. Trainer sat across from her in the big chair, the officer next to her. The early sun from the southeast slanted across behind them, casting leafy patterns across the sofa.

"Well, now, Mrs. Marshall," said Sergeant Trainer, "what do you want to tell us?"

She heard Mamma's step on the stairs. She had probably heard the doorbell. Too bad. Rina had hoped to be alone. But if it couldn't be helped, it couldn't be helped. And Mamma would have to know soon.

She handed him her signed paper. "I wanted to confess. I killed Mr. Spencer."

"What?" Trainer was astounded.

"I killed Mr. Spencer," she repeated.

He scanned the paper, his eyes narrowing. "Now, Mrs. Marshall, you're telling us you killed John Spencer?"

"No! She did not!" Suddenly Mamma was standing next to her, angry and protective.

Rina repeated calmly, "I killed Mr. Spencer."

"Caterina, shut your mouth! Are you trying to kill *me?* Have you gone crazy?"

"I've come to my senses."

"Sergeant Trainer, don't listen to this babble! My daughter is under so much strain. Let me talk to her!"

Sergeant Trainer cleared his throat and waved the paper at Mama. "Not now, Mrs. Rossi. We have to hear what she has to say."

"But it's all foolishness!"

He ignored her and looked back at Rina. "Mrs. Marshall, we'll have to ask you some questions. Do you want to come down to the station?"

"No." She couldn't bear that, not yet. "Here, please. I'll go with you later. Mamma, please go downstairs again."

Trainer said, "I must inform you that you have the right to have a lawyer present before I question you further."

A lawyer. Clint. "No, no," she said. "No lawyer."

He glanced at the other officer. The officer pulled out a card. Trainer cleared his throat again. "Now listen very carefully," he said, and began to read from the card. Finally he asked, "Do you understand?"

"Yes. You're explaining my rights. Warning me," she said. She felt far away, as though she were watching from the moon.

"Yes. Now listen carefully, Mrs. Marshall." He began to reread it, phrase by phrase, patiently making her confirm each part. Halfway through, Mamma broke in again.

"Rina, this is absolutely ridiculous!"

"Mamma, I have to do it."

"You're just trying to protect that girl!"

"I just want to tell them what happened," said Rina. "Yes,

it's for Ginny. I didn't know I would be getting her into so much trouble."

"Rina!" But this time it was a cry of despair; Mamma subsided for the moment, unable to fight Rina's calm resolve.

Sergeant Trainer studied her intently when he had finished the warning. He set the confession on the end table and said, "Mrs. Marshall, you know that a false confession is an offense."

"Yes, Sergeant Trainer. My husband is a lawyer. Over the years I've learned a bit about it."

"And you're still willing to answer my questions without a lawyer present?"

Rina looked at the paper on the table next to him. "I've come to see that it's unfair to let innocent people be suspected. It's my duty to take the blame for what I did."

"I see." He coughed circumspectly, his burlappy face neutral. "Why don't you just tell us in your own words, then?"

"But I wrote it down for you! It's all there!"

"It's better if we hear it ourselves. Start with the reason you did it."

"All right." She took a deep breath. Too bad Mamma was hearing it now. The first part was the hardest, but it was necessary. She steeled herself. "My daughter Ginny is adopted."

"Adopted?"

"Yes. As a baby. We've been a normal family, very close. But often other people don't understand. Children especially say very cruel things sometimes. You know, suggest that her birth mother was a prostitute, or something like that."

"Birth mother. You mean her real mother?"

Rina damped the ancient familiar flicker of rage. He was just trying to get things clear. She said levelly, "I am her real mother, Sergeant Trainer. I've raised her."

"Yes, of course. I see. Birth mother. Yes."

"Her birth mother is the girl who gave birth to her, and had to surrender her for adoption."

"Yes. I understand. And the other children would insult your daughter because of her, um, birth mother."

"Who was not a prostitute. Right." Rina tried to keep the weariness from her voice. "So you can see that Ginny wanted as few people as possible to know about the adoption. The same was true of us, of course, because we wanted to spare her the pain."

"I see."

"Well, the problem is that Mr. Spencer found out about it."

"Caterina!" Mamma burst in again. "That's foolishness and you know it! In the first place, he didn't know! Only Delores or Marie could have told him. Or me. And none of us—"

"Mrs. Rossi, please!" Trainer looked thunderous. "I must ask you not to interrupt or we'll have to finish this at the station."

"But it's foolishness!"

"Look, Mamma," said Rina patiently. "First of all, Mr. Spencer did know. I think Delores told him. She was so indignant about the insults that Ginny was throwing around after the cat got hurt. Maybe she thought she was defending our family reputation. But whether she told him or not, I know he knew. He telephoned me. A few minutes after six on Thursday."

"I didn't talk to him," she objected. "And he was my friend, not yours."

"You were out buying fish, Mamma." Sadly, Rina saw a glimmer of alarm join the confused anger in her mother's dark eyes. This was the worst part: hurting her, hurting Clint. She turned back to Sergeant Trainer and forced herself to go on. "He asked if it was true that Ginny was adopted, and I said yes but we'd appreciate it if he kept it quiet. I explained that she didn't like for it to be generally known. And then he said he understood perfectly." She took a deep breath. Up to this point it had all been true. "And he said he would be happy not to tell if I would deliver a hundred dollars cash to him, out at the mall."

"Rina, you'll never make me believe that in a hundred years!" exploded Mamma. Rina ignored her. Trainer's eyes stayed fixed on Rina.

"So I got my bank card and a pair of scissors, and drove out to the store he had mentioned. He got in the car with me and we drove to the bank machine. But I was just getting angrier and angrier. It was clear that he was going to keep asking for money, it wouldn't let up, and Ginny would always have it hanging over her head. So instead of pulling out my card for the automatic teller, I pulled out the scissors and stabbed him."

Mamma snorted her derision.

"It's all in my confession! And then," Rina went on, "I drove to the library book drop lane and pushed him out the door into the bushes, and came home. It was very quick. Mamma wasn't even home yet."

"Rina, you've gone crazy!" said Mamma. "Sergeant, we need a doctor! A hospital!"

Sergeant Trainer said nothing, his rough face a mask, his pale eyes thoughtful. Rina knew he was comparing the story mentally to the times and places he knew. It all checked out. It had to.

Rina added, "My big mistake was taking Ginny's scissors. I forgot her name was on them. I figured you wouldn't have her fingerprints, and the scissors are a common brand. You shouldn't have been able to trace them. But with the name, it called your attention to this house. Misdirected your attention toward her. And of course the last thing I wanted was for her to come to any harm. Keeping her from harm was the whole point."

"There would have been a lot of blood, Mrs. Marshall. How did you—"

The doorbell interrupted him. Trainer snapped, "Would you get that, please, Mrs. Rossi?"

It was Aggie, cheerful and breezy as ever. "Hi, Mrs. Rossi. I was driving by and saw the police car. Thought something interesting might be going on."

"My idiot daughter is confessing to a murder!" Mamma wailed, with a dramatic gesture at the paper on the end table.

"Really?" For an instant the hidden eyes behind those lenses took in the scene up in the living room: Sergeant Trainer and the other officer looking uncomfortable, Rina calm and resolute. Then Aggie laughed merrily and bounded up the stairs. She picked up the confession, glanced at it, then hugged Rina.

"Rina, you tiger, bless you! But all this isn't really necessary. Oh, dear, Sergeant Trainer, I'm so sorry!"

Somehow, in her enthusiasm, the coordinated and graceful Aggie had stumbled clumsily on the rug. And somehow, as she threw out her hands to catch herself, she had flipped Rina's confession into the fire. The paper caught, crackling and curling into smoke. Rina gazed at the ashes in dismay. She'd have to do it again, she realized. All over again.

Sergeant Trainer gave Aggie a long look. She said nervously, "I'm so sorry, Sergeant Trainer. Terribly clumsy of me."

"Yes," he said, "terribly."

"Tell me, Mrs. Rossi," Aggie went on, "are Mrs. Gallagher and Mrs. Deaver here? I saw their cars outside."

"Oh, God, they're downstairs! Rina, you crazy idiot, you made me forget!" She hurried to the stair railing and called downstairs. "Marie! Delores! Help me! My daughter's gone crazy!"

With suspicious speed, the two appeared. They'd probably been listening too, Rina decided, unwilling to interrupt a family crisis but hanging onto every word. Well, she'd better get used to having an unwanted audience.

"Great! Have a seat," said Aggie brightly, waving a hand at the chairs as though she were the hostess. She turned back to Sergeant Trainer. "I've found out some interesting things, Sergeant."

"A lot of people seem to have interesting things to tell me today," said the sergeant dryly. "Well, let's hear it quick."

Rina felt deflated. Why wasn't he interested in her confession? Why was he so easily distracted by Aggie?

"First let me show you something." Aggie swooped across the room and picked up Marie Deaver's handbag. With one long finger crooked under the handle, she dangled it in front of Sergeant Trainer.

"Aggie, really!" Marie Deaver looked startled.

"Just for a moment, Mrs. Deaver. I won't hurt anything. Sergeant Trainer, you probably aren't allowed to search this bag without good cause. But you can see plainly that I'm not slipping anything inside it. Now, you see I'm dumping it on this nice clean rug."

"Aggie! What's got into you, dear?" Marie hurried across toward her things.

"Wait." Aggie, still standing over the contents of the handbag, gestured her to stop. "I just want to show Sergeant Trainer something I noticed when I happened to peek into your handbag Monday. Your ID cards." She dove like a falcon toward the little heap and brought up four plastic card folders. Marie rushed toward her, but before she could reach her, Aggie had tossed the folders into Sergeant Trainer's lap.

"Here, don't you think the sergeant should have a look before you take them back?"

Marie studied the sergeant. He was frowning at the cards. She said, "It was just for a joke."

"Maybe," said Aggie. She picked up her own shoulder bag and rummaged in it. "But there are a few other things for

Sergeant Trainer to consider. First, these photographs." Aggie handed Trainer two pictures. Rina, craning her neck, caught a glimpse of the group pose Aggie had taken that first day at Delores Gallagher's, and Mr. Spencer's face in the other.

Aggie crossed to the stair railing and leaned against it. She said, "Cathy Smythe, at the check approval counter of the Thriftway Grocery, out at Eastland mall, will identify that man as Mr. Spencer, a frequent customer. And she will identify the woman who is circled in the other photo as Maybelle Darcy, who frequently cashed her welfare checks at the store."

Trainer glanced from the photos to the ID folders to Mrs. Deaver.

"It was a joke," she said again.

He looked back at Aggie. "You said that was number one," he said.

"Number two is no surprise. Several people, including you, Sergeant, can identify the same woman circled in the photograph as Marie Deaver. Number three—and this took a hell of a lot of legwork, Sergeant. I may send you a bill for the gasoline. Evelyn Price, teller at the Merchant's Trust bank in Wheaton, will identify that very same woman circled in the photo as Belinda Johnson, who frequently cashed her welfare checks at that bank."

"But Belinda is dead!" exclaimed Delores Gallagher. Mamma was frowning.

"Right," said Aggie. "But it turns out that the person who took care of Belinda's funeral arrangements forgot to tell the welfare people that she died. The welfare computer is still issuing her checks. And mailing them to Mrs. Deaver's address."

"I don't understand!" wailed Delores. "Belinda is dead! And who's Maybelle Darcy?"

"I wondered that too," admitted Aggie. "Belinda and Caroline were your maids, Mrs. Deaver. I noticed when I happened to peek into your files when I visited you. But who was Maybelle?"

Mrs. Deaver looked down at her hands, still clutching her handbag strap. Her knobby knuckles were a contrast to her well-cut suit. She always used to wear gloves, Rina remembered, even in summer. Mrs. Deaver said, "Maybelle was Belinda's cousin, I believe. Belinda was collecting her check too. That's what gave me the idea. If Belinda could do it, why couldn't I? Bobby needed it."

"I see." Aggie nodded. "And Caroline must be dead too."

"Oh! Poor Caroline!" squeaked Delores Gallagher. "I didn't know!"

Sergeant Trainer said, "Caroline White. That's the third set of ID's. Were they used fraudulently too, Ms. Lyons?"

Aggie grinned at him disarmingly. "I thought I'd leave a little work for your department to do, Sergeant."

He didn't quite smile. "Well, Ms. Lyons, if this checks out we'll have a strong case here of welfare fraud, but . . ."

"Welfare fraud!" cried Mrs. Gallagher. "Marie, how could you? Frank left you plenty!"

"Not with inflation, dear," said Marie Deaver.

Rina stared at her in puzzlement. Welfare fraud? But she used to work for the welfare department!

Delores was still dithering. "But how could you? Oh, was it for Bobby?"

"Exactly," said Marie with dignity. "He's doing so well at Shadyland. I couldn't let them take him to the state institution."

"But what will happen to him now?"

Marie Deaver, gazing at the carpet, could not prevent a tear from sliding down her cheek. Rina's shock gave way to enormous sympathy for Marie. Welfare fraud—that was terrible. But Marie had done it for her child! And Rina felt growing indignation at Aggie. Why had Aggie interrupted Rina's confession, her attempt to take care of her daughter, only to expose and blame this brave woman for attempting to take care of her son? Marie was only trying to be a good mother! Sergeant Trainer too was staring at Aggie. "You haven't explained the connection that Mr. Spencer has with all this."

Aggie tore a slip of paper from her notebook and handed it to him. "I hope you won't have to call on the people on this list. But if necessary, these three will testify that Mr. Spencer was blackmailing them. It will make Mrs. Deaver's motive clearer."

"Blackmail? John?" said Marie Deaver, suddenly animated. "Are you trying to say—no, of course not! John didn't know any of this! No one did! Why would I have told him? We'd barely met! He had no way to blackmail me!"

But then Mamma, her black eyes grim, said suddenly, "Darcy. He called her Mrs. Darcy. That Thursday afternoon, before we introduced them. And he said he'd met her in the grocery checkout line. At Eastland."

Brows raised, Delores Gallagher nodded slowly. Marie Deaver slumped back into a chair.

Sergeant Trainer said, "We did give a quick look at all the cars. And I come back to the question I was asking Mrs. Marshall earlier. There was a lot of blood. We didn't see any in our quick inspection of Mrs. Deaver's car. There had to be blood in the car, unless she'd wrapped him in towels or something."

Rina said, "My quilt!"

"What?"

"She'd just bought a quilt for her son! She had it in her car that afternoon—" Rina's hand flew to her mouth in dismay.

With a nod to the officer, Sergeant Trainer pulled out his card for the second time that morning and began to read the Miranda warnings to Marie Deaver. Rina closed her eyes and tried to grasp what had happened. She remembered Spencer's call, the cash registers in the background. She remembered Marie making a point of telling him she'd be at the grocery before the TV show. They were making a date, she realized now. And in Marie's car—no! Her intellect had followed, but emotionally Rina could not yet believe that she was not to be the one arrested. Her long night of pretending to sleep while she prepared and examined her story, her terrifying leap into the horrors of confessions and trials and prison, hadn't been needed after all.

Mrs. Deaver was saying, "Yes, I understand, Sergeant Trainer. Yes, I want a lawyer. That's all I have to say."

The images unreeling in Rina's mind had reached the inexplicable: Marie, in her white gloves, hurrying quietly into Ginny's bedroom to pick up the scissors she'd seen there earlier. Rina opened her eyes. "But why Ginny?" she demanded. A little ember of rage was growing in her heart. "Why did you try to hurt her?"

Marie looked stung. "I didn't! She brought it on herself! That boyfriend was no good. When I saw his car in the driveway that day, I decided to leave the scissors there, instead of in the river. And the rest she brought on herself too. She ran away."

"But why did you take Ginny's scissors in the first place? Why try to involve her?" Rina was sitting upright, stiff with anger.

"Bobby needs me. I had to deflect attention from myself, don't you see? The scissors happened to be handy. Rina, dear, don't be too upset. It's not like my Bobby. You couldn't love her like your own child."

Rina was on her feet, fists clenched by her side, and she wasn't sure what she might have done if Aggie hadn't snared her deftly around the waist and said, "Sergeant Trainer, you'd better take Mrs. Deaver away. Because next time she says something that dumb, I won't stop Rina. I'll join her!"

The sergeant nodded. "All right, Mrs. Deaver. Time to go."

The officer took her out. Sergeant Trainer turned to Aggie before following them. "We'll need a statement," he said.

"Okay. I'll come down to the station now."

"Strange accident that destroyed that confession," he added.

"Yes, strange," said Aggie, not looking at Trainer. She poked at the fringe of the hearth rug with the toe of her oxford. "But then, even the best detectives overlook things sometimes. Don't they?"

This time he did smile. "As long as the reporters do too." He turned to Rina. "Mrs. Marshall, in view of the fact that your written confession has been destroyed, we won't have to report the information you were giving us earlier."

"Oh, yes. Thank you, Sergeant Trainer. I'm sorry, very sorry. I just couldn't bear it anymore."

"Let's all just forget it," he said, and left too. Aggie saluted Rina and followed Trainer out.

Then there was a friendly arm around Rina's shoulder, and her mother's voice saying, "Well, tiger. How are you doing?"

Rina shook her head. "I just can't get used to the idea that it was Marie Deaver!"

Her mother shrugged. "It is hard to believe. But she's always been so defensive about Bobby, so protective—"

"I guess she was trying to be a good mother." Rina's mind moved on to the important thing. "Oh, I hope Ginny calls soon! She can come home now! But you were right, Mamma. My plan was so stupid—"

"Of course it was, *cara*. But I know you did it from love. The only problem was that you put me in a very difficult position."

"I know," said Rina remorsefully. "Having your daughter arrested for murder—oh, Mamma, I am sorry!"

"No, *cara*, not that! I mean having to think of a confession to top yours."

"Mamma!"

The black eyes snapped ferociously. "I did it while I was pretending to buy fish."

"Mamma! My God!" Rina burst out laughing.

Mamma sniffed. "You aren't the only tiger in this house, young lady."

XXII

Nick drove Ginny to Maryland in a rented car and locked Will and Sarah and pets inside briefly while he escorted her to the door. On the phone he'd heard her say, "I'll be home later today, Mom, I'll tell you where to meet me." So when she opened the door they were surprised, Rina and the grandmother rising from their chairs with looks of astonished delight. Ginny knew what she had to do and ignored the lanky figure in knee pants and white fur who was lounging in a big chair. She dropped her backpack and ran up the stairs and into Rina's arms, and they did the appropriate laughing and crying and hugging and kissing. She kissed her grandmother too. Finally she turned to Nick. She and Maggie had agreed that Rina would need a few weeks of reassurance from Ginny in order to cope with the whole truth. So Ginny introduced him as Mr. O'Connor, a school counselor who'd recommended Gogol to her, then moved to Philadelphia. "I needed to think," Ginny explained. "And Mr. O'Connor and his wife were really helpful."

Rina still looked a bit anxious. Not surprising if your daughter had gone missing and then reappeared with a strange man in tow. Nick did his best to look nonthreatening and amiable. Smiley O'Connor, straight from Mr. Rogers's neighborhood.

After a few minutes the immobile figure in the chair said, "This is the prodigal, I suppose?"

Rina looked embarrassed. "Oh, Aggie, I'm sorry! Yes, this is Ginny."

"Virginia Alice Marshall," said Ginny, looking at Maggie for the first time.

"A very good name. Pleased to meet you, Virginia Alice Marshall. I'm Aggie Lyons." She stood up with a grin and shook Ginny's hand formally, then glanced at Nick. "And you must be Mr. O'Connor, the famous friend from Philadelphia."

"Pleased to meet you," said Nick.

"Well, now that I've seen the happy ending, I'd better be off," said Maggie. "You've probably got some catching up to do, Ginny."

"Yeah," Ginny said seriously. "I've got a lot of things to think about. For starts, Mom and I are going to have some long, long talks. And Gram—well, see, I've been thinking, I'd really like to visit Europe someday. So I want Gram to teach me some more Italian, and I'm going to sign up for French at school."

Maggie nodded in delighted approval. "Busy days ahead."

"Right. And as soon as I figure out what it should be, I want to do a new self-portrait."

"Not an easy job," warned Maggie.

"Yeah, it may take a while. But the old one's outdated for sure."

They smiled at each other, then Maggie glanced around. "Hey, I thought there was supposed to be a cat."

"Yes, where's Kakiy?" asked Rina. "In your backpack?"

Ginny and Nick had worked this out on the way down. She said, "Well, Mom, I found another place for Kakiy to live."

"What do you mean?"

"Well, I've been thinking, it's not really fair. This is Gram's house too. And it's not fair to her or to Kakiy either. He's a terrific cat, and he deserves to live someplace where he's not a problem. And he likes Mr. O'Connor's family, and they like him."

"But Ginny!" Rina was concerned, Nick could see. "Are you sure? You're so attached to him!"

"Of course I'm attached to him, Mom! That's the point! Keeping him here is pretty selfish. More for me than for him. And I want him to be where it's best for *him*. See, if you really love someone, you realize that sometimes it might be best to just let go for a little while."

Maggie was standing very still, her knuckles pressing against her lips, her eyes concealed by the glasses. Nick wanted to hug her. Instead he jammed his hands into his pockets and concentrated on the others. Rina still looked worried. The grandmother said uncertainly, "Ginny, I can try. To be honest, I'll never like cats. But I can try to be more reasonable."

"It's okay, Gram." Ginny grabbed the old woman's hand reassuringly. "I know it'll be good for him, that's the important thing. They've got some great little kids who really love him."

Nick saw that Maggie still could not speak. He said, "Ginny's right. We all love him."

Ginny nodded. "Yeah, they all do. And it's not like I'll never see him again. They know he'll always be mine too, in a way. And maybe when I go away to college he can stay with me sometimes."

Rina was looking happier. A thoroughly nice woman, thought Nick. "So it wasn't just needing to think. It was Kakiy too!" she exclaimed, glancing at Nick more warmly. She seemed to know there would be more to the story, but he could almost see the fears of Philadelphia drug dealers slipping away. Leaving her cat was the most reassuring thing Ginny could have done. "That's why you went! To find him a place to live!"

Ginny hugged her. "Yes. I had to get him settled in. Kakiy will be very happy in Philadelphia."

"City of brotherly love," agreed Nick. "But I'd better be getting back now, too. I've got kids to take care of, plus a brand-new cat."

"Thank you so much, Mr. O'Connor! For taking care of Ginny, for bringing her back—" Rina saw Maggie starting down the stairs after Nick. "Oh, and Aggie, thank you too! I just wish you could stay and get to know Ginny, after all you've done for her!"

Maggie paused, one hand on the front door. "There's nothing in the world I'd rather do, Rina. But I'd better take a rain check. When you and Ginny have had your long talks, and everything's settled down again, give me a ring. I'll be here in a flash. If you want me."

"Of course we'll want you!"

Maggie's mouth twitched uncertainly, and she shook her head. "Anyway, right now I'd better get back where I belong. Rina, thanks for letting me invade your lives." She turned the knob.

Ginny ran down the steps and pumped her hand, whispering something. Maggie smiled, saluted the others, and was gone in a white flutter like wings.

Nick waved to them all and followed her out. They walked casually to their separate cars, temporary strangers for the benefit of anyone glancing out the window. But as he got in he was thinking of the whispered exchange he'd overheard at the door.

Ginny had said, "Au revoir, you old slut!"

And Maggie, grinning, had replied, "Ciao, you little bastard!"

Amazing pair. Life would never be the same.

6-19-97   ABY 9125

7-28

8-18   MR.22

8-29

9-20

1-8

4-25

5-15

6-16

3-27

5-1